Deadly
Election

To Garry' Wilma,
α Wilma,

Arthur Crandon

Very Best
Wishes,
Arthur

DEDICATION

Life throws many curved balls at you. Your closest friends and family will either help you dodge them or help you to survive the hits.

These people have kept me sane(ish) in an increasingly selfish, intolerant, mean, and depressing world.

They have given me a reason to live, to give, and to enjoy life: My amazing children, Peter, Simon, Thomas and Talia. My partner, Lance Requilme Ceniza.

Finally, as he is currently in my thoughts a lot, I dedicate this book to the memory of my Uncle George who died in London last week.

He was a solitary but kind old man who helped me in many ways – Rest in Peace, Uncle.

CONTENTS

ACKNOWLEDGMENTS

Most finished books are the work not just of the Author, but also of a team of paid and unpaid people who help to bring out the best in the raw words first written by the author.

I have received AMAZING editing and critique assistance from:

Joan Barbara Simon – www.joan-barbara-simon.com
Jane Bwye – www.jbwye.com
Su Williams – www.DreamWeaverNovels.com
Sarah R. Weldon – www.authorsarahweldon@weebly.com
Paul Headley
Tim Sargeant

And have benefitted from the advice, encouragement and suggestions of my beta readers:

Lance Requilme Ceniza
Camica Hayes
Keith Rowntree
Peter Dodd

The brilliant cover design is by
Jane Dixon Smith – www.jdsmith-design.com

ARTHUR CRANDON

.

PROLOGUE

As Virgil entered the dark cave, the crate slipped from his grasp. He stumbled to his knees. The sudden pain in his left side sapped his remaining energy. His emaciated old body crumpled onto the dusty stones. A trail of blood seeped out from under him—the close range shot had shattered his kidney and punctured his lung.

Kodama, the young officer, pointed his Nambu pistol at one of the younger men cowering in the corner.

"You! Pick it up."

The lad scrambled forward to take Virgil's place in an effort to stay alive, at least for a few more minutes. Breath came in short, painful gasps for Virgil, but he could see what was going on around him. The screams of his youngest daughter, Racquel, filled the air.

"No. Please, I beg you, no. No hurt me, please."

Her broken sobs fractured her feeble English.

She was less than ten feet from him, but there was nothing he could do for her. She lay on the ground in a state of near undress, with firm hands holding her struggling body.

The young sergeant and his three men laughed, as if drunk. Two of them held an arm each. She'd lost her blouse in the struggle a while ago and her young breasts wobbled as she struggled.

"Hold her still. How can I do it if you won't keep her still," barked the Sergeant.

Virgil's head now lay on the floor with blood dripping from the corner of his mouth. He was facing the appalling scene. The third man wrestled with her skirt, but her squirming made it difficult and he lost patience. His dagger made short work of the faded cotton fabric. Bunching the ragged clothes at one side with his fist, he sawed through the material of both in a few seconds; the nakedness of the girl was now visible to all. She sobbed with shame at her nudity, in pain—the man had cut into her side as he stripped her—and in fear.

Sergeant Hito now stood in front of the girl with his breeches around his ankles and his manhood sticking out proudly, like a flagpole. Two of the men pulled the young girl's legs apart. They didn't need telling, they'd done this many time before.

Virgil did not die soon enough. As his sight faded, he saw the Sergeant's swollen member plunge into his daughter's body—she screamed out loud in agony with every thrust until he was completely inside her. The other men cheered as their boss thrust himself harder into her, and argued over who would take the next turn.

"Look, we've got a virgin!" exclaimed the sergeant, pointing down to the blood seeping from the violated girl.

It took him just a couple of minutes to finish.

"That was a tight one," he said, smiling.

He wiped himself on the discarded skirt as one of the others, a shorter, fatter man took his place.

After twenty minutes all four men had used her body and she lay curled up. She raised her head to see the now lifeless body of her father, and sobbed even louder.

"I sorry, father, I so sorry," she wailed.

CHAPTER ONE

General MacArthur kept his promise and returned to the Philippines late in 1944 with nearly two hundred thousand American troops. They hunted down the remaining Japanese soldiers. Many of the invading troops held gold and other treasures, looted from all over Asia. The disgraced General Yamashita was in flight, hiding these treasures wherever he could, digging holes in the ground, filling the basements of deserted houses, or finding a secluded cave.

The American rescue was too late for Virgil and his village. It would be another week before the liberating yanks paraded through the streets of the historic Spanish-style town of Vigan to the cheers of the war weary locals.

Lieutenant Kodama surveyed the bloody scene.

"Quickly, get them into the cave. Search the forests—we can't let any of these scum get away."

His men carried the limp remains of the men, women and children inside, piling them up like animal carcasses next to the neatly stacked wooden cases. A few of the men broke off and went into the forests to make sure none had escaped.

The weary soldiers were in luck, the village still had a cow and a few goats. The smell of the animals roasting over the smoldering remains of the village huts was exciting the soldiers. They had not eaten well for more than a week.

Before dawn broke over the hazy tops of the Cordillera Mountains, some of the men busied themselves blocking up the cave entrance and dragging down branches from overhanging bamboos for further concealment. Within an hour they were on their way, any evidence that they were ever there was now walled up in the cave.

They made slow progress through the lush tropical jungles of the Northern Philippines. Kodama spoke quietly with his sergeant

"Do you think we can make it to Subic? There's no point trying to get to Manila—the Americans are already controlling Manila Bay."

"Maybe we can find a small boat in one of the small harbors in Tarlac and take our chances—the Yanks are moving fast—if we don't get off the island soon we'll have no chance."

The dense vegetation opened out onto a small road running alongside the sea. They could see the beach a hundred yards away. The troop crouched down and scurried across the road, regrouping in the shade of some large rocks and coconut palms at the top of the beach.

The sergeant gathered them together.

"We have to stay off the roads. We've no idea how far the Americans have got. We'll move along the shore using the rocks as shelter. Try not to be seen, the locals attack us or contact the enemy, and we cannot take chances."

Four hours later, as they skirted San Fernando, La Union their luck ran out. The sun was at its hottest now—these temperatures didn't suit the conscripted soldiers.

The American commandos spotted them a long way off. An abandoned barn close to the road proved an excellent vantage point. As the Japanese moved past on the shoreline below, the American commander called out.

"Halt and surrender!"

Lieutenant Kodama managed to get a shot off in the general direction of the building before the Americans cut him down with rapid fire.

All the other Japanese dropped to the ground or behind trees when then heard the American shout.

"Don't shoot, don't shoot!"

The youngest recruit stood up and started walking toward the building with his hands in the air.

"Traitor!" screamed the sergeant as he lifted his rifle and shot the boy in the back of the neck. The startled lad fell forward gurgling as he breathed his last.

The Americans needed no further excuse. The few Japanese had no chance; there were twice as many Americans. Hand grenades landed between the rocks that were sheltering them. All the Americans had to do was sit and wait for a few seconds. They saw the effects of the blast before they heard the noise—body parts were thrown out into the open—then it was quiet. The allied soldiers approached with caution, rifles ready. They needn't have worried. There was no life in the bloody remains strewn over the beach and the road.

The allies quickly dug a deep pit. The unmarked grave by the side of the road was left undisturbed for nearly seventy years.

Senator Enrique Consuelo was tired and irritable.

"Where is she?" he demanded of the first maid he saw.

"Sir, she's in garden. Shall I fetch her?"

"No, just tell her I'm home, and tell her to come up to me later."

The maid nodded and ran off as the weary politician climbed the stairs.

As he walked into the spacious, thickly carpeted bathroom, the scent of lavender reached him. Glimmering scented candles surrounding the heart-shaped Jacuzzi caught his eye. Steam rose from the warm, silky, oil-laced water. He smiled, both in anticipation and remembrance.

Thoughts of that exciting evening just a few weeks ago came to his mind.

His partner was frequently away—he made the most of her absences. As he looked at the foaming bath, he could imagine the three young girls who were his guests that evening. This had been a particularly enjoyable encounter. He smiled fondly at the memory. Regular exercise and a good diet gave him plenty of stamina, despite his advancing age. Over two hours he satisfied them all. Thinking of their eagerness, the softness of their young skin, he was again becoming aroused.

The room was cool and the air was scented. Pastel beige drapes bordered the panoramic windows—very stylish but relaxing. Carefully removing his brown leather shoulder holster with the pistol still inside, he donned his silk robe. He draped the gun holster over the back of a chair near the window. Music pervaded the background from speakers hidden in the walls—Celine Dion's *My heart will go on*.

The elegant, stylish surroundings were largely paid for by the Senator's business interests including smuggling, illegal gambling, prostitution, and more.

Bending slightly, he selected a quality bottle of Langhe Nebbiolo, an old and fine red Italian wine, from the rack in the alcove by the door. The Senator prided himself on his knowledge of fine wine. He had an enviable collection that he thoroughly enjoyed.

After uncorking it and pouring himself a generous glass—he was too impatient tonight to decant it and let it breathe—he gazed for a couple of minutes out over the fish pools in his private garden. Before him were well tended lawns between beds of roses and bougainvillea. Ornamental palm trees provided shade for the small wooden chairs and tables spaced around the symmetrical enclosure.

He disrobed and eased himself into the spacious tub, touching a discreet button on the side. The quiet motor beneath responded with a hum, bubbles emerged from nozzles in the bottom and sides of the tub, gently massaging his legs and back. He sank into the depths of the bath, closing his eyes.

Consuelo was tough, very tough. Certainly not someone you would want as an enemy. He had a deserved reputation as a ruthless warlord, but was very bright, with admirable political skill. So far, he had shown much better judgment than his predecessors.

Despite his ruthlessness, he believed he was a good man and, in truth, he was not *all* bad. He could be generous and thoughtful when the occasion demanded.

He took care of his staff like a benevolent grandfather, often paying long term employees unofficial 'pensions' and shouldering medical and funeral expenses.

Serious health problems had caused him to re-evaluate his life, but he still believed it was his destiny to become the President of the Philippines before he left this world.

The bubble jets were now up to maximum strength, the gentle massage was very pleasant.

The bathroom boasted moldings in Italian style with the most expensive gold plated imported fittings. Chloe, his partner, had a good eye for design. She was a beautiful, intelligent girl less than half his age. As always, she had organized the scented candles for the room and arranged for the bath to be drawn.

After soaking for thirty minutes, he slowly rose through the bubbles, dried himself and put on his robe, then settled into his favorite armchair. Chloe arrived with an inlaid wooden tray with chamomile tea—part of his strict health regime. The Senator was a diabetic; he had nearly died from an episode two years before. Ever since then he'd followed medical advice and felt fitter than before his collapse.

Chloe had an admirable body. The flimsy gown she wore accentuated her curves. The sash was loosely tied at the waist. The Senator admired her and wondered if she was wearing anything under the robe. He was about to find out. As she came over to him and sat on his lap, the gown fell open to reveal her naked body. Her legs opened as she sat astride him.

"I've missed you so much," she whispered.

She smelled wonderful, fresh flower tones, just as he liked. As she opened her legs wider he saw that she had shaved herself in anticipation. She looked very fresh and inviting.

"I see you have missed me, too," she smiled, looking down at him.

He was still aroused from his earlier thoughts, and now became fully erect and ready. He smiled as his robe parted and she took hold of him.

"This is what you need, sweetheart," she breathed softly into his ear as she raised herself slightly.

She held him, moving him up and down between her legs until natural lubrication eased her efforts. He was quite large, but he slowly slid into her. As the full extent of him filled her for the first time in many weeks, he thrust hard against her. She moved forcefully to grind herself against him for several minutes. He held her tightly to him as his juice flowed. She felt the gush and tensed to receive it. It felt good.

After a while they sat down to talk and drink tea. Chloe was a bright girl with a degree in communications. In terms of his trusted associates and staff, she was near the top. She was a useful sounding board for his ideas and he took her advice seriously. His commitment to her was long term—she was the mother of his two young children.

Despite his earlier health issues, he was now working at a pace that would have exhausted a man half his age.

Chloe made it her job to ensure he relaxed whenever it was possible. She knew what he was like, but was faithful to him. It was nearly two weeks since she'd seen him. She missed his strength and security.

There were two large packed cases by the door of the bedroom.

"Good job," he said, smiling at her. "You've packed already. You must've known I was in a hurry."

"You always are these days, sweetheart, no time for me anymore," she pouted playfully.

"We'll have more time soon."

Before she could reply, he shouted for guards to come and get the bags.

Five minutes later the car was outside with its engine running, the Senator waiting in the back. She jumped in beside him and the driver shut the door behind her smartly. They were on their way to the local airport. Within an hour, they were in the air and halfway to Manila.

"Can't you keep her any steadier?" Consuelo barked at his harassed young pilot, as the small plane took yet another dive into an air pocket.

"Sorry, sir," replied the timid young man, the most junior of the Senator's three pilots. "We're so light this trip, we're being blown around more than usual. The wind is quite strong."

"I know that."

He made his way back to his seat and his sick bag. The tail end of a typhoon was still creating strong winds, causing turbulence for the small sixteen-seater plane. The Senator felt queasy as the light aircraft bobbed about in the face of the gale.

Jagged ridges of the Cordillera Mountains in the north of the province below looked dangerously close. Razor-like peaks resembled the edge of a saw and seemed to go on forever

It was a relief when they touched down at Manila domestic airport sixty minutes later. The black Ford Expedition was waiting for him on the side of the runway. Consuelo ran down the exit stairs as soon as they were unfolded. The driver opened the door wide, ready to receive him. Before pouring himself into the plush black leather on the back seat of the car to wait for his wife, he took a few seconds to wave at the small group of photographers gathered at the airport entrance.

"Welcome home, sir," said the driver, an older man and faithful servant for more than twenty years.

"Thank you, Edward. I'm glad to be back. Is Simon at the house yet?"

"Yes, sir. He arrived the day before yesterday."

Simon, his 'secretary' and general fixer, had been taking care of some election rigging in the Southern Islands.

The Senator and Chloe arrived at his Manila mansion just before two p.m. after the short drive through the busy traffic. Their Manila home was set in a tree-lined gated community in Bel-Air—the Philippine elite lived here. The two lanes of the dual carriageway within the village were clean and smooth. Tall coconut palms adorned the central reservation, interspersed with mature banana plants. A lone road sweeper lazily dragged his trolley along the dusty path.

The car turned smoothly left as the electronic gates parted to allow them in. Even in a street of outstanding homes, theirs stood out. Painted white with a red tiled roof, the twenty two room mansion was imposing.

"Who will be coming tonight?" Chloe asked as they made their way to the bedroom.

"It's really just a thank you party, an early celebration," he replied. "My top people in Manila will be here. We want to be discreet about this meeting, so I told them to make sure they drove right through the gates and to use cars with tinted windows."

"Well, you can leave it to me," she smiled. "I'll make sure it will be a night to remember." Enrique knew what she meant.

There was a knock at the door and without waiting a slim lad entered the room. They'd asked Jake to 'do' them this afternoon. He pushed in a small trolley.

Nodding courteously at the Senator and his lady, without a word, he set out his tools on a small table next to the Senator's chair. He set about trimming and tidying, and touching up some of the white roots, which were now becoming more prominent after each trim. The Senator continued to chat with his wife but was careful in his choice of conversation with Jake there.

Jake served as hairdresser and beautician-in-residence. He'd lived with them for seven years and was almost part of the family. The Senator liked him very much; his feminine affectations made Consuelo smile. Jake was gay or 'bakla'—the local name for 'lady boys.'

He would've been a very beautiful woman with his high cheekbones and slim build; he liked to wear short dresses and was never short of admirers. After the hair treatment, Jake gave the Senator a deep neck and shoulder massage then moved to Chloe.

The Senator stood up abruptly as Jake prepared his stuff. Chloe took this as her cue that their private moments were now over and it was time for business. They quickly embraced one more time.

"Thanks for everything, pussycat. I've got a lot to do before the party, but I'll see you later."

She smiled and released him, then sat down to enjoy Jake's attention.

Today was Thursday. Consuelo preferred to be in the province at the weekend and usually travelled back to the Capital on Monday. But this time, as the election was approaching, he stayed longer to consolidate his support. One of the final meetings of the campaign was going to take place at his house that evening. It signified that the end of his battle was near.

He was not a military man, although he liked to cultivate the image of being a tough guy. His bid for the Presidency was well organized—he was running a military-style campaign. The loyal team he had built around him was astute and experienced, he controlled them tightly.

The sprawling three-story house had a well-equipped conference room, converted from its former use as a snooker room when he bought the place ten years ago. Next to the conference room there was a small but comfortable private office. Simon was outside waiting for him and rose smiling as he entered.

"It's good to see you, sir," he said, accepting the Senator's outstretched hand and shaking it briskly.

They sat in black leather chairs on either side of an antique coffee table.

Simon was maybe ten years younger than Consuelo. He was also taller and slimmer than the portly man. When the Senator recruited him, Simon said he'd retired from his air force career at forty-five and spent a few years as a mercenary in the Middle East. He kept his pilot's license and sometimes flew planes for the Senator.

In the beginning, the Senator had reservations about employing him, but a recommendation from his Chinese friend, Bin Xu, a newly rich 'commodity broker' with whom he had done many clandestine deals, persuaded him. Simon was a solitary figure. He didn't mix with the other staff, but was exceptionally efficient. Consuelo had learned that he was one hundred percent reliable—his initial misgivings eventually faded.

Simon began his briefing, consulting his notebook.

"How are things in the South?" asked the Senator, his face breaking into a hint of a smile.

The other man looked up.

"Fine sir, fine. We'll get sixty percent out of Cebu and better in Davao."

Consuelo knew his aide was being optimistic, but he took that for granted. Simon continued.

"You need to ring the Governor of Palawan. He'll help us, but he needs a personal word from you."

The Senator nodded.

"And this evening?"

"Everything's prepared, Senator. Everyone you wanted to come has accepted. There's no agenda; you told me it was to be informal, no?" He looked up quizzically at the Senator, who nodded curtly.

"I met with two of the Bishops and the Vice-President, discreetly of course, and they're very happy now. They asked me to pass on their thanks to you. I don't think we will have much trouble with the Church, and the VP will be here tonight."

"What about the Mayor of Makati, is he happy now?"

"Yes, he's a happy man. I took care of his little problem for him."

"I know, I read about it in the newspaper,"

Both men chuckled.

Being a journalist was a dangerous occupation in the Philippines, especially if you were stupid or brave enough to criticize powerful men. You became accident-prone very quickly. Marvin, a popular young journalist, formerly an announcer on a local radio station, raised allegations of financial impropriety surrounding the Mayor on his weekly show. A killing would create too much bad publicity and suspicion, but three masked men paid a visit to his home during the day while he was at work. Marvin's wife was in the hospital right now, seriously injured, but she would live.

The two strolled next door to the spacious conference room with its large windows that filled the room with natural light. Simon squinted at the change in the light as they walked in. The room would comfortably seat twenty, but there would only be about twelve people there tonight.

Some of the attendees were Manila based but others were making their way by plane and car.

"Everything that you asked for has been done. I'm sure that everything will go well tonight," said Simon.

"Well done, you do seem to have everything under control."

"Of course, Sir" the other man replied, eyes still on his notes.

"I'll take a rest now and see you later."

The Senator didn't wait for a response and headed towards the bedroom. Simon made his way to his own, smaller office down the corridor, and locked the door.

Simon was in it for the money, but he respected his boss, and prided himself on his cool efficiency in his work. The Senator's former friend, President Bautista, was extremely unpopular. She wasn't standing for re-election although she'd only served one term. A not so small fortune sat in foreign banks waiting for her—she was keen to get out while she still could.

She'd thrown her support behind Consuelo's closest rival, Senator Cruz. This was a poisoned chalice for the poor man, but there was nothing he could do about it.

Senator Consuelo's power base was in Abra, Northern Luzon. He had spent a lot of time cultivating his image there. After all, the people respected strength. In the last few months however, because of his Presidential bid, he had worked with highly paid advisers from the local media and the church. He had managed to ensure that, to most of the country, he seemed somewhat softer and more intellectual.

He was now cultivating a more statesmanlike, benevolent persona. It was working so far. He was slowly climbing the popularity charts, but there were still many days to go. He just had to keep his nose clean and his election machine well-oiled and supplied. To date, he had spent more than twenty million dollars and he knew there would still be more to pay. His resources were diminishing, and this concerned him. Distracted, he shook himself back to reality when Simon called him.

Simon had, as instructed, arranged for the most important guest of the evening to arrive early. The well-dressed man strode the short distance from his car to the front door, which opened as he arrived, two bodyguards following at a distance. He was dapper, slightly overweight and shorter than his host. Dyed black hair made him seem younger than his sixty years.

The Senator wore his best smile and stood with an outstretched hand. Vice President Ramos looked up, returned the Senator's smile and warmly clasped the outstretched hand with both of his own. The former television presenter had been used and abused by his former friend, the President, and was counting down the days until the election.

"Welcome, my dear friend," enthused the Senator, continuing to shake the man's hand a tad longer than was necessary.

He led him through to the small office next to the meeting room where he offered him the nearest chair.

Consuelo wasted no time

"The President has taken a tighter and tighter control on the media. It'll be one of my first acts to give them back their independence. I want you to be part of it."

The VP looked up.

"I'd like you to take over as the Chairman of the Philippine Broadcasting Company."

The PBC controlled and/or regulated the growing number of television and radio stations in the country. As a former and still well-known broadcaster, Mark Ramos would be back in a world he was familiar with—and at the top of it. The Senator knew that this was an irresistible offer.

"And to emphasize how important I consider the media to be, you'll also be a special Presidential Adviser."

The Vice President couldn't hide his delight. He thought he'd get the Chair of the PBC but not the elevated status of special Presidential Adviser.

"You'll have my full support, my friend," he gushed, reaching forward to clasp Consuelo's hand firmly once again.

It was a win-win situation for the Senator. Ramos' support was now assured. He had put him into a situation where he could do little damage, and he certainly didn't intend to take any advice from him. The Vice President got up from his chair.

"This calls for a drink."

The two men sat and drank like old friends. The Senator nodded at the appropriate places while the Vice President rambled on, condemning the current administration, blaming others for his situation. Consuelo had heard it all before. After twenty minutes or so the Senator made his excuses, he had to prepare for the party. He left the Vice-President with a large glass of whiskey, and the rest of the bottle close by.

The meeting would start at six. Simon made a point of insisting that they should be on time. This would likely be the only meeting of the group before the election—or probably ever. They all had their work to do for the Senator in their own way over the coming days.

Other guests started to arrive after thirty minutes. Uniformed catering staff met them at the door offering water and juice. Large amounts of alcoholic drinks would flow after the short business of the day was over. They were shown into a plush drawing room to await the arrival of the others.

Simon ushered them into the boardroom. The Senator, and a slightly groggy Vice President, stood by the door to greet them. Everyone at the party was a well-known public figure. There was already an air of celebration, exactly what the Senator was trying to achieve. He stood to speak and the room fell silent.

"Dear friends, we're nearly there, nothing can stop us now. I know many of you have already worked hard on my behalf and I thank all of you."

He raised his glass. Around the table, the others toasted each other. He looked around the table making eye contact with his guests as he spoke.

"You know, when I started my campaign, many people said I had no chance. It's thanks to you and other like-minded people who've recognized the need for change that I've gotten to where I am now."

The serious tone of his speech caused the room to fall silent, as the Senator had intended. He had their full attention

"I must give you a word of caution; we enter the most dangerous part of the race now. Many people will try to stop us, to expose any skeletons, real or imagined. Please be on your guard for these last few days. Then we can all relax as we reap our rewards."

He raised his glass again.

"Here's to success," he proclaimed.

The assembled guests cheered and again toasted each other. When the chatter in the room subsided, the Senator resumed.

"I want to pass you over now to my good friend, the Vice President of the Republic of the Philippines."

Vice President Ramos stood to speak, as pre-arranged. He was an imposing figure and an accomplished speaker, even when under the influence of alcohol. He put his arm around the Senator, hugged him, and smiled—that said it all really, but more was expected.

"I'm among friends here tonight so I can be frank. We all know that the country needs the kind of man we've pledged to support as the next President. Unlike the present incumbent, this man knows about loyalty, he's a man of the people and has the interests of the country as his number one priority. In a couple of weeks we'll be celebrating our victory."

Ramos went on to praise Consuelo effusively for another five minutes and ended by telling the assembled dignitaries that if there were any problem he could assist with, all they had to do was pick up the phone. He finished by giving them his private cell number. There was light applause and a brotherly pat on the back from Consuelo as he stood to take over.

"As a humble country politician, I'm proud to be in such distinguished company tonight. My vision for our great country is one of prosperity and equality—and to regain our dignity in the eyes of the international community."

There were somber nods around the table.

Consuelo introduced Simon, who stood and smiled. The Senator made it clear to them that Simon was available at any time of day or night. He'd call each of them daily with updates on the campaign. Simon shook his boss' hand, and the Senator sat down.

Simon outlined the weak areas, where the campaign needed support. The Church was not yet solidly behind the Senator—he needed the Bishops present to work on that. The Archbishop of Manila had made public comments about Consuelo's links to illegal gambling, which in truth, funded half of his enterprises. Public denials helped but somehow over the next few days the Archbishop must be persuaded to be less vocal in his opposition.

The Catholic Church in the Philippines was strong politically and had a lot of popular support, holding firmly to early Catholic ideology inherited from the time of the Spanish occupation. The only way to end a marriage was by annulment, apart from killing your spouse. Both were equally popular but the latter choice was usually cheaper. With little danger of prosecution, it was widely practiced.

Most of the national daily newspapers had come round to endorsing Consuelo—newspaper owners, editors and senior journalists all benefited from the largesse of the Senator. The major television channels stayed mainly neutral as the incumbent was not standing again and they were not prepared to support no-hopers even if urged to do so by the Office of the President as she would be gone soon.

The army was solidly behind his campaign. They had never been very comfortable with a woman in charge. Consuelo asked the military men present for a list of senior officers who supported him. They would ensure the military vote went his way. Each of them would receive a discrete phone call from Consuelo and an early Christmas present.

The National Chief of Police started to write a similar list. Police General Estrada had served for thirty-five years in the police, after a short military career. He was six months from retirement and this election was going to provide a substantial boost to his pension fund. The Senator promised better pay and conditions to the Police, especially the recruits who received very little. It was easy to sell Consuelo as the new President to his men.

The Mayor of Manila, Manuel Decena, had also suffered under the current leadership. The President had taken away control of planning decisions and building permits. This meant the loss of a major source of income. She had also taken away the lucrative issuance of business permits. Consuelo would return both of these to him under his new administration.

Mayor Decena had already received some 'compensation' from Consuelo. He would deliver many thousands of votes from those who lived and worked in the nation's business capital. Thanks to the support of the Mayor, the Senator's face—an airbrushed, much younger looking version—smiled out at the daily commuters from thousands of public buildings, the sides of the major thoroughfares and public billboards all over the city.

Harry Chua, one of the richest men in the Philippines, had supported Consuelo through his Senatorial race and bankrolled him for a large share of the election costs. His family fortune dated back to the Marcos era. His father had been one of the disgraced President's closest cronies.

Consuelo's and Harry's parents had been good friends, but were both dead now. Nevertheless, family loyalty meant everything to a Filipino. Consuelo generously thanked him for his support, a gesture meant to convey to the meeting that money was no object for the campaign. They could all rely on rich rewards at the end.

The Senator spoke again.

"I will need the help of each and every one of you to implement the policies our country so desperately needs."

The group was politely silent again.

"I know you all share my beliefs and visions, and I know I can rely on you all to play your part."

He looked around the table solemnly, then his expression changed and a broad smile graced his face.

"Relax, enjoy yourselves tonight, you are among friends. Tomorrow we'll start to work in earnest as we come down to the wire, but tonight we'll play."
With perfect timing, the door burst open. Attractive serving girls wheeled in a lavish buffet of hot and cold food. Wine and spirits with mixers and ice arrived on two further trolleys. Gradually the guests wandered next door to the more comfortable drawing room with sofas and coffee tables—and open bottles of whiskey and brandy on every table. Chloe joined Consuelo; he smiled as he gave her a quick hug.

"Good job," he whispered in her ear. "Is the entertainment arranged?"

"Of course it is. I selected the girls myself, and they're all sexy."

He laughed.

"I knew I could rely on you, as always. Well done. Have the electricians gone now?"

She nodded.

"I've checked the rooms and everything is fine."

He kissed her firmly on the lips.

"I couldn't manage without you,"

"Thank you, sweetheart. I love you so much."

She meant it.

The party was in full swing now. Dance music was playing, apparently from the ceiling, and the mood was set. Some of the guests were always in the public spotlight and rarely got a chance to let their hair down. They took full advantage of the opportunity.

Well before midnight, young, pretty girls appeared and mingled with the guests. Chloe had contacts in many places. She was often called on to supply 'company' for the Senator's guests. Tonight she had done an admirable job. All the girls were stunning, and all the more appealing in their scanty outfits.

The happy guests soon paired up with attractive partners, then moved slowly to the space in the middle of the room that had become the dance floor. Two security guards in plain clothes kept an eye on the proceedings, looking out for anyone who was tempted to take photos with their phones. It did not take long for the alcohol and dim lighting to have its desired effect. The Senator was pleased to see kissing and groping going on in different corners of the room.

Several of the girls were down to their panties now and all inhibitions had been lost. Two of the girls, one with a large butterfly tattoo high up on her inner thigh, were completely naked and one had Harry Chua's manhood halfway down her throat.

As the evening wore on the guests disappeared off in the direction of the bedrooms with a girl, or sometimes two. One bishop left the party early. Consuelo and Chloe decided that they could take the opportunity to make their excuses and slip away.

The other bishop was one of the last guests to leave the room. He befriended a young slim serving lad who he later escorted to his bedroom.

The sun had risen over the house and was beating down on the lush, green lawns by ten a.m. There'd been monsoon rains a few days before, so the air was fresh and humid. In the patio area beside the house, the Senator and Chloe entertained those who'd managed to get up for breakfast. The chefs had been busy, a hot buffet breakfast awaited them on the patio, and a pleasant scent drifted over from the rose beds. The various 'partners' were long gone.

When they left the house, each guest drove away in a brand new black Ford Expedition, a personal gift from Harry Chua. Harry was also in the business of cultivating friends and he was a very generous man. He had to be to maintain his influence.

By early afternoon, Consuelo was feeling the effects of the hustle and bustle of the last few days. He retired to his bed, with Chloe. She was tired and pleased when the Senator suggested they rest for a while. They climbed into bed and snuggled into each other. Chloe stared at his face. His eyes were closed.

"Are you awake, darling?"

He replied in the affirmative straight away and opened one eye.

"Are you pleased with how the party went?"

He nodded.

"Yes, it was all I could have hoped for. You did a very good job."

She smiled.

"I wish you'd let me help you more. I'm quite capable you know."

"Yes, I know, sweetheart, I just want you to have an easy life."

He was too tired to care how patronizing that sounded, but it was enough to provoke her.

"I do have a brain and a lot of experience, you know. I was doing quite well before I met you."

Even in his semi-conscious state Consuelo now realized he'd said the wrong thing.

"Of course, I know that sweetheart," he said. "I'm sorry. I'll give you more responsibility if you really want it."

"I do," she replied. "Let me show you what I'm really capable of. Trust me, please! You know you can. Let me take care of more things for you. I could organize your press conferences and your press releases. I'm sure Simon has more important things to do."

The Senator then realized what was going on. He had sensed just a little hostility, maybe even jealousy, growing over the last year or so towards Simon. The man had indeed assumed a greater role in the Senator's life with the run up to the campaign, and Chloe resented it.

"Alright, sweetheart. You can prepare my press releases, starting tomorrow, but don't send anything out before first letting me check it."

"Of course, sweetheart."

She knew he wouldn't go back on his word and went to sleep happy.

As usual when the Senator was busy, Simon took charge of his phone. He politely fended off the many people who wanted to see him. He enjoyed making people feel important when they rang, but only allowed through those whose business was a benefit to the Senator. In spare moments he amused himself reviewing the photos taken in the guest bedrooms during the previous night by the hidden cameras put there earlier in the day by the electricians.

Simon only let one person through the net today. She was an elderly lady who had worked for the Senator for most of her life. She looked even older than her advanced years as she emerged from the small group using a walking stick and moving unsteadily. Her husband was dying of cancer, he urgently needed an operation. She was desperate and turned to Consuelo as her only hope. There would be smiles, tears, and camera clicks as he solved her problem, very publicly. She was lucky that the election was so close.

He was sitting in the garden with his usual entourage when the stooping old woman approached him. He rose and smiled broadly, then bade her sit down next to him.

"What can I do for you my dear, tell me how I can help you?"

She looked forlorn and upset, and could hardly hold back the tears. Consuelo leaned forward to calm her. He took her hand as she spoke.

"I am sorry to trouble you, sir. You've been so good to me and my family over the years. My dear husband has taken to his bed, sir, he has liver cancer. The doctors say they must take it out straight away or he'll die. I don't know what to do."

She looked up pleadingly into his eyes. This was all good stuff for his image. His photographers quietly snapped away in the background.

"I'm so sorry, my dear. You're like family to me and I'll do anything I can to help. How much do you need to get your husband the help he needs?"

She forced a smile as he looked into her eyes. "The doctors want five hundred thousand pesos to make him better, sir."

He held her hand tightly,

"You don't need to worry about it anymore, mother. Go home and look after your husband."

She had tears in her eyes now.

"Simon is going to give you a letter to take to the hospital. It will tell them that I'll personally pay all his medical bills. I promise you they'll get him taken care of."

The old lady began to cry openly. Consuelo led her gently to Simon who guided her inside, where he would write the letter. His secretary and photographer travelled everywhere with him and made sure the media were well informed about his generosity.

The Senator planned to return to the province later. His family would go back with him this time. It was a good time for the public to see 'family photos' of him with his lady and their children.

Chloe brought her own entourage with her. Her beautician and interior designer would be with them on the plane, Enrique told her she could redecorate their bathroom to give her an added incentive to come. He needed her to be smiling and happy on this trip, and she didn't want to be bored while her husband was busy politicking. Three of her girlfriends came as well to keep her company while the Senator was busy.

The Senator spoke quietly to Simon in a corner.

"Did you see the photos taken in the house last night?"

Simon nodded.

"Please follow up everyone who was at the party, make sure they're ok, and check if they have any concerns. If any of them are wavering or trying to bargain for more money get back to me straight away, we must have unity now. Anyway, we have some leverage in case any of them want to rock the boat."

Both men smiled.

The plane set down smoothly at Benguet airport. As usual, cars waited to whisk everyone off to the Estate. The children ran to the gardens, laughing happily, while maids carried suitcases upstairs to the bedrooms. Chloe and her party made themselves comfortable in the garden with glasses of chilled wine.

Consuelo was already busy with Simon.

"Who've we got coming tonight?"

Simon referred to his notebook.

"The usual boring bunch, sir. The most important Mayors and Vice-Mayors will be here—and a few Councilors."

Consuelo planned to take it easy the next day, he knew he would be having a late one that night. He used to enjoy being 'one of the boys' but he now found Provincial matters boring and the company of these small-minded men tiresome.

A large table was set in the garden. It was a warm night, with a breeze rustling through the coconut palms above.

The ten politicians waited for him around the dining table. They had already started on the third bottle of Johnnie Walker Black Label when the Senator entered the room. They rose to applaud him as he made his way to the head of the table.

Mayor Eddie Bautista from Narvacan was a distant relative. It was an effort to be nice to the boorish man, but the Senator was adept at concealing his feelings.

"I can guarantee you ninety percent in Narvacan my friend," said Bautista proudly, slapping the Senator on the back.

Consuelo hated that, but smiled through it.

"I have made sure that they are all behind you, they will do as I say," continued the Mayor.

He was happy for the chance to brag in front of his peers. The Senator played the game.

"What would I do without you, Eddie?" He laughed. "Why, I would probably lose the whole election!"

Bautista was not very bright and the sarcasm was lost on him. Everyone laughed, including Bautista.

"But why only ninety percent, my friend? How could you let ten percent of them get away?"

The laughter continued and the tone for the evening was set.

Cooks delivered hot local delicacies to the table, and made sure there were was plenty of whiskey and brandy throughout the extended meal. Consuelo enjoyed the evening more than he thought, but he was glad when the last of them left after midnight and he could go to his bed.

The next morning he slept late. He was just about to start his lunch when Simon entered.

"Sorry, sir. There're three lads outside asking to see you."

"Any idea what it's about?"

"They wouldn't say, sir. They said it's a personal matter, but they don't look like they're begging for money."

The Senator was intrigued.

"One of them used to work for you, sir. Darwin. He worked in the gardens."

"Ok, show them in. I'll give them a few minutes."

Consuelo was feeling good and sensed there might be another photo opportunity here. Maybe there was a chance to get his photo in the final edition of the Philippine Star.

CHAPTER TWO

The hidden cave in the mountains remained undisturbed for more than sixty years. No one dared to live in the remote area for a long time. Stories that the inhabitants of a whole village had disappeared mysteriously were passed down through generations. Only the brave dared to venture anywhere near the cursed area. However, over time the memories dimmed, and finally a few brave younger souls re-inhabited the area.

One morning, during the rainy season, three youths were foraging for food. To catch their breath, they rested in a shallow dip close to the base of the nearest mountain; the area was new to them. One of them spied a crack in the rock face filled by what seemed to be piles of loose rocks and covered by overhanging foliage. On either side there was solid rock.

At nineteen, Darwin was the eldest. Benny and Pedro were both seventeen. The younger boys looked to Darwin for leadership.

"This looks interesting," said Benny, trying to scrabble over the rocks.

"Well, we don't have anything else to do," said Darwin. "Let's clear away the rocks; there may be something behind."

The younger boys looked at each other, Darwin could read their faces.

"Oh, come on, don't be such babies. Don't worry about those stories. They're just old wives' tales. There're no ghosts. Let's get on with it, are we men or boys? There are three of us. Nothing's going to happen."

Bolstered by his confidence the other boys moved in and started to help. After fifteen minutes, they discovered that the rocks were blocking a narrow entranceway between the cliffs leading into a small cave. By noon, they had cleared a gap. As they squeezed their heads through the opening they could see a larger space beyond the rocks.

They cleared the narrow entrance until there was a space which they could squeeze through. It was pitch black inside and the air was musty—their bravery didn't go as far as to venture into the dark and dismal chasm just yet. They sat on the larger rocks nearby to eat their snack.

The boys discussed what they might find inside the cave. Pedro, the youngest, offered to go back to the village for torches.

"Don't talk to anyone about this," said Darwin. "They'll ask too many questions. We don't want anyone knowing, at least for now."

The boy ran through the forest. As he scampered through the dense undergrowth, his young mind thought about the possibilities, what they may find in the cave. There was no one around as he entered the village. Most people were sleeping in their huts to avoid the mid-day sun. There was very little change in their day-to-day life— the nearest shops or towns were many miles away.

Over the years, the population had risen and there were now five families, about thirty people in all. Pedro sneaked into his family house—a simple one-room shack. His father was asleep in the corner on a straw mat. Pedro quietly picked up some kerosene torches stored at the back of the lean-to shed. He found some matches in the kitchen and then crept out of the village and hurried back.

He was soon back at the cave entrance. The boys lit a torch and made their way into the cave, scrambling over the remaining rocks.

As the light dimmed the atmosphere became tense. None of the boys wanted to show it to their friends, but they all knew of the legend about the area and each had fears. They progressed in silence and stayed close together, taking confidence from each other. Darwin led, trying not to show his trepidation to the younger boys.

Ten yards into the cave they found the bones.

"Look, do you think they're human?" said Benny.

"Maybe it was a dog or a wild boar?" said Darwin.

As they lowered the torch to illuminate their find, they suddenly recoiled. There was no doubt. It was a human skeleton, small, probably a child. Their fears returned in a rush. They were more afraid and nervous now. Standing close together, they paused for a few seconds, not sure what to do, and then inched back towards the cave entrance and safety.

Darwin, as the eldest, tried to set an example to his comrades. He forced a smile.

"Don't worry, that one's been dead for a very long time."

Pedro and Benny didn't move.

"I'm scared, kuya," said Pedro.

Tears welled in his eyes. Despite his seventeen years he was immature. He tugged the shirt of the elder Benny and they backed up towards the entrance.

Darwin, despite his bravado, was not going to stay there alone. He moved to follow his comrades out of the cave, but as he turned, a metallic glint caught his eye.

"Wait up," he called out. "There's something there." He peered further into the cave and inched towards the

28

metal glint, carefully skirting the small bundle of bones. As he moved further in, with his colleagues warily following, he began to make out the outline of more skeletons lying along the walls and ledges. Their eyes were becoming accustomed to their surroundings and the dim light. They gained confidence as the walls and ceilings became more defined. The sight of human bones was not new to the boys, and in itself gave no fear—it was their tribe's tradition to preserve the bones of their ancestors and keep them wrapped up in cloth.

It was obvious that whatever had taken place there happened a long time ago. Whatever worries remained were overshadowed by anticipation and curiosity. They gave little thought as to why the skeletons were there. Tribal fights were common, although not as frequent as they used to be. There were often deaths or serious injuries from ambushes and village or family disputes

The sparkle that caught Darwin's eye was slowly becoming clearer. The torch illuminated the deeper recesses of the cave as Darwin moved forward warily. There were many large wooden boxes stacked further back in the cave. He called to the others.

"Hey, quick. There's something over here."

They ran over to him, their fears now overtaken by curiosity.

The boys were now only fifteen feet away and they could make out the glinting outline of the coins. The broken box, with its content spilling out onto the floor, was an amazing sight. Dozens of coins of different sizes lay on the floor around the box. Even through the covering of dust and dirt, it was possible to see that the coins were almost certainly gold. The boys stared at each other. They pulled the sides of the damaged box apart and shinier coins erupted from the widening gap.

"Oh my God!" exclaimed Pedro.

All three boys stood looking at each other, their mouths open.

"Come on, let's see what we've got."

He started pulling at the side of the next box; more bright shiny coins cascaded onto the floor. They managed to open a couple more of the boxes—more coins, mostly Spanish Doubloons, were revealed. All the boxes they opened contained the same. The boys stood in awe as they stared at the coins lying scattered around on the cave floor.

"Are these real?" Benny asked.

He picked up a handful of coins and let them trickle through his fingers—they made a metallic clinking as they struck the coins already on the floor. Pedro picked up a coin and bit it theatrically—he didn't know why, but he had seen it done in the movies, and they did taste very real, he thought. There were many more boxes neatly stacked further into the cave. Their young minds couldn't begin to consider the magnitude of their find and how their lives were about to change.

The air was thin in the cave.

"Come on, let's get out before the torches burn out," said Darwin. Each boy scooped up some of the coins, and then they made their way back to the exit, still awestruck from their discovery.

They sat at the cave entrance to consider their find.

"Let's get back to the village. The Captain will know what to do," said Pedro.

The other two looked at each other.

"Are you crazy?" said Darwin. "Do you think if we tell anyone in the village about this that we'll ever see any benefit from it? They'll take it over straight away and we won't get a single peso."

Benny nodded in support. Pedro felt stupid, and became defensive,

"Well what are we going to do? We can hardly walk into the shops that buy gold in Benguet City with cartloads of gold coins, can we? Even if we did, they would rip us off."

"Exactly," said Darwin. "We can't handle this on our own, but we've got to be careful. How can we make sure we get our fair share?"

They sat and thought for a while. Darwin's father had been killed three years ago in a tribal fight, so Darwin was taking care of his mother and his younger sister. Two years ago, he worked for the local Senator who used to be the Governor of Abra and still lived close by in Benguet. The Senator seemed a kindly man and had occasionally chatted to him if they passed in the garden. The Senator would help. He would know what to do.

"I have a suggestion," said Darwin. "What about the Senator? I'm sure he'll help us."

The two nodded in agreement, they could think of no alternative.

"Well, we'd better go straight there. It would be dangerous for us to carry the coins around in the village," said Darwin, standing up. "But we have to put everything back as we found it, hide the entrance again even better than when we found it."

Everyone knew Darwin at the Estate. He could get them through the gate, and then he would find Marcos the head gardener. Marcos was from their village. He could take them to the Senator. They had a few of the coins in their pockets to prove their story.

The afternoon sun was easing up as they trudged towards the highway where they would catch a bus for the thirty-minute journey to the Senator's Estate. Buses were frequent at that time of day, so they didn't wait long. It was nearly full but the air-conditioning was a welcome relief.

The magnificent Estate house and gardens were set at the top of a small hill on the left hand side, and the surrounding land encompassed a working farm. The Senator grew tobacco which provided local employment. The upper slopes were covered with immaculately landscaped gardens and walkways, magnificent palms and mango trees.

In the hills at the top of the Estate were the remains of ramshackle abandoned gold mines. There was gold in the hills, but not much, and it was difficult to mine. The bus dropped them at the bottom of the drive, together with several tourists. It was a short walk up to the Estate, to the first security gate. In front of them at the top of the drive lay the impressive house. There were three sets of barriers before you got near the inner sanctum where the Senator lived. Armed men guarded each entrance point, although they were mostly young kids, too inexperienced to use the old and dirty weapons they were carrying.

Darwin and his companions were lucky. One of the guards at the first gate was Butsoy. He was not much older than Darwin, and knew him well. He smiled as the boy approached.

"Hello, young Darwin," he said. "What brings you and your friends here today?"

"Oh, it's just a friendly visit to see Marcos. We've brought him some food from the village."

He showed Butsoy the bag that contained the scrappy remains of their lunchtime meal. Butsoy seemed satisfied. He opened the gate, and then resumed the card game with his colleagues.

It was quite a walk to the vegetable gardens where Marcos would be found at that time of day. He had a hut and a small rest area in a quiet corner away from public view. A thought occurred to Darwin as they made their way through the fruit trees.

"We must be careful with Marcos," he said. "He means well, and he's a good friend, but when he has a drink he can't keep a secret."

"We daren't tell him," said Benny. "Everyone will know."

The boys stopped. They had to decide what to do before meeting the old man.

"I know," said Darwin. "I'll tell him I want to see if there are any jobs because we need work. He'll believe that."

"Yes, but we don't want him there when we talk to the Senator. He'll think it strange that we ask him to leave," said Benny.

Darwin thought about this for a moment.

"I'll say I want to ask the Senator for a loan, and I'm embarrassed to do that in front of him."

The other boys nodded in agreement.

Marcos was resting in his hammock between two young coconut trees in a quiet corner of the garden. The old man's main job was to provide vegetables for the estate's busy kitchen. The boys spotted him a long way off and made their way through bitter melon vines and tomato plants until they reached the small coconut trees.

"Hello, Darwin. It's been a long time."

Marcos climbed out of his hammock and clasped the boy's hand warmly. He already knew Darwin's friends as they'd often visited him there.

"I know, I'm sorry that I don't get to see you more often my old friend, but I don't always have money for the bus fare."

"Oh yes, I understand, but I hope you haven't come here to borrow money from me. I can barely get by as it is."

"No, no," Darwin quickly assured the old man.

"I know that, my friend, I wouldn't even think of borrowing from you. We want to see the Senator, I really need to work now, and so do my two friends."

He glanced at the others.

"I'm also hoping that he will lend us a little money. We're really desperate, my mother can't cope, and my uncle is getting worse."

Marcos nodded.

"Well, if you catch him in the right mood he'll help you. He can be generous if it suits him. You're lucky, he's at home today. I'll take you up there and we'll see if he has time to see you."

They waited while the old man disappeared into his hut and changed into a presentable shirt and pants, and then started to make their way back towards the main house.

At the bottom of the roadway leading up to the private rooms, was the second security check. Marcos was a well-known and trusted employee and the three guards opened the gate as he approached. Another three guards were stationed at the door before the stairs. One of them pressed a few buttons on the intercom, and in a few seconds Marcos and the boys were on their way up to the residence.

At the top of the stairs, the room opened out into a large carpeted area with two sets of settees and armchairs, each seating six. Behind them were several dining sets of different sizes and a row of three computer stations along the wall with large monitors. There was a large well-polished black grand piano in one corner.

Simon greeted them at the top of the stairs.

"It's not often we see you up here, Marcos."

Simon liked the old man, and they often chatted in the garden.

"I am sure you remember Darwin," the old man said.

"Of course. How are you young man?"

He shook him firmly by the hand.

"How can I help you?"

Marcos butted in.

"The boys are shy, sir, but they want to have a word with the Senator if he's free."

"Ok," said Simon. "He usually has time for loyal and trusted employees. Let me go and see what I can do."

"Thank you, sir."

Simon soon came back into the larger reception area and shepherded the group of four into the smaller dining room. Consuelo, without rising, and chewing on his last mouthful of vegetables, motioned them to sit down. Simon waited unobtrusively in the corner of the room.

The Senator glanced up from his meal and looked at Darwin, smiling.

"How are you, son?"

"I'm fine, sir. Thank you for taking time to see us."

The Senator nodded.

"You're welcome; it's nice to see you again."

"If you don't mind, sir, I have a delicate matter of great importance to me and my family that I want to talk to you about."

The Senator was used to opening statements like this and was a bit disappointed. He wondered how much money the boy wanted. Darwin spoke quietly and directly to the Senator.

"Sir, please may we talk privately with you? This matter doesn't concern my good friend Marcos."

Marcos looked up, surprised, but held his hand up.

"No problem, I have work to do anyway."

Darwin leaned towards Marcos and put his hand on the older man's arm,

"Please don't be offended, my friend. I'll tell you about it later." Marcos rose quietly and left the room, squeezing Darwin's shoulder in a supportive gesture as he went. Darwin glanced up at Simon, who was standing in patiently in the corner.

"Simon can be trusted, son. Is it ok if he stays?" Darwin didn't want to push his luck or upset the Senator so he nodded in agreement.

Now that the matter of who could stay was settled, the Senator was keen to get to the bottom of the mystery.

"How can I help you?"

Without saying a word, Darwin took one of the coins and laid it on the table. It was one of the shinier ones which recently fell out of the box. The Senator stopped chewing his food mid-mouthful and stared down at the coin. He moved his plate to one side and picked it up for a closer inspection, and then he raised his eyes to the expectant Darwin.

"Where did you find this?"

"It was in amongst some rocks close to my village."

Consuelo sat back and thought for a while.

"Do you know what this is?"

"Maybe it's an old Spanish gold coin?" said Darwin.

His two companions sat quietly, still in awe of their surroundings and the Senator. They were happy to leave the talking to Darwin.

The stories of the Japanese retreat through the Cordillera Mountains were well known. Sometimes, people came across small coins, daggers, or jewelry that had been dropped by the hastily retreating soldiers.

The Senator lifted the coin in his hand, trying to guess the weight by its size. It was bigger than any he already owned. He looked up.

"It's a fake, it's too heavy. Probably made of lead and coated. It's not worth much but I'll give you 1,000 pesos to help your family out."

He took a 1,000-peso bill from his pocket and put it on the table.

Darwin stared at it without saying anything, and then stared out of the window ignoring the Senator's gesture. He wondered if he was right in coming here, but he'd gone too far now. There was no-one else to turn to.

He put his hands in both pockets and pulled out two fistfuls of coins that made a small pile on the table. He glanced at his friends and indicated they should do the same. When they'd finished a small mound of about sixty coins were in front of them.

"We found them in a small cave in the mountains, a couple of miles from where we live. There were a lot more of them."

Consuelo nodded, still expressionless, and sat in thought for a few moments. Darwin went on to tell him the whole story. He listened with growing interest.

"Who else knows about this?"

"We kept it to ourselves. There was no one we could trust in the village. You were the only person we could turn to for help."

"Are you sure no one saw you while you were clearing the entrance or blocking it up again?"

"The cave is in a very remote area. We've never even been here before, it was just by accident that we were there today," Darwin reassured him.

The boys told him the whole story; the skeletons, the coins on the floor, and the many large wooden crates that they had left behind them in the cave. The Senator listened quietly with absolute attention. He picked up a coin and rose from the table to examine it by the window.

Consuelo considered the situation for a moment. "How did you find it?"

"We were lucky," chirped Pedro. "You can't even see the entrance until you're right up close. We just happened to be passing, and then it took ages to clear it."

Darwin looked at him as if to say 'leave the talking to me'.

"It hadn't been disturbed for years. We made sure it looked that way again before we left."

"If you boys have discovered it then surely someone else could?"

"It's possible, I guess," conceded Darwin, "but not very likely".

The Senator made up his mind up.

"Have you eaten?"

In fact, the boys were very hungry. Their meager lunch had been a long time ago and they told the Senator that they hadn't. Consuelo nodded at Simon, dutifully standing in the corner, who was listening intently to every word. He didn't have to say anything. Simon let himself out quietly and returned a few minutes later. The boys scooped up the coins and put them in their pockets.

"Can I keep one?" the Senator asked.

Darwin agreed.

A short while later the door opened and two maids came in carrying plates of food the like of which the younger two boys had never tasted. They tucked in hungrily and put all thought of treasure aside. Consuelo stood up.

"Excuse me for a while, boys. I need to think about this and work out the best thing to do. I'll be back in an hour or so. Enjoy your meal."

He left the room with Simon following.

Consuelo had to think quickly. His campaign for the presidency was in full swing and burning money, a lot more than he had budgeted for. Here was an opportunity to refill his coffers—quietly and secretly, if he was careful.

After a quiet discussion in the corridor, Simon strode off with a clear purpose. The Senator opened a door on his right and entered a small room with a meeting table and six chairs. It was minimally but tastefully decorated, with black and chrome furniture, very modern. Consuelo sat down at the head of the table to make notes.

He didn't look up as Brian and Tom entered the room. They were two of his most trusted bodyguards, both ex-special forces. Brian was British and had served in the SAS for six years; Tom was American, and earlier in his career had been an officer in an elite American Marine Force Recon unit.

Between them, they had served Consuelo for more than twenty years. Brian was nominally head of security for the Estate, and mainly stayed in the province while Tom was in charge of Consuelo's personal security and often travelled with the Senator. Everyone knew that their roles and responsibilities went beyond that.

They were both very large framed; you would certainly want them on your side in a fight, but they were not stupid. Consuelo valued them for their brains as well as for their more sinister abilities. The Senator carefully explained the situation to them.

"These are our objectives, lads" he said. "One; find the treasure. Two; secure its transport to the safety of the Estate."

News of the find could leak out very quickly. Many people would try to deprive the Senator of at least a part of the windfall, if not all of it.

The Senator wrote out an agreement that the treasure should be split equally four ways between him and the boys which would allay their fears. While they talked, he copied out three further identical agreements.

The boys finished their meal. It was rare that there was food left over on the table when they finished a meal, but today they could not finish all that was put before them. They were feeling pleased with themselves. The Senator sent in beer. A little later he rejoined them. He sat down in his usual place at the head of the table.

"This is what we'll do. We have to act quickly to protect ourselves. We don't want someone else to find the gold, do we?"

The boys nodded.

"You'll go back with a couple of my men so that they can check it out, then we'll move the gold here for safe-keeping. I know places where we can sell it and we'll split the money four ways. How does that sound?"

He looked at them expectantly.

Darwin could not conceal his delight.

"Thank you, sir. Thank you very much, sir. Yes, that'll be fine."

The Senator produced the papers for them to sign. They didn't read them; the two younger ones could not read anyway. After putting their marks at the bottom on the single page they each passed a copy to the Senator. Darwin gave a cursory look over his, before signing. Consuelo offered them some more beer and asked them to wait.

Simon came to fetch them thirty minutes later. He led them through some passages to a small graveled courtyard enclosed on three sides. Brian and Tom were waiting by the door.

"Hello, lads," said Brian.

The boys were shy with the large foreigners, but they all shook hands. The men tried not to look intimidating and failed. Although they appeared unarmed, this was deceptive. Their Berretta pistols were concealed in the inside pockets of their flak jackets, along with various knives and daggers.

The group piled into the old Chevrolet Tahoe that waited with its engine running in the courtyard. The car was dark green, almost black. It'd seen better days, but it would blend in well with the forest on a dark evening. Simon jumped into the driver's seat and off they went. Darwin and his friends took the middle seats with the two men filling the back; all of them were quiet as they set off.

After about ten miles, Darwin spoke.

"Pull off here, it's not far now."

They were just outside the village of Santiago. Simon looked around; he wasn't going to leave the car on the side of the road. He found a nearby clearing and parked the car as far off the road as he could, under the shade of two large trees. When he was satisfied that no one could see it from the road he turned off the engine.

They prepared for the trek. Eagerly, Darwin led them up the gentle incline through the dense undergrowth; there was no path to follow. Simon remained behind with the car. After the others had gone he sat down on the grass with his back against the car and lit a cigarette. He took his phone out of his top pocket and began texting.

Soon the ground leveled out, the undergrowth thinned and the going got easier. After about fifteen minutes the undergrowth opened out on their left and they moved towards the foothills.

Following a small stream, they soon reached the concealed entrance and the boys set about clearing while the men quietly scouted the area to ensure they were alone. Brian and Tom were well trained in surveillance, but so was Paul.

Paul Rowntree was an old soldier. He left the Australian Army when he was forty-five, after a stint as a Corporal in Special Forces. At sixty-nine, he was still very fit and hiked several times a week in the mountains. In all, he'd spent nine years in Special Operations based in New South Wales and had acted as a mercenary and a bodyguard to some very rich people. He was camped out near the top of the larger hill on the right hand side.

He always enjoyed the outdoors and was out that afternoon walking the hills, looking out for wildlife. He lived in the nearby village of Santiago with his beautiful young Filipina wife, Lucy, and their son Dennis, who was twelve. Paul was through and through a military man and he missed the army life. He was reasonably happy with his life, but it hadn't turned out how he'd expected.

Since leaving the army, Paul had worked a few protection and security jobs, but they dried up as he got older. He'd also tried his luck at several business ventures, all of which had ended in a failure, some at great expense. He tried to be a good father but wasn't naturally inclined to parental responsibilities, and as Dennis grew up he tended to treat the boy as a recruit under his command rather than as a son.

He first spotted the group when they broke cover to follow the stream; he followed their progress with interest. They were moving furtively, looking around to make sure they were alone, he thought that was odd. He captured their progress with his telephoto lens along the way. Instinct and training told him to lay low and observe.

Brian and Tom scouted the area and returned to the cave entrance. By then the boys had cleared enough of an opening for them to squeeze inside. The men followed the boys through the gap with a struggle. Their powerful flashlights lit up the cave.

"Wow, look at all those bones," said Benny.

They could see many more skeletons now.

"C'mon, let's check out these boxes."

Brian and Tom moved over to the stacked chests.

Everything else was just as the boys said. Brian and Tom counted the boxes. Then they opened six more at random. In every box gold coins glinted and sparkled.

"Let's see what's further on in."

Brian took Darwin by the shoulder and guided him forward.

"Make some tea ready for when we get back," he said over his shoulder.

The cave narrowed, and then opened out beyond a bend to the left. A wide gulley came into view on their right. Darwin trod carefully along and around the edge following a narrow walkway running along the wall on the left. He peered beyond into the dark depths of the cave and hesitated when the pathway widened a little.

The first thing he knew about Brian silently moving up close behind him was a powerful arm around his neck squeezing his throat, stopping his breathing. His surprise gave way to fear and pain in less than a second as a six-inch blade slid through his tee shirt and between his ribs, piercing his heart. The silent murder took five seconds— thankfully, he felt little pain. There was no time for any resistance. He flopped like a rag doll into Brian's arms.

Brian was careful not to get any blood on his clothes as he pushed the lifeless body into the gulley. At that point it was deep enough that the body could not be seen unless you really leaned right over. There was not much blood on the knife but Brian wiped it and replaced it into the depths of his jacket. Casually he made his way back to join the others.

They were standing around and examining the boxes and their contents as Brian returned. No one had started to make tea.

"Where's Darwin?" asked Pedro.

"He's taking a piss. We didn't find any more treasure," said Brian as he sidled up to one boy in a casual manner while Tom positioned himself next to the other. At Brian's imperceptible nod, in a synchronized movement they grabbed both boys around the throat and stabbed them expertly. Their co-ordination was perfect, as if rehearsed. There was no sound except for a low splutter as they sank to the floor. Their eyes were still open but their faces were blank.

They dragged the boys like sacks of potatoes and dropped them over the edge into the deep gully to join their friend. Without looking back, they moved out of the cave and began restoring the rocks and camouflage to the entrance.

A flask of tea and some sandwiches appeared from Brian's rucksack. They planned to be there for a while. Nearby were some rocks where they could sit and wait.

Paul was still observing them. Clearly, the men were going to hang around for a while so Paul, way up on the opposite hillside, also made himself comfortable. He moved slowly, always being careful to remain unseen.

About two hours after the men and boys left him, Simon received the call from Brian he expected.

"We're all set."

"Any problems? Is it all true?"

Yeah, it's true, and no, no problems. The problems are in a pit at the back of the cave. We won't be seeing them again."

Simon started the engine, backed out onto the road, and headed back to Benguet. His phone rang.

"Yes, sir, it's all true, and we don't have to worry about the boys."

"Ok. See you back here, the truck will be ready."

Paul sat in his makeshift hide. He was puzzled. Why were Brian and Tom the only ones to come out of the cave?

Dusk was approaching and the men lay down and rested, taking it in turns to stay awake. They moved about a hundred yards away from the entrance and into the bushes, just in case anyone came along. Paul was glad the infrared vision on his binoculars gave him a clear view of their position. Brian and Tom nodded off occasionally as they rested beneath the branches. Paul did not.

At about two a.m., Brian's phone rang. He answered curtly and then stood up and prepared to meet the truck. He shook Tom awake and left him there as he departed down the hill. Paul followed Brian's progress as far as he could until he disappeared. He usually went home earlier than this, but he was fascinated with the scene and determined he would stay until it had played out.

Brian reached the road in ten minutes; it was easier going downhill. He settled into the bushes so as not to be noticeable, until a familiar three ton Elf truck approached. Simon was driving but there were four other men, two in the cab and two riding in the back.

The four men jumped out and began to clear the undergrowth and bushes so that the truck wouldn't be visible from the road. Tom was nearly finished with clearing the cave entrance as the men appeared. Without a word, they all helped to finish the job and then disappeared into the cave.

Brian and Tom watched from the back of the cave to make sure the workers didn't venture further inside. They didn't want the men to see the bodies. One man had brought tools and nails to repair the boxes.

After about twenty minutes, the three pairs of men emerged from the cave carrying boxes between them. In a silent line, they proceeded down the hill. Paul had a clear view and took more photos.

Over the next two hours, Paul counted twenty-three boxes being carried from the cave. Finally, the entrance was concealed and the men trudged back down the hill. The roads were quiet at this time, just a few commercial vehicles travelling through the night. The slow returning truck laden with boxes didn't attract attention. They only passed one or two other vehicles on the whole journey.

Paul waited until dawn and then made his way home. He went the long way around. He didn't expect them to come back, but he had to be sure.

CHAPTER THREE

Lucy was making breakfast as she heard Paul come through the gate. She wasn't worried when she woke earlier to find he wasn't there. Paul often stayed out all night on his mountain hikes. Anyhow, nowadays she preferred to be on her own.

The infatuation she first felt for the much older man had gone years ago. Nevertheless, she was relieved when she heard him open the gate. At his age, although he was still fit, he might not come home one day. They were no longer close, but he represented security and a safe, if modest, future.

"Hi, sweetheart," he said, as he smiled and kissed her briefly on the lips. She made his usual cup of tea and started to cook bacon. He seemed thoughtful.

"Are you ok?"

"Yes, I'm fine, love," he said as he took his hot tea from her.

"That bacon smells good. Any chance of some baked beans?"

Without a word, Lucy took a tin from the cupboard. She poured them into the pan with the bacon. That was how Paul liked them.

"Not much going on last night. At least it was cool; I managed to get some sleep."

"That's good," she replied automatically, while buttering two slices of bread.

Dennis came down into the kitchen just as Lucy was making Paul a second cup of tea. He didn't realize his father had been out all night until he spotted the hiking gear by the door.

"Oh, you went out last night, Dad?"

"Yes, just down the road up to the top of the ridge, nothing special. I couldn't take you, you've got school today."

"I know, I know."

Dennis loved to go out at night with his dad, but he couldn't argue. Paul never took him on school nights.

Paul had begun to feel his age recently. He excused himself and went upstairs to sleep for a while.

At around noon he woke, and after a few moments he remembered the events of the night before. After showering and shaving, he came downstairs to find his son on the computer in the study playing a war game.

"Sorry, son, I need the computer for a while. I need peace and quiet."

The boy was disappointed to have to finish in the middle of a battle with friends, but he knew better than to argue with his father. As Dennis left, Paul shut the door.

Lucy was preparing lunch, but she heard Paul come down the stairs. She wasn't going to disturb him during what she assumed was one of his regular sessions browsing for porn.

Paul settled down and linked his camera to the computer. One by one, he downloaded the photos into a password protected folder. His military training taught him the value of security. He didn't know who the younger boys were, but he recognized Brian and Tom straight away.

Paul was a frequent visitor to the Senator's house and he knew the Senator's brother, Tony. The Senator liked to cultivate relationships with foreigners. Paul knew Brian on first name terms as they had a similar background and a few common friends.

Was there another way out of the cave or were they still in there? He was intrigued by the boxes. What was in them? A few hours earlier, just as light was beginning to creep over the horizon, the truck, laden with boxes, arrived back at the Estate. The workers were tired, but their night's work was not done. The guards opened the double gates when the truck approached.

There were a series of isolated farm buildings beyond the fruit orchards, about a quarter of a mile from the main Estate. They formerly housed the Senator's racehorses – a passing fad that ended many years ago. The furthest one housed old farm machinery. They stopped right outside. Two men jumped off the back of the truck to open the doors.

They moved all the old bits of machinery to one side, and stacked the boxes as far into the corner as they could. Brian and Tom helped them, it would be light soon. Simon drove them back to the house as dawn was breaking.

A private dining room close to the kitchen was set up for the recently arrived workers. Brian and Tom brought them in. Breakfast appeared—they were being treated well. The Senator slipped into the room an hour later, and they all rose but he motioned them to sit down.

"Come on then, tell me all about it. I want to know how it went last night."

"The lads were brilliant," said Brian. "We got it done with time to spare; they were almost as good as soldiers,"

The others laughed.

"Any problems?" asked the Senator.

"No, everything went smoothly. We actually finished a couple of hours ahead of time."

"Well done. Your efforts will be handsomely rewarded."

He said no more, but when they'd all finished, he produced four fat envelopes and handed them out.

"You must never tell anyone about last night, not even wives or girlfriends," he said solemnly. "I'll look after you boys, you know that. There'll be plenty of work in the future, and more bonuses, but no one must know about last night. Don't let me down. You'll regret it if you do"

They were not quite sure what the Senator meant by that, but no one dared to ask him.

"You've done well. You can go and spend some time with your families now."

They took that as a hint they should leave, and backed out of the room nodding as they left.

Simon made sure that none of the men knew each other. They all came from different villages. None of them would live to collect their 'bonus', Consuelo's orders were that their 'disappearances' should start within days.
In the village fifty miles away, the families were becoming concerned. Daniel, Darwin's uncle was reassuring the boys' mother. The boys sometimes stayed out all night hunting, or fishing. They would probably turn up later—hopefully with a good catch.

"Stop fussing woman. He's a man now, he can look after himself. He's probably catching lots of fish and doesn't want to come home yet."

"Maybe,"

She didn't sound very reassured.

"He's never been out all night before."

"Don't be silly woman. He's with his friends. He's alright,"

She brightened a little.

"I guess you're right," she smiled.

The Senator was drinking his mid-morning coffee when his phone rang. Simon answered it.

"It's someone called Michael for you, from Manila. He says he's returning your call."

Consuelo put his cup down and took the phone.

"Hi, Michael. Thank you for calling back. How's the jewelry business these days?"

The Senator was a frequent customer in a boutique store in Greenbelt and had become friendly with the owner, Michael – one of the most qualified and experienced appraisers in Manila.

"Not so bad, sir, not so bad, and how's the election business?"

"We're quietly confident Michael, and I think we'll be alright. Listen my friend, I need to you come here and value some jewelry for me, but this must be kept very secret. I don't want anyone, especially the press, to get wind of this. I need you to come up here straight away and to keep this to yourself. I have a plane waiting for you at the domestic airport. You will be very well rewarded, but you must come right now."

"No problem, Senator, my assistants here can cope. I can be on my way in twenty minutes."

"Good man. I'll see you later. Don't tell your staff where you're going, though."

"You can rely on me, sir. I won't let you down,"

Twenty minutes later Michael was in a taxi and on the way to the airport. He arrived early in the evening, and by seven p.m. he was in the garden with the Consuelo having dinner.

"Thank you for coming so quickly, Michael. I really do appreciate it,"

"It's no problem, sir. It's a pleasure to help you. It sounds quite exciting."

Michael did not want to seem pushy, but he was curious. What did he have to value? Why the need for secrecy, and more importantly, what would he be paid? When the meal was over, the Senator opened the subject.

"I've got something special to show you, but I want you to see it tomorrow when you're fresh."

Consuelo put his hand on Michael's arm conspiratorially.

"You will be amazed. I can assure you it'll be worth the wait."

Brian and Tom managed to grab some sleep, but were disturbed by a phone call from the boss late afternoon. As soon as dusk began to fall, they made their way to the barn again. They crept along the hedgerows and bushes so that no one would see them. Many vehicles coming and going from the deserted barn could attract attention.

"This lot must be worth an absolute fortune," Brian said, as they lifted one of the heavier boxes between them.

"I guess so. What d'you reckon, twenty million dollars?"

"More like thirty million, I think. Just think what we could do with that."

"Yeah, that's right. Luxury forever; never having to work again."

"Except we'd spend the rest of our lives looking over our shoulder, waiting for the boss to send someone to kill us!"

Brian laughed.

"It's nice to dream, though, isn't it?"

His colleague nodded. They took a break and got out their flasks.

"We don't do so badly, really, I suppose,"

"No, I suppose not,"

"And so we should for what we do!" Tom nodded.

"How long do you think you'll keep this game up, then?"

"Oh, I have a plan," Tom said, mysteriously. "How about you?"

"Yes, me too. I want out of this game as soon as I can. A couple of more year maybe..."

"Oh well," he said. "In the meantime..."

Tom stood up and picked up another box. They finished by midnight and headed back for a late night meal and a couple of hours sleep.

It was still dark a few hours later. The sun would rise in an hour or so. Simon was already waiting with a 4 x 4 in the courtyard behind the kitchen. The Senator and his guest appeared a few minutes later. Simon opened the back door and the two men climbed in. They set off for the barn. As they arrived, the doors swung open.

The sight that greeted was incredible. All the old machinery was stacked tidily at the sides of the barn and in the center, arranged neatly like a display of vegetables in a supermarket, were many wooden crates. Each one was open. Thousands of glistening coins reflected the bright glow from the lamps placed around the barn by the bodyguards earlier.

Consuelo gasped. It was much more than he'd imagined. Michael stood transfixed; the Senator brought him out of his trance by gently guiding him forward and giving him a large notebook and several pens. Michael had also brought testing chemicals and equipment.

Both men walked forward in wonderment. Up close, they stooped down and picked up various coins.

"Is this what I think it is?" Michael asked. "Yamashita's gold?"

"I think so, but I need you to confirm that it's genuine and tell me what it's worth."

Michael was recovering now and thinking of the fat fee he could charge, not just for his professional services, but also for his discretion.

"An accurate valuation will require about a week," he said, mentally beginning to clear his schedule for the next few days.

Consuelo laughed.

"It's ok, I only need a rough estimate, and I can give you three or four hours."

Michael raised his eyebrows. His valuation would be very rough, but he wasn't going to upset the Senator.

"Ok, I can test the purity of the gold but I need much larger scales to weigh it."

Simon was dispatched to find scales while Michael set up his equipment. He quietly started his work.

By mid-morning, Consuelo and Michael were on their way back to the house. Brian and Tom were busy covering up the gold.

Michael smiled at Consuelo.

"I suppose there's no point in asking about the provenance of the gold—knowing where it came from would assist in a more accurate valuation."

The Senator grinned.

"It really is better that you don't know. If I told you I would have to kill you."

Both men laughed at the joke, but Michael didn't realize just how serious the statement was. They arrived back at the house and sat in the garden with coffee and sandwiches.

"You could never sell this on the open market of course, but if you could, in one go, you could expect about this much."

He handed Consuelo a slip of paper on which he had written the sum of sixty million dollars. Consuelo smiled; the Presidency was his without a doubt. Simon joined them then. He was carrying a black briefcase which he placed before the Senator and opened. The Senator took out bundles of American dollars. Michael's eyes were wide.

The Senator carefully counted the money back into the case and handed it to Simon.

"Simon will give you this when you get to Manila."

Michael grinned as he shook the Senator's hand. The case contained two hundred thousand dollars.

"I'm sorry but I have no plane available today. Is it ok if Simon takes you back by car?"

Thirty minutes later they set off.

After passing through San Fernando, they reached the open countryside.

"Is it ok with you if we visit my fish supplier, he's just five minutes off the road?" Simon asked.

Michael was lost in thought, but nodded. He asked Simon to take him to the Shangri-la Hotel in Makati where he intended to eat the best food and sleep with the most beautiful women he could pay for.

They turned off the road onto a dirt track that was overgrown and obviously little used. They climbed the side of a hill, travelling slowly along the bumpy road. Michael got a little concerned.

"Your fish supplier certainly lives in a remote place."

"Yes, he likes his seclusion, but his fish is delicious. I'll get you some."

The track petered out just before the land started to rise up more steeply. There was a dense thicket of trees rising up ahead and the vehicle stopped just short of the incline.

"Come on, it's a short walk up the hill."

Michael sighed but followed. Simon strode off ahead with Michael struggling to keep up behind.

After a few minutes, they came to the edge of a cliff with a sheer rock face falling away maybe two hundred meters down to the secluded valley below.

"Come and see the view," Simon said, striding towards the cliff.

Michael followed but was afraid to get close to the edge. Simon turned around and made as if to walk past him.

Michael didn't feel the knife blade enter his neck and wondered for a second why his neck felt wet. As his mouth filled with blood, the pain shot through him. He couldn't shout or move and felt himself falling to the ground. Before he hit the ground, he was dead.

Simon searched the body and removed all forms of identification. Why should he make things easy for the investigators, if ever there were any? He hauled the body close to the edge and tipped it gently over. It fell into a deserted gulley full of large boulders. This was a difficult area to reach; the body was unlikely to ever be discovered.

The casual stroll back to the car took just five minutes. He dialed a number on his phone—it was answered in two rings.

"I'll be back soon, love, let's try to get a couple of hours to ourselves tonight."

He listened while the other party replied.

"Yeah, I guess these have been a tiring few days. Anyway, it's not long now, eh? Keep your chin up—we'll soon be away from it all."

He laughed at the response and closed the phone.

The sun was setting as Paul started walking along the highway on his way back to the foot of the mountains and the cave. He would still leave it another day or two before exploring the cave, but he was curious as to whether Consuelo's people had been back. It was early evening as he crossed over the main road about a mile from Santiago.

A very smart black Ford Expedition sped past him on its way to Benguet. Paul recognized the Senator's secretary, but Simon didn't notice Paul. His eyes were fixed on the road.

Paul walked on a further five hundred yards before turning off the road towards the hills. There was some traffic now; this was what passed for a 'rush hour' in the area. No one saw him leave the road as he set off through the undergrowth. There was a path worn where the men had carried the boxes. Paul chose to walk about five yards parallel to this track; he didn't want it to become even more obvious. Luckily, it petered out when the route became rockier.

Before he had gone five hundred yards, his eagle eyes noticed movement halfway up the hillock on the other side of the valley, maybe a quarter of a mile away. He made his way through the valley and up the side of the mountain. As he approached, he saw a group of men. They were calling out a name as they searched the bushes

Paul showed himself and approached the group. He knew many people in the local villages and they recognized him.

"Hello, Daniel. Are you ok?" Daniel had a stall in the market in Santiago selling produce the village had collected in the mountains. Paul could see that something was wrong; Daniel was trying not to cry.

"It's Darwin, my nephew, and his friends. They've been away from the village for a long time now. They haven't been home for two nights."

Daniel was a sick man. He was recovering from a stroke and still couldn't walk well. This worry was not helping—he looked ten years older than when Paul last saw him only a few weeks ago.

"I'll look out for them on my travels."

Paul remembered the three lads who had gone into the cave. He was hoping that the two events were not connected.

"Thank you, my dear friend," said Daniel, clasping Paul's hand tightly. Paul pulled it away gently and set off back into the trees. He took a different direction; he didn't want the group to see exactly where he was heading.

The men were well away from the area by now but he scouted around before approaching the entrance, just to be sure. Then he checked the markers, he would know if anything had been disturbed.

Simon was back at the estate. It was not every day that you killed a man and made a hundred thousand dollars. He never enjoyed killing, but had become used to it. It didn't bother him much.

He ate a quiet dinner in the kitchen before going to his room which was on the third floor. He walked the corridors, checking the other rooms; he was alone on the floor. After quietly closing the door to his room he opened his phone and pressed speed dial one. Someone answered the phone in two rings. Simon spoke first.

"It's ok."

The phone went down at the other end. Two minutes later, a thin figure noiselessly climbed the secluded back stairway to the third floor and made its way along the corridor. Simon's door was unlocked and the figure entered without knocking and shut the door carefully. It didn't open again that night.

The next day, Consuelo prepared to receive a guest. The sleek white jet arrived at his private airport just after noon. The black, heavily tinted car was waiting to take him to the house.

Alexi Khalid was a frequent visitor to the Estate. He and Consuelo were close business associates. He was the brother-in-law of the President of Afghanistan; many people said he was the power behind the throne.

Probably in his early fifties, he had a disarming smile and an air of innocence. Most people put him at around forty. He had a bulging waistline; in the West he would be considered 'portly'. A neatly trimmed thin beard adorned his slightly chubby face and his long hair was tied at the back with a bow. His hair was dyed jet black. He was an imposing character who would be difficult to forget.

The Senator had phoned Alexi yesterday—both men were used to seizing opportunities quickly when it was necessary. This time the request had been quite unusual.

"Do you want to buy some gold, Alexi?"

"I know you have some gold mines there, my friend, but I thought you got rid of that domestically. Don't tell me you are doing so well you are trying to export it now."

"I wish, Alexi, I wish. No, I just came into a bit of good fortune, that's all, and I want to share it with you."

"That's intriguing my friend. Do tell me more."

"Well, let's just say that I was lucky enough to find some treasure that somebody left behind, many years ago."

Alexi was an educated man. Consuelo wondered if he would pick up on his meaning.

"You mean you have found Yamashita's gold?" He sounded incredulous. "How much did you find?"

The Senator didn't feel comfortable discussing this further on the phone. The lines were supposed to be secure, but you could never be sure.

"Why don't you come and see for yourself?" Consuelo suggested. He knew the man would come.

"Ok, I will. Can I fly down tomorrow?"

"Of course, it will be great to see you."

"Are you serious about selling the gold?"

"Oh yes, for the right price."

Alexi laughed again.

"You'll never change, my friend. I'd better bring an appraiser with me then."

They finally agreed that Alexi would come early the next day. Consuelo would send a car to fetch him from the small local airport, as he always did. It was just arriving back at the Estate with its V.I.P passengers.

The guards opened the gates in advance for the arriving car—this was one visitor you did not stop. They saluted as the car drove through. The Senator was waiting by the door with his family. Putting his arm around Alexi's shoulder, Consuelo guided him into the palatial dining room reserved for special occasions and special guests.

"It's been too long, Alexi. We've not seen you here for nearly a year."

Consuelo guided him to his seat, next to his favorite wife, Yasmin, who had already taken her seat. The Senator sat down beside Alexi.

"You know, I am going to be the next President of this country soon, my friend."

"I do read the papers, and it does look like you stand a good chance of getting there."

"It's in the bag, nothing can go wrong now."

"I'm sure you are right, Enrique. I've always known you would get there eventually."

The Senator put his hand on the Alexi's arm.

"When I'm living in the Presidential Palace we'll be able to do a lot more business together."

"Yes, I expect we will. Power opens doors, to be sure."

"Now listen, my friend. That is why I need your help. Elections cost money—lots of it. I need to turn this gold into money, American dollars, quickly. Don't worry, the price will be fair."

Alexi sat back.

"My dearest friend, you know I'll do anything to help you, but of course it will depend on what is on offer and the price."

"Of course, of course."

The six-hour flight was beginning to take its toll on the guests. Alexi excused himself; he and his entourage needed to rest before dinner. Consuelo took the opportunity to catch up with calling his campaign managers.

The first call was to the Mayor of Manila, Manuel Decena. The man could help to deliver the large Manila Civil Servant and workers vote.

"Hello Manuel, how's it going?"

The Mayor responded smartly.

"It's going well. I've met with the labor leaders, and as many civil service heads as I could. They all know things are going your way now, and none of them wants to back a loser. There's just one thing, Senator."

Consuelo expected this and laughed

"Ok, who do we need to pay off now and how much is it going to cost?"

"Hehe, you know what I need already, the mark of a natural leader."

Both men laughed.

"Enough of the flattery, my friend. Give me the details."

"Ok, the transport services union leader wants ten million pesos to endorse you."

The Senator whistled.

"Wow, he thinks highly of himself, doesn't he?"

"Well, that's true sir, but he is very influential among his three hundred thousand members."

"Yes I suppose you're right. Ok, you can promise it to him. I'll get it to you in a couple of days."

Mayor Decena immediately picked up his phone again and dialed the number of the transport services union leader.

"I have good news for you, he has agreed. The Senator will give you five million for your support."

"Well done, Mayor, and thank you."

The deal was done.

Consuelo continued down his list of calls. It was nearly dinner time now, the guests started drifting downstairs again and within an hour they were gathered in the dining room. Consuelo again sat next to Alexi.

"So, when will I see this amazing find of yours?" Alexi spoke quietly. Their discussions were not for the whole table to hear.

"Let's relax and enjoy ourselves, Alexi, and I will take you to see it right after dinner."

"That will be fine, thank you. I will need to leave no later than tomorrow evening."

"That'll be good timing as I have to get back to the election work."

Simon drove the two men, together, with one of Alexi's guards and his appraiser to the barn. Brian and Tom had transformed it again. The door slowly swung open and the Aladdin's cave of treasure was revealed. Alexi was taken aback. He hadn't expected this and couldn't disguise his amazement. The Senator smiled—he had never seen Alexi at a loss for words before.

"My friend, how on earth could you find so much treasure? There must be tons of gold here."

The Senator put his hand on the man's shoulder.

"Good fortune comes to those who deserve it," he said. The appraiser set to work, going through very similar steps to the ones that the now deceased Michael had earlier taken.

The next morning, Alexi and his wives descended the wide staircase, deep in conversation. Consuelo could see them from the drawing room where he sat enjoying the first coffee of the day. He wondered which one of his wives he'd slept with last night, maybe both? *I guess there must be some advantages to being a Muslim*, he thought to himself.

He waved and called; Alexi and the girls looked up and acknowledged him. They came across the hallway and joined him in the drawing room.

"Can we go and find Chloe?" asked Yasmin, looking pleadingly at her husband.

"We're going to be very bored if you men start talking about business and stuff."

"Yes, of course you can."

"She's in the bedroom with the kids, go on up, she's dressed. She'll be pleased to see you," the Senator said.

The girls made their escape.

After a couple of moments, Alexi opened the subject.

"That was quite a surprise last night, Enrique. I have never seen such a sight. So much gold in one place boggles the mind."

"I thought you would be surprised."

"How much of it do you want to sell?"

"All of it."

Alexi raised his eyebrows.

"Whew, that's a lot of gold to move. How much do you want for it?"

The Senator gave him a figure.

"I'm sorry, I can't pay that much for it," Alexi said, trying to look regretful.

In fact, Alexi received a report from his appraiser very early in the morning. He knew that the price the Senator wanted was cheap.

"Look my friend, you know the gold's genuine, and you know it's worth a lot more than that. You're getting a real bargain. I'm only doing it because I need the money for my election, I need it quickly, and I need to do it without any fuss. There are few men in the world that could do this, but I know you're one of them."

"Well, ok, the price is good. I will give you twenty million dollars now and the other forty million when I get the gold."

The Senator nodded.

"How will we transport the gold? Small amounts are easy to deal with, but such a large amount may present a problem."

"I've already thought of that," Consuelo confirmed. "There would be too much interest if we tried to move it by air or by sea, and I couldn't trust the local customs officers, there is far too much money involved. What if we deliver to your embassy in Manila? You could fly it out from Manila airport. Use your status here—you have diplomatic privilege."

"I guess that might work. I can get the rest of the money to the embassy in a few days, and then we could do the swap. Let's work on the detail over the next few days. We have a deal."

They shook hands.

Consuelo was passing Simon's room just before lunch. Jake, the hairdresser, was coming out with the remains of Simon's early lunch. When he was not busy with haircuts or make up, Jake helped in the kitchen. As soon as Jake was gone, the Senator spoke to Simon.

"Alexi will take it all, but we need to deliver it to the Afghan embassy in Manila."

Simon was lying on the bed. He sat up and nodded.

"I'll tell you when. We can get Brian or Tom to bring it up. In the meantime, please brief them about it."

"Ok, that's fine, sir. I will."

The Senator shut the door and was off down the corridor before Simon finished speaking.

All was quiet at the Estate when the convoy of four cars left for the airport at midnight. Alexi's car pulled up alongside the plane, and they waited for the Senator to arrive. The tiny airport was nearly deserted, just a skeleton crew.

Two of Alexi's staff brought out four slim black cases and loaded them into the Senator's car. The two men hugged and shook hands, and Enrique watched as his friend climbed the steps.

As the plane rose into the night sky, they set off back to the Estate. The Senator drove the first car. After passing through the gate he slowly followed the road around the left hand side of the house and up the incline.

At the top of the hill was a derelict four-story structure. It would have included an entertainment complex, with restaurants, bars, parking and accommodation. He abandoned the project seven years ago; criticism by the powerful Catholic Church would cause problems to his political ambitions.

In places, iron bars, now rusty, stuck up from the unfinished concrete floors.

The basement area, designed as a store for liquor, was accessible through one staircase. A reinforced metal door at the bottom of the stairway blocked the entrance to the storage rooms beyond. Vents to allow airflow rose through the ceilings and upwards emerging through the grass.

The Senator drew up to the secluded structure well after midnight. He used a small flashlight to guide his path through the now dense grass and small bushes. It would have been manicured lawns and exotic trees by now if the project had been completed.

The padlock on the door was new. The old rusted one had been recently replaced in anticipation of the new use for the structure. The Senator ordered that an additional padlock be put on the door. He kept all the keys—he would maybe later give a set to Brian.

Beyond the padlocked door was a corridor with two rooms off on either side. All of them were empty, the walls and floors unfinished and dirty.

He brought the three cases down one by one; he did not want to lose his footing on the narrow stairs. He piled them in the far corner of the first room on the right, and then checked all the rooms before he locked up. For good measure, he found an old sheet and threw it over the cases. One case was still in the car; he would need money for his campaign.

It was nearly two a.m. when he slowly drove back down and quietly let himself into the house. Chloe would be asleep. Consuelo saw the light on in his study. Simon was there poring over some sheets of handwritten figures.

"Hello sir, just finishing off the day's accounts." Simon had free run of the Senator's office.

"How are we doing?"

He didn't really need to ask. He kept very good accounts in his head.

"Well, we should make it through to the election, but we'll need the rest of the money from Alexi to make good our post-election promises."

The Senator smiled—the timing couldn't be better.

"Thanks, Simon. Go get some rest now. We have another busy day tomorrow."

CHAPTER FOUR

"Are you going to the mountains tonight, dad? Can I come?" Dennis asked, when he saw his father preparing.

"If you want to help you can come and act as a look-out but you'll be on your own for a couple of hours. Do you want to do that?"

The boy's face brightened and he ran back down the stairs.

"Thanks dad, that's great."

Dennis was impatient to get going. His father told him that he had a 'special mission' tonight. Dennis would play an important part. He rushed his food and waited outside, impatiently, for his dad.

After following the highway for nearly hour, they reached the spot. Paul guided them away from the road, and they sat down in a grassy clearing about twenty meters away.

Paul made sure his son was well hidden, then set off for the cave. The part-trodden path was still there, but it had rained so it was not as visible as before. It didn't matter, Paul knew his way now. Twenty minutes later he reached the cave. Everything seemed quiet and deserted. It took him thirty minutes to remove enough debris from the entrance to squeeze past and into the cave.

Inside, the stones underfoot were slippery, he trod carefully. The light dimmed further in, but his flashlight helped. He inched his way inside, pausing until his eyes became accustomed.

"Hello—is there anyone there?"

There was no reply. As he moved fully into the cave, the eerie sight greeted him. Old bones now lay in uneven piles along the sides of the cave and lined the bottom of the wall like some macabre decor. He carefully recorded the scene and moved on.

Two years in Afghanistan had taught him many lessons, especially about exploring caves. This training served him well now. Had any traps been set? Were there any unwelcome surprises? The *Indiana Jones* movies came into his head as he moved forward.

Further into the cave the floor was dry. It widened on the right, with a floor area cleared of rocks and debris. There was a large bare space, but there were scrape marks on the floor. He quickly realized that this was where the boxes came from.

Something bright caught his eye among the tiny rocks. He bent down and picked up the coin, wiping it on his shirt. It was small compared with the coins already taken, which was probably why earlier visitors had missed it. Paul polished it on his shirt until it was shiny. The detail was still very clear. He knew immediately what it was. After placing it on a ledge to photograph, he put it in his pocket.

He sifted through the dirt and debris on the floor of the cave and found several coins of different sizes.

As he moved further into the cave an unpleasant smell slowly became apparent. He knew that smell—it brought back discomforting memories and he was immediately on his guard. Time in the front lines of many jungle and desert battles meant he knew well the smell of rotting flesh.

He moved along quietly, following the wall into the widening cave. The stench was very strong now. The deep gulley opened up on the right. He covered his face with his handkerchief, but it wasn't helping much. Warily, he peered over and shone his torch down. The sight that met him was straight out of a bloody horror movie.

Sprawled out on top of each other were the decaying bodies of the three young men. They were fully clothed, but their exposed flesh was partly eaten away by the grateful rats and maybe other animals that called the cave home. With the flesh mostly stripped from the skulls, they grinned up at him through empty eye sockets.

Paul had seen death and destruction in his time; he had caused much of it himself. Such scenes held no horror for him but these boys were only a few years older than Dennis was. He made his way out of the cave as quickly as he could. There was nothing he could do for the poor boys. They'd obviously been murdered. There was no point alerting the local police, they would do nothing, especially if they knew the Senator was involved.

In his colorful life, he had killed many men, but in his opinion they all deserved to be dead and he lost no sleep at night on account of their deaths. This was different, however. Young lives had been snuffed out like candles— for greed. He felt angry. He couldn't let this go. He had to do something.

Outside the cave, he rang his son to check that everything was ok. Dennis was dozing off, but tried to sound alert when he spoke to his father. Yes, he was fine and no one had come along.

Paul set about resealing the cave entrance and began the trek back down the hill. They would soon be on their way home. They could still get most of a night's sleep. Tomorrow Paul would give the matter more thought. It was his way to sleep on things before making decisions, it gave him a clearer perspective.

Dennis was dozing when his father reached him. They were both tired and spoke little on the walk home, which thankfully was downhill. When they arrived, they crept in through the back door so as not to wake Lucy and went straight to their beds.

After breakfast the next morning, Paul retired to the shaded gazebo on the other side of the garden with his manila folder. He printed all the photos and put them in the paper file. Lucy brought him his second cup of tea and silently put it on the table in front of him. He was engrossed in his work and didn't acknowledge her, but she was aware that as she approached he angled the file away from her. She was used to his games and thought little of it; he could keep his secrets.

Paul had known the Senator and his family for more than ten years and was no stranger at the Senator's Estate. Over the years, he had learned what Consuelo was like; if Paul was to benefit from this situation, either for the boys' family or for himself, he needed to be careful.

There was no way he could bring Consuelo and his men to justice without risk to himself and his family, but he did think there may be a way to get some compensation for the villagers and, of course, something for his troubles.

He would not be too greedy. The Senator could live with his demands and still achieve his objectives. He could build in enough layers of protection so that when he approached the Senator, the man would have no alternative but to agree.

He had a mission; it was like the army days. Not even his family could know, that could put them in danger, and he really needed protection and insurance of some sort. How could he achieve this? He could always try to bluff Consuelo, but he knew that the man was a street fighter by nature and skilled in such games.

He'd led a very exciting life in the Special Forces and as a bodyguard – he missed the controlled risk-taking and the adrenaline rush of putting bold plans into action. This time he had a good moral reason for his plan. That added to his confidence.

At sixty-nine, this would be his last adventure, do or die, he thought. Realistically he did not have many years of quality life left; he was already beginning to feel his age more and more each day.

Paul packed up his paperwork and moved back into the house.

"Can we go into town this afternoon?" Lucy asked as he walked into the kitchen.

"Yes, sure sweetheart, if you want to."

It fit in with his plans anyway. Lunch would be ready in a couple of hours, and Lucy was cheerful now as she went about washing the salad vegetables. He disappeared into the computer room, mug in hand, and shut the door emphatically as if to say, 'Do not disturb'. Dennis, who had risen from the sofa in the hope of spending time with his dad, sat back down to watch television.

Maybe it's his age, she thought. *Maybe internet porn is all he is good for now.* He hadn't touched her in a couple of months. She didn't mind really, but it hurt her pride that he hardly ever showed interest now, unlike many men who had made their interest obvious. Lucy was an attractive woman.

The computer clicked and buzzed as it powered up. He began a lengthy description of the events, and then he expertly inserted photos.

He named the participants and their relationship to the Senator. Details of illegal activities by the Senator were included. He knew 'where the bodies were buried' for many of the 'deals' the Senator was involved in.

His military training and intelligence gathering abilities meant he always kept his eyes and ears open. Over the years, he'd heard and seen many things that maybe he should not have. This document could explode the Senator's political ambitions.

He enhanced and enlarged the photos wherever he could and by the time he'd finished he had a professionally presented twenty-five page report. He reread the whole thing three times, each time adding a bit more detail until it was twenty-seven pages long.

Traffic was bad as usual on a Saturday afternoon. As they made their way to Benguet, Paul grew impatient. He dropped his family at the mall and then found a parking place close to the National Bookstore in the City Centre. The store was packed with giggling schoolgirls. He selected six large padded envelopes, two rolls of carton sealing tape and two reams of best quality bond paper.

His short military career hadn't provided him with a very large pension and in a country where you had to pay for education and medical care his meager income didn't go very far. Up to now, Paul and his family rarely took holidays and led a frugal lifestyle. Better times were just around the corner, he kept reminding himself.

His next visit was to the computer shop. He bought two sets of ink cartridges for his printer and put them in the trunk of the car, then strolled down the street to McDonalds.

Over the years, he'd started many assignations and brief affairs here. Lucy knew of some of them, there had been many fights in the past, but Paul was good at hiding his tracks and she only knew the tip of the iceberg. She no longer bothered to ask. Although cordial, there was little real affection left and they were leading separate lives.

He arrived back at the mall late in the afternoon. Lucy and Dennis were waiting for him in Shakey's Pizza as arranged. Dennis was relieved; his Dad was in good spirits.

"So what have you both been doing?" he said, putting his arm around his son.

Dennis loved it when his dad was in a mood like this.

They were relieved to see him relaxed; it was not often he was like this. Paul waited until there was a lull in the conversation,

"I think it's time we all had a holiday. Where would you like to go? How would you like to visit Uncle Bill?"

Paul had a younger brother, an engineer working in Vietnam. They had sometimes talked about going to see him, but Paul always said that they couldn't afford it.

"That would be brilliant, when can we go? Can we go tomorrow?"

Paul and Lucy both laughed.

"Maybe in two weeks," he replied.

He looked over at Lucy,

"Would that be ok with you?"

"It would be great. Dennis will have the time of his life."

They soon cleared the City Centre and headed for home. Paul's purchases were well hidden under the tarpaulin. He would sneak them into the house later when Lucy was getting Dennis ready for bed.

When Lucy called Dennis upstairs, he slipped into the garage to retrieve his purchases. This time he locked the study door. It was unlikely that Lucy would come down again, but he wanted to be sure. She rarely walked in on him when the door was closed, but tonight he could take no chances.

He cleared his desk and started printing out the reports, setting the printer to photo quality. Each page took more than thirty seconds to print; his printer would be busy for nearly two hours.

While the printer was working away, he prepared letters to his intended recipients, leaving a big space at the bottom. He carefully attached one of the gold coins to each one with scotch tape before stapling them to the report. He placed ten further blank sheets on top for extra padding – he didn't want anyone to be able to feel the coin inside.

On the table in front of him now sat six identical packages. He placed one further envelope in his top drawer and locked it. He couldn't leave these packs in the study, Dennis was very inquisitive. While there was no one around, he packed them carefully in a carrier bag and hid them in the back of the car.

Consuelo wasn't the only wealthy and influential contact that Paul had developed over the years. His expertise as a military man had been sought in the earlier years by wealthy politicians, businessmen, police and military.

He was well known to a handful of powerful people who were not on Consuelo's side. Indeed, there were many who would love the opportunity to damage the Senator (either physically or politically, or both). He went through his address book considering who would be the most appropriate and trustworthy of his connections. If something went wrong, these packages would be hand delivered by one of his Manila lawyers.

If anything happened to Paul or his family, they would arrive on the desk of two senators, two high-ranking Generals, the Chief of Police for Makati, and a well-known Bishop within hours. Armed with the evidence in the packages, any one of these could bring Consuelo down. If they worked together there would be no way out for the Senator. He told them that if they were receiving the package it was very likely that he was dead, and begged them to take care of his family as best they could.

Over breakfast the next day, Paul told his family he was going to Manila.

"I will only be away for a couple of days," he said. "Embassy business."

Lucy smiled to herself. This was always the reason he gave for going to Manila—sometimes it was true.

He usually took the overnight bus from the road outside his house just before midnight. It would arrive in Manila at around seven a.m. the next morning. Lucy didn't mind him going on his little trips, she liked him being away. It was a relief for her. She didn't have to be on her best behavior, or make sure she kept her cell phone with her. Most importantly, while Dennis was at school for five or six hours she was free to meet friends. She smiled inwardly at the prospect.

Paul started to pack in the early evening. Lucy dutifully laid out all his clothes on the bed as usual, but he liked to pack himself. She gave him enough for three days, just in case, but he was likely to finish his business in two. He was anxious to get back to visit the Senator. An hour later he was waiting on the dusty road for the night bus.

Over the years, Paul had dealt with many of the best law firms in Makati City. The packages would be his protection. He addressed each package to a different lawyer, with the envelope addressed to the final recipient inside. The instructions were very clear. If he didn't make contact with that named person in the firm twice a day at a specific time, after an hour's grace period, the packages were to be dispatched to their final recipients. In a few months or so, when Paul felt safe, he would collect them.

He enclosed a sizeable retainer and a promise that much more money would be forthcoming when, if all went as planned, he later came to collect the packages. If they had to deliver them, the recipient was instructed to reward the lawyer substantially. He told them they must deliver the packages themselves, not to use a courier or junior staff. They must also make sure that it was the named recipient who opened the package, not some secretary or assistant.

The packed bus reached Manila soon after dawn. Paul's taxi took twenty minutes through the heavy traffic to get to his usual hotel, the Makati Palace on P. Burgos Street. Once there, he didn't stay long. He left his case in his room but chose to carry his backpack, with the valuable letters, with him. By nine thirty, he was out on the hot and bustling streets again looking for a taxi.

His first call was to Ruth Aquino, a woman he had known

from the province. She visited Baguio City (about two hours' drive from where Paul lived) every month to buy gold to resell in Manila.

They first met many years ago. She was selling antique guns for a town Mayor in Ilocos Norte. A military contact referred her to Paul and he matched her up with a wealthy collector in Indonesia. They both did well out of the deal and became friends.

Paul needed the coins to be tested, and he knew she had the equipment to do this. He had no doubt that they were genuine but he wanted to know the quality and carat of the gold. He would cut a small, unrecognizable piece off, and give her a story about it being part of some broken piece of jewelry he inherited.

He had another and more important purpose in seeing her; he was hoping that she would introduce him to someone who could buy large quantities of gold without asking questions. He was glad he lived in the Philippines. Only in a third world country like the Philippines where regulations and laws could easily be ignored could such deals be done.

She was a healthy widow in her fifties, and was tougher than she looked. Her husband, a seaman, died years ago. She had two children who were both now abroad with their own families. Her husband left her well provided for. She owned a house in a respectable part of Manila.

The house stood out as being very substantial and well-built for the area, with high walls and an impressive gate. The taxi dropped him outside and the driver sped off, disappointed with his tip. Paul pushed the doorbell and waited. After a few moments a handyman opened the gate. When he saw that Paul was a foreigner, he waved him in. He was obviously expected. Paul strolled up the short drive, admiring the well-kept flowerbeds and lawns on either side. It reminded him of his own garden.

Ruth was waiting for him by the time he reached the front door.

"Hello, stranger," she said, smiling warmly and kissing him briefly on the lips.

"Yes, it's been a long time. Life gets so busy. I don't get the time that I used to."

"It's ok, I've been busy too. It's like that these days," she said, letting him off the hook lightly. She took his arm and guided him into the living room. He sat in a comfortable armchair while Ruth went to the kitchen. In less than a minute, she was back with a tray of tea and biscuits. After pouring the tea she sat down next to him.

The room was clean, but cluttered with expensive furniture. Old and fading family photos covered the walls. Interior design was not important to Ruth.

"How're the family? Dennis must be quite big now? Eleven? Twelve?"

"They're fine. Dennis is twelve now, he's a big lad. He can beat me at football."

"That's just you getting older, my dear."

Paul laughed and nodded.

"Maybe you're right."

There was a convenient pause.

"I need your help, Ruth," he announced.

He took a white folded napkin from his pocket, and handed it to Ruth.

"What's this?" she asked, opening it up.

She carefully picked up the piece of gold.

"I've inherited some old bits and pieces from my aunt in Brisbane. There were some old bits of broken metal amongst the jewelry—we think its gold, but I would like to know for sure."

Ruth held it up to the light and rolled it between her fingers. She refolded the napkin with the gold inside and put it into her pocket.

"I'll need to test it. I have my chemicals outside in the shed. Can I do it tonight?"

"Yes, that'll be fine. I can call back tomorrow." There was silence for a few seconds.

"You can stay here tonight if you like."

She was looking straight into his eyes, her meaning was crystal clear.

Paul and Ruth had a history. A few years ago, she'd called on Paul unannounced. He was alone in the house; Lucy had taken Dennis to Manila to visit her mother after one of their quarrels. It was early evening when she arrived on the bus and Paul offered her dinner. The plan was that after dinner he would drive her to a hotel in Vigan, but after they finished a bottle of wine she ended up staying.

After dinner, they sat next to each other on the couch. Paul was a tall man with large hands, which Ruth remarked on. After a few drinks; she asked him if he was large in other areas. He took the hint and kissed her. She gasped with surprise at his size as she put her hand inside his pants, finding that he was stiff and ready.

They were both tired by the time they set off for Vigan the next day. They made love three times. She laughed when he begged her not to tell Lucy. She assured him she just wanted fun and would be discreet, but playfully said that she would expect a repeat performance next time they met. Paul had forgotten this, Ruth, obviously, had not.

She leaned in towards him and they kissed. Paul hadn't expected this, but he was happy to oblige. After a few seconds, he broke away.

"I thought you'd forgotten."

"Of course not. I've often thought of you, and I'm glad to see you again."

He stroked her hair; her head was nestling into his shoulder now.

"I have to get my stuff and check out of the hotel. I have a couple of other jobs to do as well. I'll be back by about seven o'clock."

"That'll be fine. I'll have dinner ready for you."

The Makati Palace Hotel was in one of the 'red light' districts. Paul sat in the bar observing the goings-on in the still busy street below. Pretty young and slim girls (and boys) walked the streets engaging the many foreigners in conversation in the hope of selling their services. The police turned a blind eye for a monthly 'retainer'.

He checked out of the room and was relaxing before returning to Ruth, he just had one drink. 'Brewers droop' was one thing he did not want tonight; it had been a while and he hoped he would be able to rise to the occasion. He left just before six-thirty. Paul was never late for anything if he could help it. The taxi ride was about twenty minutes, so he took the opportunity to call his family. Dennis answered after three rings.

"Hi, Dad," he said excitedly. "When are you coming back?"

Paul smiled with pleasure; at least someone missed him.

"I'll be home late tomorrow night, son. I'll be there when you get up in the morning."

"Yay!" said his son, he put the phone down and ran into the kitchen to get his mother.

"Mom, Dad's on the phone," he shouted up the stairs when he discovered the kitchen was empty.

A few seconds later, she came down the stairs and picked up the phone. "Hello, Paul."

Paul sighed inwardly—it used to be 'hello sweetheart' but in the last year or so, he'd noticed a change. He made a mental note to buy her flowers on the way home.

"How are you? How's the business going?" she continued.

"It's fine, I'll come home overnight tomorrow night."

"Ok, that's good. Dennis misses you a lot."

And what about you? Do you miss me? Paul thought, but he didn't say anything.

"I'll see you at breakfast."

"Bye for now, then," he said.

The phone clicked at the other end.

He arrived at Ruth's house on the dot of seven. The traffic was heavier than usual. Again, she opened the door as he approached. This time he got a longer kiss on the lips as he walked in. Ruth led him by the hand into the lounge, where there was a wooden tray on the coffee table with an opened bottle of chilled white wine, two glasses and a bowl of potato chips.

"So, tell me what you've been doing with yourself? It's been a while."

She smiled at him.

She wore a flowing dress that finished just above the knee. A little young for her age, but she carried it off well.

"Nothing much changes. Dennis is growing up, and I'm getting old, but apart from that there's nothing exciting."

"And Lucy?"

Paul saw no reason not to talk to Ruth about Lucy— there was no one else he could talk to, maybe it would help.

"She's fine, but she's distant lately, things between us are strained. Maybe it's just that I'm getting old, maybe she has a lover."

Ruth laughed.

"Maybe she has, she's much younger than you."

"Don't remind me."

"She's very lucky and she knows it," said Ruth reassuringly.

"Maybe, but it's been a while since she showed it."

She sat closer to him and held his hand.

"Come on, dinner's ready." She guided him to the dining room, and then disappeared into the kitchen. There was a lit candle in the middle of the table making the scene intimate. After a few moments, she reappeared with two bowls of soup. Did she remember that Paul liked oxtail soup or was it a coincidence? He buttered the French bread while he waited for his soup to cool.

"You know, I did have another reason to see you, apart from the jewelry," he said.

"I know, you owe me a fuck. That's not a problem at all." They both laughed, but she had made her point and he knew what was expected of him tonight.

"That's not what I meant, but, of course, I am more than happy for…well, you know."

Paul hoped that he really didn't have a problem with that.

"I have a connection in the province that needs to sell a lot of gold quickly, for cash. Do you have any connections you can trust who might help?"

"How much gold are we talking about?" she asked.

"Several million US dollars' worth."

She whistled. She knew he was serious; Paul wouldn't waste his time on a joke like this. She knew Paul was well connected to Senator Consuelo and other politicians.

"I think I know someone who can help. I'll ring him first thing in the morning and we'll go and see him."

"Can you tell me a bit more about your contact?"

"He's a German. I've known him and dealt with him for a long time."

Paul had mixed feelings, he was glad it was a foreigner, but a little bit unsure of Germans. Oh well, he thought. Let's go and check him out.

"That sounds fine. I'm looking forward to meeting him."

They finished their dinner and again she led him by the hand—this time upstairs. Ruth shut the bedroom door and they kissed passionately. She pulled him over to the bed and pushed him down. As she lay down beside him, he felt her hand opening his pants.

"Hmmm, I'd forgotten how big you were."

He appreciated the compliment.

"Well, I've not forgotten how sexy you are," he said, putting his hand inside her dress and stroking her nipple— he was pleased to find no bra. Her 'massage' was making him very stiff. He would have no problem tonight.

Paul rose early the next day. Ruth was still asleep. He

quietly dressed and let himself out of the house, leaving a note: 'Gone for a run, see you in an hour.' He let himself back in later to find her preparing breakfast.

"I've made an appointment for us to see my friend Herman after lunch. His office is about two hours away on the other side of Manila."

"Oh, that's great. We can travel when you're ready and have lunch there before we meet him."

"That would be nice. By the way, I've tested the gold you gave me. It's very good quality- nearly twenty two carat, and it's very old, quite intriguing really."

She looked at him waiting for a comment. She didn't get one.

"How much more of this do you have? I'd love to see some of the pieces. Do you want to sell them?"

"Sorry, Ruth. I wouldn't part with them, they mean a lot to me."

"Are you sure? I could give you a really good price, as a friend."

He shook his head. It was time to change the subject.

"That's great work on the gold, Ruth, thank you very much." That was clearly the end of the matter. She took the tissue with the gold pieces out of her pocket and put it on the table next to his mug.

"Oh no, Ruth. That's fine. Please keep the scrap. Maybe it's worth something to you for your time and trouble." Ruth smiled and took them back. In fact, she knew it was worth about thirty thousand pesos which made her very happy.

Ruth's trusted German contact, Herman, dealt in large quantities of gold and other precious metals.

His compact offices were on the twenty-first floor of a prestigious office building in Quezon City.

The German Embassy was in the same building. Security was very tight and that was why Herman had his office here. They emerged from the elevator to face his office. It was just across the hallway on the right. The discreet sign on the door announced that he was a 'Mining engineer and consultant.'

Herman wasn't involved in mining these days; he made his money in other ways. Being a 'fixer,' he had a closely protected reputation for matching willing sellers and buyers in any commodity and in any quantity. He and Ruth had known each other for years; they had done a lot of business in the North of Luzon. Herman admired Ruth; she had survived and prospered for twenty years in a difficult and dangerous business.

Ruth rang the doorbell, A good looking and smartly dressed secretary opened the door. She was small framed and slim—maybe about thirty years old. Paul and Ruth were shown in and took a seat on the couch. The desk was uncluttered with just an open page a day diary, and three phones tidily arranged in the center and corners.

The brilliant white walls were bare, apart from framed certificates proclaiming business registration and various permits.

There was a small kitchenette behind the reception desk; the secretary disappeared inside. Another door, slightly ajar, led to the only other room. After a couple of minutes and without asking, the secretary, who had introduced herself as Cheryl, emerged with coffee and mini scones.

Ten minutes later the well-dressed German emerged beaming with a confident smile. He was immaculately groomed; a small moustache and a bald head seemed to suit him. He wore a light business suit with matching shirt, tie and shoes. Paul was immediately reminded of Hercule Poirot.

He approached Paul and warmly shook his hand.

"I've heard a lot about you, Paul," he said, in nearly perfect English.

This was the truth. When Ruth rang him earlier in the day, he asked many questions. Herman was very cautious who he dealt with, so he made discreet enquiries of his own.

He briefly embraced Ruth in European fashion, kissing her on both cheeks,

"Come in, come in," he said as he ushered them both into the inner office. The secretary followed them in discretely and placed their coffees on the table. Tasteful pinpoint lighting was set into the white suspended ceiling.

They remained standing while Ruth effected proper introductions, then Herman indicated they should sit down around the table.

"I'm sorry, Herman. I have another appointment. I'll just leave Paul in your capable hands."

Ruth made her excuses and left, after tactfully refusing another cup of coffee, arranging to meet Paul later in the day. Paul made a mental note to cancel that arrangement. He was going to be busy for the rest of the day and didn't intend to stay another night in Manila.

The men faced each other and spent a few minutes in small talk. Paul eventually decided that it was time to get down to business.

"Thank you for seeing me, Herman. Did Ruth tell you why I wanted to see you?"

Herman smiled politely and nodded. He had a calm manner, and spoke quietly, as if he were considering carefully what he was about to say, which he was.

"You know, I've been in business here in the Philippines for twenty years and have a few select clients that I've dealt with for years. I rarely accept new clients. I only agreed to see you because Ruth recommended you and because you are a foreigner. I checked out your background before you came."

He sat back and waited for a reaction

"Well, thank you again for at seeing me. I presume that as I'm sitting here drinking your coffee, I checked out with your contacts, so maybe we can talk about some business now?"

Both men relaxed, but Paul was impatient to get down to business.

"Next week I'll have gold coins with a value of between two and three million dollars. I need to liquidate them quickly and quietly. Is this something you can do?"

Herman raised his eyebrows; the welcoming smile was fading from his face now. This was business.

"I can do it. I'll need a quarter of the purchase price as payment. It's not all for me, there are transport costs and many people to pay off along the way."

Paul nodded. He was prepared for this and bartering about the price was not the thing to do in these situations.

"That's fine, as long as I can stay with you until the payment is made."

Herman thought for a moment, and he decided that this wouldn't be a problem. Paul's presence might even prove useful.

"Agreed," Herman said, now with a hint of a smile.

"You can leave everything to me. I have a couple of associates who'll be interested in the goods, so I'll contact them later today. When the gold is available we'll meet outside Manila. I'll tell you where later."

Paul accepted the need for discretion at this time—he would have expected no less.

There was one more job to do before returning to the province; it wouldn't take him long. After a few moments he hailed a taxi and set off for the post office, As soon as Paul left, Herman got to work and within an hour he had a deal. By early evening Paul was finished. The bus station at Cubao was packed when he arrived there just after eight. He had a long wait, the next bus left at ten minutes past ten. The going was bumpy and very noisy for the first hour until they got out of Manila and onto the bigger Northern Luzon Expressway.

Things were going well so far; his plans were falling into place. There was little else to do in the bus, so he tried to work out how much gold was in each box (assuming they all contained gold). He'd estimated the size of the boxes. Guessing they may be about half full, he crosschecked the results against the estimated weight. As a professional soldier, he could make a reasonably accurate guess at how much an ordinary man could carry.

The gold rate was at an all-time high now because of the uncertainty of oil resources and the weakness of the American and European currencies.

He got back to considering his plan. If the Senator was backed into a corner he could be dangerous. Paul's experience and contacts wouldn't be able to help him, but he had a strategy. He only needed to deprive Consuelo of a small proportion of his treasure. He gambled that the Senator would decide that it was not worth the risk of killing him just to protect a relatively small amount of his windfall. He hoped that the Senator would be in the province and that he could meet him the day after tomorrow. Things had to move fast now, before the Senator spent all the money and became the President.

He'd forgotten to take his camera to Manila, but he'd worked out how to deal with that, it would not be a problem. All it needed was another trip to National Bookstore and one other place. He could easily do that while Lucy was shopping.

Just after midnight, the bus passed through Tarlac and Paul was fast asleep with his notebook in his lap. He arrived home as dawn was breaking and he was hungry. No one else was up, so he quietly made himself some cheese on toast and tea, then he fell asleep on the sofa watching football. When Lucy woke him at noon, he felt refreshed and hungry again. After a quick shower, he sat down to chicken curry and rice with his family.

"How was your trip? Did you have a good time?" Lucy asked, to make conversation.

"Actually, it was very good. I have some plans which will solve our financial problems. I met some people in

Manila, and if all goes well we won't have any money issues soon."

"That's nice."

Lucy tried to sound a little enthusiastic, but failed.

Paul sensed her mood.

"I know I've tried some things in the past which haven't come off, but this time I know it will. I'll be able to tell you all about it in a few days, but I can't yet. We can put Dennis in the best school, take a nice holiday, live wherever you want. Wouldn't that be great? Please be patient, sweetheart."

She put her hand on his shoulder.

"If that comes off, Paul, I'll be very happy."

Lucy was nearly at the end of her patience with his moods, his pie in the sky schemes, and his lying—she had nearly had enough. She kept quiet for now, though.

On the way to Benguet they discussed the afternoon's plans. Paul was distracted—in his head, he was going through his planned meeting with the Senator. He phoned the Senator's brother but there was no reply or call back yet.

Lucy took Dennis with her to the hairdressers; Paul was pleased as this gave him at least three hours. After he made his purchases in National Book Store, he went as usual to McDonalds. The restaurant was half-empty so there was plenty of room. He easily found a space where he could put two tables together for the space he needed.

When he finished he stood back and reviewed his handiwork. Six very neat, well wrapped packages. His final job was a visit to the local Post Office, then he set off to pick up his family. He checked the glove compartment and saw with relief that he hadn't forgotten his camera; he was going to need it.

Lucy bought a bottle of wine on Paul's instructions; she sensed that Paul was still in high spirits. It was a welcome change. She'd noticed that his mood had improved over the past week or so. She fleetingly wondered whether he had a new girlfriend, but decided that it wasn't likely. She was pretty certain that he really was past that sort of thing.

CHAPTER FIVE

Before breakfast Paul was already calling Consuelo's secretary to make sure the Senator was at home. Simon was in his office and working when the phone rang.

"Hi, Paul, how are you?"

"I'm great, Simon, how about you?"

"Well, apart from being too busy because of the election, I'm fine,"

"Is the Senator there today? I've got something I'd like to discuss with him. I don't need much of his time, maybe thirty minutes."

"I'm sure the Senator will make time for you, let me just go and ask him. I'll ring you back in ten. Can you tell me what it's about?"

Paul laughed.

"Need to know basis right now, mate, I am sure you'll find out later but I really need to see him today. Tell him it'll be good for him."

"Ok, my friend. I'll get back to you."

"Maybe he wants to make a donation to my campaign fund," the Senator mused. "Everyone likes to be on the winning side, what do you think?"

"I don't think so, he isn't known for his generosity, quite the opposite, but he did say it was important that he see you today."

The Senator smiled.

"Ok, well I guess we'll have to see him to find out."

After ten minutes Paul's mobile rang.

"It's fine, Paul. The Senator will be happy to see you,"

There was little time left now before the election, but Consuelo had everything under control. A meeting with Paul would be a pleasant distraction for an hour. The day after tomorrow the results would be announced—he'd wait in Manila, and he'd be President Elect by lunchtime or soon after.

Paul set off after breakfast. Dennis and Lucy were with him. He'd drop them at school first as it was close to the Senator's Estate.

"I'll come and pick you up after lunch. I'm going to pay a call on the Senator."

She smiled and nodded.

Lucy took Dennis straight into the assembly hall of the school where prayers were about to begin. She gave him a big smile and a kiss as he struggled to escape and join his friends. When she released him he sped off without looking back. Lucy made her way outside, away from the gossiping mothers, and made a call. In a couple of minutes she was in a taxi on her way to the old Spanish quarter of Benguet, to the Venturers' Inn.

The old tourist inn had been built in the time of the Spanish occupation, maybe two hundred years ago. Its architecture, newly renovated, was beautiful. The small red bricks were being cleaned and repainted. It had been an imposing building in its time. The current owners were restoring it to its previous splendor.

"Good morning, stranger."

Maria, the wife of the owner and a good friend to Lucy, came out from behind the reception desk and greeted her as she walked through the ornate paneled door into the spacious reception area. She beckoned Lucy through to the small private dining room at the back. Maria called out for coffee and the two women sat down to catch up on gossip.

"It's been a couple of weeks," said Maria. "I was beginning to think something was wrong."

"No nothing's wrong, except that he's been so busy with this stupid election that he hasn't had time to see me. I've missed him so much, and it hasn't helped that Paul's been acting strange lately."

"What do you mean 'strange'?"

"It's difficult to say, but he seems more pre-occupied, he doesn't complain so much – perhaps he has another woman."

The two girls laughed.

"I hope he has, it would make things a lot easier for me."

Her friend nodded.

After thirty minutes, he arrived. He was the real reason why Lucy was there. Tom was wearing very plain tourist clothes today—he wanted to blend in as much as he could. Without stopping at reception, he walked through to the room where Lucy and Maria were having coffee. Lucy had her back to him and was startled when she felt his hands on her shoulders and his kiss on her neck. Maria laughed.

Lucy turned around to kiss him properly. Maria discretely turned away silently while the two lovers reacquainted themselves. Lucy told him earlier on the phone that she had at least four or five hours so they weren't in a rush. Tom sat down beside Lucy and greeted Maria.

"Thank you for making the time for me at last, I'm so grateful," Lucy said sarcastically, but playfully.

"I'm sorry sweetheart, it'll be over soon, I promise, and then we'll be able to have a lot more time together."

Tom was a different kind of man than her husband. Apart from being much younger, he was kinder and more considerate.

She met him at a Christmas party thrown by the Senator a few years ago. She went with Paul, under protest. She didn't want to be anywhere with him at that time. They'd fought about a week before over texts from a woman that she found on his cell phone and he'd hit her. It'd shocked both of them to the core. She considered leaving him, but there was Dennis to consider. She calmed down as the bruising on her cheek faded; it didn't show under the make-up.

Paul had too much whiskey, as usual, and was getting louder. Lucy felt uncomfortable and told him she wanted to go, he ignored her. She stood up and told him she was going to get some fresh air and then walked off without waiting for a reply.

Making her way through the gardens, she paused and strolled amid the roses and orchids. There were seats by the ornamental fishpond. She sat down and allowed the tears to flow. Tom was strolling in the garden as part of his security duty. He could hear her from twenty yards away and approached her. The leaves crunching underfoot alerted her to his presence and she turned her head away, but try as she might, she couldn't stop the crying.

"Are you ok?" Tom had asked.

She didn't reply right away, but he sat down and tried to comfort her. After a while she told him of her woes. He listened patiently and caringly as she unfolded the story of her unhappiness. Tom knew Paul, and was not surprised at what she was telling him—he'd never liked the man. She managed to pull herself together after thirty minutes and went back inside, but he rang her the next day to check if she was ok. She agreed to have coffee with him and that's when it began.

They had been seeing each other for three years and were deeply in love. Tom planned to take Lucy and Dennis away from her overbearing husband, forever, as soon as he had enough money. That time would be very soon.

Maria knew about the affair right from the start. Her husband, Bruce, had been in the US military and was a good friend of Tom's, and the small hotel was an ideal place for them to meet. They were usually there about twice a week and had once managed a weekend away when Paul was 'on business' in Manila.

"I've got work to get on with, I'm afraid," Maria said, discretely, as she slipped the heavy key to Lucy. "The Hotel is catering a dinner for local bankers later in the day; there's a lot to do."

"That's fine, Maria. Thank you so much"

Lucy kissed her on the cheek. Maria rose and left the two lovers to their time together. She knew why they were there of course and didn't wish to keep them chatting any longer than courtesy demanded.

Lucy and Tom slowly climbed the stairs, hand in hand. The hotel had only three levels, and no elevators. The keys were old-fashioned metal ones, not the electronic plastic ones. The room had an oversized bed, fresh flowers and elegant, sophisticated decor. Lucy laughed when she spotted the box of chocolates on the bed, a nice touch by Maria. They were not in a rush today. They lay on the bed fully clothed kissing and caressing for more than thirty minutes.

"I have some news, sweetheart. I've earned a lot of money lately; the boss paid me very well."

"Good for you,"

"No, it's good for US. I've got enough money now to give all this up and go away with you."

He was watching her reaction closely.

"Do you still want to do that, sweetheart? We'll never have any financial worries again."

Lucy grinned broadly and held him very tightly.

"It's what I've wanted for so long, my darling. Of course I want to—anytime you like, anywhere you like."

She clung to him for a long time until she felt his hand sneak up the front of her short skirt and his fingers move slowly under the edge of her tiny panties.

Lucy always made Paul wear a condom on the infrequent occasions they made love. She told him she was frightened of getting pregnant again. In reality most of the time she was quite safe, but she was aware that she might not be Paul's only bed mate and was frightened she might catch something.

She had no such concerns with Tom. She gave herself to him with no concern for protection. It didn't occur to her to consider whether she was his only sexual partner, and anyway, it was early in the month—there shouldn't be a problem. She wanted to feel him inside her without any barrier. This was one pleasure that she shared with him alone and she had grown to enjoy and anticipate it.

He was younger and stronger than Paul was, not to mention bigger, and he lasted a lot longer. Their lovemaking sessions often left her a little sore but she loved having the soreness as a reminder.

After they were finished, they lay back in the bed.

"I've missed you so much, sweetheart."

"Well, there is no need to miss me anymore, my darling." She looked at him quizzically.

"Can you be ready in a week?"

Her mouth fell open.

"Is this for real? Is it really going to happen?"

He held her tight.

"Yes it is. I'm making the plans now. All you need to do is go and pack your stuff."

She didn't know what to say. She'd often wondered if this day would ever really come.

"Oh, sweetheart, thank you, thank you, thank you." She buried her head in Tom's chest.

"In a few days I'll give you money for tickets and expenses. We can be away very soon."

Her mind was in a whirl. There would be so much to try to do in the coming days; she'd have to be very careful. Dennis could be a problem. She would have to say they were taking a holiday and would deal with the situation when she was away from Paul. The dust would eventually settle and all would be ok.

They slept for a while. Lucy was happy when she awoke and realized she was in his arms. He came round after a few moments to find Lucy kissing him and gently rubbing him. There was plenty of time for another session before they had to go.

When Lucy got the call from Paul she was dressing.

"I am sorry darling, I am going to be longer than I thought," he said. "Do you mind catching the bus home with Dennis? I'll see you later."

"That's fine Paul, don't worry, take your time," she replied. She was glad for more time on her own. Paul sounded drunk, which was normal when he spent time with the Senator. They left the hotel at five-minute intervals just to be safe.

Paul arrived at the Senator's Estate just after ten. The guards knew him well and opened the gates immediately. Simon was sitting on the patio outside the entrance door to the Senator's apartments having a late breakfast and a cigarette.

As Paul approached, he smiled, stood up, then beckoned him to come and sit down.

"Welcome, my friend," he said and shook Paul's hand vigorously. "Come and have some breakfast."

As he sat down, Simon gestured to a nearby maid to bring coffee and pancakes for Paul, ignoring his protests. He sipped the coffee.

"So, how's life treating you?"

"Not so bad, mate, not so bad. Still struggling along,"

"How are Lucy and Dennis? Are they ok?"

"Yes, they're great," Paul replied. "We are going on holiday soon,"

"That's good for you," said Simon. "I cannot remember the last time I had a holiday."

After a few moments, Paul pushed his plate away. Simon took that as a signal he was anxious to meet with the Senator. He knew Paul was not one to waste time.

The receiving area at the top of the stairs was deserted except for a maid tidying and dusting. Simon led Paul through to the meeting room and motioned Paul to sit down, then went to find the Senator.

Consuelo greeted Paul warmly, like an old friend, as he entered the room. Simon nodded to both of them and left the room, quietly shutting the door behind him.

When they were alone, the Senator sat back, smiling expectantly at Paul.

"Thank you for seeing me, sir. It must be a very busy time for you. I can't turn on the television without seeing your handsome face. You seem to have it in the bag. I'll soon have to call you Mr. President."

Consuelo laughed politely.

"I think you've had a lucky break recently to improve your finances, Senator. I thought I would come to wish you well. It must have come at just the right time."

The Senator's smile gradually changed into a half quizzical and half-wary expression. Paul smiled at him and waited for a further reaction.

"I don't know what you've heard, but money is tight at this time, Paul. Election expenses are crippling me. Have you come to make a donation for my campaign?"

Paul ignored the question.

"You know, we're all feeling the pinch. I can hardly manage on my pension and I'm too old to do much work now. I was hoping you could help me out."

Consuelo was not used to getting requests for money, even in jest, from foreigners and he was feeling uncomfortable.

"I'm sure you're not serious, Paul. I've known you for years, and you always seem to be doing ok. Your pretty wife seems happy. Why would you need money?"

"Well, the truth is I want a lifestyle change. I've never really liked it here in the Philippines and I've decided it's time I took my family to live elsewhere, maybe Malaysia."

The Senator had no idea where this was going.

"You've come at a bad time, Paul. You know I would help you out if I could. Maybe after the election I'll be in a better position."

"Oh, don't worry Senator. I'm not going to ask you for more than you can easily afford. I only need about four million dollars."

The Senator laughed nervously.

"I know everyone believes I am a rich man, but the truth is I'm hardly getting by right now. My pockets are nearly empty with all the money I have to pay out. I'm sure you're joking about the four million dollars, Paul, but where are we really going with this? I know you're not a man to waste time with jokes."

Paul sat back in his chair.

"Senator, you and I've known each other a long time and you're right, I don't waste my time. I'm quite serious. I know you've recently come into a nice fortune, and I understand why you must keep it secret. You may have difficulty explaining if anyone asked, no?"

The Senator stared at him, stony faced. This was an unexpected turn of events.

"I only need a small part of it—you'll still have plenty left for your politics, easily enough to replenish your coffers and reward your people."

"Paul, you know that rumors abound in this country and at times like these. I just can't help you right now, my friend. I couldn't give you four thousand dollars, much less four million dollars."

His tone was much sterner now and he was becoming irritated. His instincts were telling him that something was wrong and he would have to tread very carefully.

"Oh, that's ok," said Paul. "It doesn't have to be in dollars, gold doubloons will do."

He took the shiny gold coin from his pocket and placed it in front of the Senator, who stared at it, his face still expressionless. For emphasis, Paul took more of the coins from his pocket and put them on the table. The Senator seemed at a loss for words.

"Don't worry, Senator, your secret's safe with me. I promise you, I really don't want to cause you a problem, I just need a little of your good fortune. I know about the coins from the cave close to Santiago. I know your men emptied the cave of its fortune and killed the lads who discovered it."

Paul opened his briefcase and brought out a brown folder. He spread its contents on the table. The Senator stared at the photos.

"How the hell did you get these?"

The senator was trying to remain calm. He examined each photo, trying to work out how much trouble he could be in if these things became public. Paul's camera had automatically timed and dated each photo.

"Senator, I'm a very professional and careful man. The cave site is still intact and no one will find it for probably another twenty years and by then nobody will be able to put the pieces together. You and I will be long gone.

You've known me for years. You know I'm not a blackmailer. I see no reason why we can't complete this one and only transaction without ill will. I'll never bother you again. I think you know you can rely on my word."

The Senator considered Paul's words while he looked at the photos. Paul sat back in his chair to give the Senator time to take it in. There were so many names and accusations in there as well as the cave and treasure issues, and the accuracy of the timelines would be difficult to challenge.

A proper investigation could ruin him and he knew it. There were photos there of Paul handing the packages to a smiling postmaster, as if he were presenting him with an award. There could be no doubt that what Paul told him was true. Paul pointed out the post office photos and explained what he'd done. He told the Senator everything except the names of the people who would receive the packages if 'things went wrong', as he put it.

"Paul, you're nearly seventy years old. What if something happens to you naturally? I could still be in trouble."

"Lucy knows all about the packages. She'll make sure they don't get delivered unless you do something silly. She has very clear instructions, and so do the attorneys," he lied.

While he was examining and considering the papers the Senator regained his composure. He handed the papers back to Paul with a little smile.

"You know, Paul, even if someone tries to use this, there is nothing here that pins anything directly on me," he tried to sound confident.

"Well, I'm not so sure, Senator. If this got into the wrong hands, it could ruin your chances at the Presidency, or of hanging on to it, and probably put you in jail as well."

They both knew there were other considerations. With this information there were influential people who'd come looking for the treasure for themselves.

Consuelo was already thinking of angles and possibilities. A plan was formulating in his mind, but he had to buy himself some time to think things through.

Over the years he he'd been the subject of several other serious blackmail requests. None had resulted in any loss to him. Two had resulted in payments, but he always made sure he got the money back, usually from the dead hands of the blackmailer. There were a few more blackmail attempts that were more modest and mostly related to his philandering. Consuelo usually fobbed the girls off with a token payment.

Consuelo at last sat back. He'd read the document three times. He knew what he had to do, he just had to work out the details.

"Let's, for a moment, explore the possibility that I may be willing to avoid any...inconvenience."

Paul smiled, he had the Senator hooked now. He could take his time to reel him in.

"How much money do you want?"

"I've already told you," Paul said impatiently. "Four million dollars. Please don't insult us both by trying to haggle over the figure. Don't forget, I saw what came out of the cave. I counted the boxes. It doesn't take a genius to realize that what I'm asking for is a small fraction of what you now have."

Paul wasn't prepared to bargain. His deal was the only one on offer. He thought this tough stance would impress the Senator.

"There will be no more demands. You'll never hear from me again. You have my word. The lawyers are instructed to deliver all the packages to you unopened once I am safely abroad and give them the all clear. Senator, I am not your enemy and I mean you no harm. You can rely on me to do as I say."

"It looks like you have me over a barrel," the Senator said, resignedly.

"Let's suppose that I agree to this. The gold is no longer here, it's in Manila," he lied.

However, this seemed reasonable to Paul. He was willing to accept that it wasn't a delaying tactic.

"I can make arrangements for you to pick it up tomorrow. Is that ok?"

Paul nodded. He wasn't sure what he'd expected, but it all seemed to be going too smoothly. Then he reassured himself, how could it go wrong? His planning had been impeccable. It was going so well because the Senator knew he had no choice. He was simply being reasonable, just as Paul knew he would.

"Don't worry, Paul. This is business, it's not personal. I would probably be doing the same thing if I were in your position."

He stood and held out his hand smiling. Paul shook it nervously, but with some relief.

"There's no reason for us to fall out over this. We've known each other for a long time, we can trust each other. Please stay and have lunch with us, and anyway, I have to go and make some phone calls to make the arrangements for your meeting tomorrow. I can't be there of course, but I'll ensure that all will go smoothly."

Paul was pleased with his days work. Everything the Senator suggested seemed reasonable.

"That's very civilized, Senator. I've always enjoyed your hospitality, so why not?"

The Senator picked up the photos and papers on the table and unlocked the door.

"Come on through, Paul, let's have a drink."

The Senator took his arm and guided him back to the lounge area. Consuelo led him to a set of sofas with a large screen television. Paul settled himself down to watch the European football that was currently on the TV. Consuelo made his excuses and left.

He went straight to his private study and called for Simon and Brian. While he was waiting, he rang his head of security and told him that Paul mustn't be allowed to leave the Estate. He must be shadowed at all times discretely, and forcibly detained if he attempted to leave.

The Senator knew Paul's favorite drink—whiskey and American ginger ale. He had a large bottle of Johnnie Walker Black Label sent in to him while he waited in his study for the others.

Paul soon relaxed and became engrossed in the football, enjoying his whiskey. Two young men—probably off duty security guards, he thought—wandered in and sat down to use the computers.

He rang Lucy to tell her he was with the Senator and would be staying there for a while. Meals and drinks with the Senator usually went on for hours; she should catch the bus home with Dennis. She didn't mind at all—more time to do some shopping, she said. He settled back down to enjoy the football.

CHAPTER SIX

The Senator ignored Brian and Simon as they entered; he was writing notes. Tom followed them a few seconds later. Without a word, he sat down with the others. The Senator's tone sounded important and urgent.

The Senator laid the photos and report out on the table without a word. Brian, Tom, and Simon cast their eyes down to the table. It took them just a couple of seconds to realize what was in front of them.

"What the hell is this?" Simon asked sharply.

He picked up the report and started to read it, then passed the pages around. The Senator was angry, he shouted as he thumped the table.

"How could you let this happen? You're supposed to be professionals."

He looked accusingly at Brian and Tom.

"I thought you checked the area—obviously it wasn't thorough enough. Paul was happily snapping away and recording everything. How could you have been so sloppy?"

Tom was the first to speak.

"Senator, we couldn't have expected that someone like Paul would be there. It's literally a chance in a million. He must have been miles away in the hills with a telephoto lens."

The other two nodded their agreement. Their boss calmed down a little.

"The most important thing now is to deal with it, quickly and effectively."

When Brian put the papers down the Senator gave them all the details of his meeting with Paul.

"Where does this leave us, Chief? Are you going to pay him?" asked Brian.

"Of course not. I can't afford to give in to even one demand. He'll not get a penny. Look, we've handled stuff like this before. It's a problem, Brian, but we can manage it. By nightfall all will be fine. Don't worry. I've decided what we're going to do."

The men knew the Senator. He was not a man to bluff. If he said he had a plan, then he had a plan.

"We have to move quickly, though. I've worked out what we need to do. As long as we all play our part things will be fine."

He briefed them for their tasks, told them to report in to him regularly, and sent them off.

Tom waited until he was on his own, well out of sight of the Senator, then called Lucy.

"Hi, sweetheart, please listen carefully, there's a change of plan. Don't worry. Everything will be fine so long as you trust me. Please listen carefully. This is extremely important. You remember Brian, my colleague, don't you?"

Lucy confirmed that she did.

"He'll be calling on you in an hour or so. There's nothing to worry about, I promise you. All you have to do is act surprised and go along with whatever he says."

"What's going on, Tom? You've got me worried."

"Lucy, you've got to trust me, there really is nothing to worry about. I won't let you down. No harm will come to either of you. Just go with Brian if he asks you to, and please—this is very important—make sure that you bring your passports with you when you leave, ok? Promise me you won't forget."

"I promise, sweetheart, but please tell me what's going on. I'm really worried."

"I'm sorry my angel, I can't talk now. Please just do as I say. I promise you that the three of us will be safe and together soon."

"I made up my mind a long time ago that my future was with you, sweetheart. I love you and trust you. I'll do anything that you say."

"Thank you my darling. I have to go now, but I'll see you soon. I love you."

Simon was the first to leave the compound, with two armed guards in an old Range Rover. It was a short drive to the Post Office. The Postmaster had been there for twenty-five years. He knew Consuelo's father when he was first the Mayor of Benguet, then Governor of Abra.

Consuelo phoned the old man while Simon was en route. When the black four by four drew up outside the quiet post office, he was waiting for them. He walked out to greet the visitors. Simon didn't drive this time; he emerged from the passenger side smiling with an outstretched hand. The Postmaster scurried to greet them.

"Welcome, my friend, welcome. It's so good to see you, and I am always pleased when I can do anything to help the Senator."

He was nearly bowing. Simon motioned for the guards to stay in the car. He wouldn't need them. He walked with the old man through the side door of the decrepit building.

The Postmaster hadn't yet recovered from getting a personal call from the Senator a few moments earlier.

"How are you, my friend?" Consuelo had asked. The Postmaster recognized the voice of the Senator straight away.

"I'm fine s...s...sir," the old Postmaster managed to splutter, trying to contain his surprise. "I'm honored to hear from you sir. Is there anything I can do to help you? Anything at all?"

The Senator squirmed. He hated sycophants, but on this occasion he was very glad to have such an obedient one in this position.

"Tell me, did you get a visit from a tall, old white haired foreigner a day or two ago? He would have brought in some packages to be sent on to Manila."

"Oh, yes sir, we did. We wouldn't forget that because there aren't many white men in the city and because of the photos he had insisted taking. I've never before had a customer insist on taking photos of handing over parcels to me—very strange."

"Are the packages still there?"

"Oh, yes sir, they are. The Manila pick up is only twice a week. They won't go until tomorrow."

"Ok, my friend, you've done a good job. Now, it is essential that you look after those packages, one of my men will be over shortly to pick them up."

Without hesitation the postmaster replied. "Of course sir, no problem, sir. You know I would do anything to assist you and your family. My father always did whatever he could to—"

The Senator cut him off. "Don't worry my friend. Your help is very much appreciated. Your family's long record of helping us will never be forgotten."

"Oh, thank you sir," said the old man as the phone went down at the other end.

At the Postmaster's beckoning, two young lads came over from the counter area and placed the packages into a large sack. Simon kept half an eye on the boys to ensure that they put all the packages in. When they were finished, Simon carried the sack to the car.

The Postmaster stood beside him smiling expectantly and then feigned surprise when Simon produced a small brown envelope stuffed with one thousand peso bills and handed it to him. It went straight from Simon's hand into the inside pocket of his jacket in a single movement. He was still waving and thanking Simon as the car sped away.

They were nearly home when another four by four sped past them on the opposite side of the road. Brian was in the passenger seat. He nodded at Simon as he went past. With Brian were two local uniformed police with holstered guns at their sides. Consuelo owned the local police just as he did the local military and officials.

Simon got off at the main entrance to the house and carried the sack into the study. Consuelo looked up from the papers he was poring over with some of the local election officials.

"Are you sure you got them all?" he asked, his gaze returning to the table.

"Yes, sir. I watched over them, they're all there."

The Senator glanced over to a cupboard in the corner.

"Put them in there, please."

Simon did so. The Senator walked over and joined him, quickly checking the cupboard before shutting the door and locking it.

"Good job, Simon. There goes his little protection scheme."

He would incinerate them later on. There was no rush. They were under his control now. Consuelo smiled confidently. *One down, two to go*, he thought.

Brian and his men were halfway to Santiago. Paul's house was set back off the road by about a hundred yards. It was a detached, concrete built two storey building just a little bit American in style. Once they turned off the road and onto Paul's drive, they would be able to park up under the large trees that Paul cultivated to provide privacy.

Brian could now see the house up ahead on the left. The gates in the high wall were open. Lucy never had the paranoia about security that her husband had. She had probably just arrived back from school with Dennis, Brian guessed, and left the gates open for Paul, thinking he'd be arriving later. They parked up on the left hand side just before the garage; two of the men jumped down and shut the gates behind them. Nobody was going to be leaving the house for a while.

Lucy and Dennis were in the back garden, but Lucy heard the arriving car and was already coming around the side of the house. She smiled at Brian as he walked towards her, then she saw the other men had closed the gates behind them and gone straight into the house without a word.

Lucy moved as if to side step Brian and follow them into the house but Brian caught her arm and gently but firmly pulled her around to face him. She was startled; she knew they were coming, of course, Tom told her, but she still had no idea what they were here for.

"Brian, what's happening? Why are those men going in the house? What's going on?"

He steered her away from the house and pushed her down gently into one of the wooden seats placed against the garden wall. He sat down beside her and placed his hand firmly on her arm.

"Please don't be concerned, Lucy. There's nothing to worry about. You and Dennis won't be harmed."

Lucy looked bewildered.

"Why should we be? What's going on Brian? Where's Paul?" She looked at him pleadingly.

Brian took a deep breath and paused. Things would go more smoothly if he could keep her calm.

"The truth is, Lucy, Paul got himself into a bit of trouble with the Senator, and the Senator believes Paul has something here at the house that he wants. It's nothing serious. I promise you, if you can just keep calm and help me we can clear it up today."

Lucy still looked bewildered. She thought for a few seconds.

"Where's Paul?"

She started to take her mobile phone out of her pocket but Brian reached over and snatched it from her hand. She looked frightened.

"I'm sorry, Lucy, I can't let you call Paul yet. Please don't be concerned. You'll see him soon."

"Please, Brian, tell me what's going on? Is Paul ok?"

Brian smiled at her as he pocketed her phone.

"Please try to relax, then we can get the job done quicker. We just have to find out if what we want is in the house, then we'll take you to the Estate, and you can join Paul there. He's fine, really. He's drinking with the Senator. I'm sorry I can't tell you any more right now, but believe me, everything will be fine, just keep calm, and try to relax."

Lucy knew better than to argue further with Brian. She kept trying to remember that Tom had told her everything would be ok.

"Let's go into the back garden and relax while my guys do their work."

He helped her out of the chair and guided her through the door to the back garden. Dennis was kicking a football against a wall completely unaware of the drama. Brian and his mom appeared around the side of the house and sat down in the small white plastic patio chairs at the side of the garden.

Lucy tried to rise, but Brian again put his hand on her arm and spoke firmly.

"It's better that you don't go in the house until they've done their work, Lucy. Don't worry, they won't break anything."

Lucy was far from being reassured, but she had no choice but to sit back down. They sat in silence.

Inside the house, the men were thorough and professional. As they searched the house, they carefully lifted the carpets and rugs, and replaced them afterwards. Envelopes, boxes, and packages were opened and resealed carefully where possible.

The door to the office was locked, but it was not a strong lock—the frame cracked easily after a hard push, with little damage to the door trim. Lucy heard the noise as the door gave way and started to say something to Brian, but she stopped herself.

The men pulled out every cupboard and drawer, and checked every crevice before packing up the computer. Paul was a tidy man, all his files, folders, and file boxes were neatly arranged on shelves around the walls, which made them easier to look through.

There was one small locked drawer under the computer table. They forced it open and removed a thick brown envelope.

"Put the computer equipment in the back of the car," said the senior officer.

Without a word, the computer, printer, scanner and some other bits were removed to the back of the car and stacked behind the seat. The senior man brought the envelope to Brian.

He examined the contents. He had already seen identical documents at the Estate. He looked over at Lucy.

"Do you know what this is, Lucy?"

He handed her the first page.

"I've no idea, Brian. Paul keeps a lot of stuff from me. I've never seen that before. What's Paul doing, Brian? Is he in trouble? Are we in trouble?"

She managed to conceal her agitation from Dennis who was still playing close by. However, despite Tom's assurances, she was now close to tears.

Lucy often worried that one of Paul's dubious moneymaking schemes would get them into trouble. As a foreigner, he should be very careful, she warned him. Even if his schemes were legitimate, that was no protection in the Philippines; the corruption went right to the top. Most officials were effectively above the law, and they could do what they wanted. Whatever Paul was up to, it involved the Senator and she knew that was dangerous.

Dennis was still happily playing in the back garden. Lucy kept checking on him. She could see him through the open gate, but she didn't want him to realize that there was anything wrong.

Brian considered the papers and photos for a while and seemed satisfied. He put them back in the envelope and tucked them neatly into his jacket pocket.

"Wait there for a moment, please." He stood up and strode around the house to the front door. The house looked relatively untouched. He was pleased that his men had been careful.

Lucy was waiting anxiously in the garden

"Ok, Lucy. You can go in and get ready now,"

She called Dennis, who still had no idea what was going on, into the house and they both changed. She was hoping that, whatever the problem was, it would soon be over.

Paul was enjoying the football match, and the whiskey. Consuelo came back to join him and noticed that there was about four inches gone from the bottle. He settled down in one of the comfortable chairs next to Paul.

"Are you ok with the whiskey, Paul? Is there anything else you need? You must be hungry by now, let's have some food."

The Senator guided him towards the door. At this point, Paul was unsteady on his feet.

Consuelo's small meeting room had been turned into a dining room; steaming bowls of rice and fish covered a side table.

"I asked Tony to join us. I knew you wouldn't mind."

Tony rose, smiling, his hand outstretched.

"How are you, Paul?"

The three men settled down to the meal. The Senator had thoughtfully brought the whiskey bottle through and he poured Paul another drink as he sat down.

"How's Dennis doing at school?" Tony asked.

"He's fine, Tony. He misses his holidays in the Old Country. We don't go there as often now that my mother's dead."

"Oh, I'm sorry Paul. I didn't know your mother had passed. Is your father still alive?"

Paul shook his head. "He died many years ago, so there's no reason to visit anymore. There's nothing for me there now."

"What about your family? Surely your brothers and sisters miss you, especially now that your parents are gone."

Paul looked sad. "There's just the one brother, Tony. I don't have much contact with him. We do not have big families in Australia like people do here."

"Oh, I see," said the Senator, glancing at his brother. "I didn't realize."

"I don't miss the place at all. I love Asia and want to finish my days here."

After lunch, the three men went back to the sofas in the lounge area and drank more whiskey. Thirty minutes later the Senator made his excuses and told Paul he would be back soon. Tony stayed there drinking with Paul.

Tony had spent thirty years in Canada and loved to gamble. He and Paul often went to casinos together.

Tony, of course, knew about the gold but was astonished when his brother told him earlier of the surprising events of the day. The Senator needed Tony's help for the next part of his plan.

At Paul's house, Lucy and Dennis appeared in the front garden, dressed and ready for their trip to Benguet. Lucy felt more composed now. She kept remembering Tom's reassuring call.

It was a tight squeeze in the large four by four but they all got in. Once they were on the main road, Brian received a call from Tom. Lucy felt even more reassured when she overheard Brian talking to Tom. Yes, they had made a thorough search and found the envelope and yes, Lucy and Dennis were with him and would be joining Paul and the Governor for dinner.

As they entered the city, the car took a turn to the left, which surprised Lucy.

"Don't worry. We're meeting at the Benguet Plaza Hotel for dinner."

Lucy looked pleased. This must be a celebration of some sort, she thought.

The Benguet Plaza Hotel was the most prestigious in the city. They parked up in a garage at the back of the hotel and entered through a side entrance, leaving the guards in the car.

Tom was looking for the Senator, he had to work fast. He caught up with his boss in the garden.

"Excuse me, sir. Brian rang me. He wants to get back here. He's asked me to go down to the hotel and take over."

"That's fine. You know what needs to be done."

The Senator walked away, preoccupied.

The friendly staff escorted Brian and his party into a small private dining room. As the waitresses went back and forth bringing in the food, the guards slipped quietly into the room and sat down to eat in the corner.

Lucy remembered her cell phone.

"Can I have my cell phone back now please, Brian?" Brian made a show of checking his pockets and then apologized. "I'm sorry, Lucy. I've left it in the car. I'll go get it."

Tom was walking into the hotel at that moment and met Brian just as he was on his way to the garage. Brian was surprised to see him.

"What are you doing here?"

"The old man sent me to take over. He said you had better things to do at the estate."

They both laughed and walked out to the car together.

"I told Lucy I was coming out to get her phone. I didn't want a scene in the restaurant, so you better look after it now."

He passed it to Tom.

"Just destroy it once the job is done."

When Brian returned to the dining room, Tom was with him. Lucy was relieved to see Tom, but tried not to show it.

"Change of plan, Lucy. I'm needed back at the ranch. Tom will look after you, and we'll meet up later."

As soon as Brian disappeared, Tom passed Lucy's phone back to her. Tom and Lucy sat in silence pretending to eat for a few minutes. She was so relieved to see him, and she wanted to hug him so badly, but Dennis and the guards were there. It was important that they didn't suspect.

Tom winked at her and stood up.

"Ok lads, let's go. You can bring the car around to the front."

They got up slowly and shuffled out of the room. A few seconds after they had left the room, Tom slipped out quietly after them telling Lucy to wait there with Dennis.

The guards left by a small exit door next to the main entrance onto the quiet main street. No one in the street took any notice of them or the third man, Tom, who followed a few seconds later. They slipped down a side alley to the right of the hotel. The alley was narrow and dark, but there was a light above the small door into the garage.

Tom followed them as they approached the car. They were only a couple of yards inside the garage and were struggling to see in the dim light, so they moved very cautiously. The guards knew what was supposed to happen tonight so they showed no surprise when Tom told them to check the back for the large plastic sheeting they would need to wrap up the bodies.

The first guard was leaning over into the back of the SUV when Tom brought the hatch down on him with great force. He heard the man's back snap and watched for a second as he writhed, half in and half out of the car, and moaned quietly. He was barely conscious and didn't offer any resistance as Tom's large and powerful hand closed around his throat. It took just a few seconds for his body to go limp. Tom moved away from the car before he could be certain that the job was complete because the second guard was coming around the front of the car looking very confused.

He had seen some of what had happened but was in front of the vehicle and could not see the back. From his viewpoint, it looked as if his comrade had fallen inside. Before he could react, Tom was at him and a five-inch blade pierced his uniform. Blood started to ooze out around the blade, which was now embedded in the man up to the hilt. He sank to his knees, still bewildered, and then fell forward motionless, his eyes wide open in horror, staring at the ceiling.

Tom heard noises from the back of the car and turned his attention to the first guard who had started gurgling, unable to move. He took a short wire from inside his coat and held the wire tight around the guard's neck. It drew blood as it cut into the flesh, but more importantly it cut off his air supply. In thirty seconds, he was dead.

Both the guards were small and slim and Tom had plenty of space to work on the garage floor. Just to make sure no one would disturb him, he bolted the two doors. He laid out the sheets and wrapped each man like a parcel with the binding twine.

He then piled the neatly wrapped bodies into the cargo area of the SUV and covered them with a blanket before closing and locking the hatch. He checked around the floor thoroughly to make sure that there was no trace of blood, and then rang the Senator

"It's done, boss. They're both dead."

The Senator smiled, thinking that Lucy and Dennis were now disposed of and there was just Paul to deal with. *Two down, one to go*, he thought. Tom went to fetch Lucy and Dennis. He was still puffing from his exertions when he walked into the room.

"Is everything OK?" Lucy asked.

"Yes, fine sweetheart, just sorting something out."

Lucy looked behind Tom

"Where are the guards?"

"I sent them back to the Estate by bus. I have other things to do. Come on, it's time for us to go."

Lucy and Dennis followed Tom as he strode briskly out of the restaurant. He held the back door of the car open for Dennis. Lucy walked around the car and let herself into the passenger seat.

Dennis was tired and he dozed as they pulled out of the garage. Tom and his mom spoke quietly as he slept.

"Tom, what's happening today? It made me so scared," Lucy said, staring at him like a startled rabbit.

He smiled at her and put his large hand over hers.

"It's all ok, sweetheart. Just a change of plan, that's all."

She continued to stare at him, a bit more calmly now.

"Look, sweetheart, a few things happened at the Estate today. We have to bring our plans forward, that's all."

After a couple of seconds, she remembered her husband.

"Where's Paul?" The frightened rabbit was back.

"He's fine. He's drinking with the Senator and they plan to go to the casino later. Don't worry about this afternoon. That was just a bit of a misunderstanding. Everything's fine now."

She trusted him but was not sure whether to believe him. For now she decided it would be best if she kept quiet.

"We have to bring our plans forward and it'll be easier anyway with Paul kept busy. You have to leave tonight."

To Tom's surprise, Lucy nodded. She had prepared for this.

"When you told me to bring the passports I realized. I trust you, darling. I know you'll look after us."

"Of course I will, sweetheart."

He still had hold of her hand and he squeezed it gently now.

From the inside of his jacket he pulled a large wad of money and put it in her hand. It was all one thousand peso bills and must have been more than an inch thick. She had never before dreamt of such an amount. While she was still staring at it, Tom put a sheet of written instructions in her lap.

"I want you to go to Singapore. I'll meet you there."

Her mouth was still open as he slowly pulled out of the garage. Lucy regained her composure after a couple of minutes and put the money and the note in her bag. The bus terminal was set back off the main road a little way out of the city. It wasn't busy at that time of the evening, but buses were leaving every thirty minutes for Manila.

Ten minutes later, as Lucy and Dennis were boarding the bus, Tom approached the Benguet Infirmary. It was the largest hospital in the City, being six stories tall. It loomed ahead on the right.

The Senator owned the building, but rented it out to a consortium of doctors. He made a point to ensure that the head of security at the hospital was one of 'his' men. He had earlier called the man to give him instructions.

The incinerator burned non-stop twenty-four hours a day. Some waste materials, especially anything infectious, had to be disposed of quickly even in the middle of the night. It was unusual, however, for a private car to turn up late at night with large packages. The security chief made sure that no one else was around as he directed the driver to back up to the noisy furnace.

As soon as the car pulled to a stop, Tom popped the hatch lock and the security Chief lifted the cargo hatch. He helped Tom to remove the "packages" and cast them into the fiery opening. The men carried out their grisly work in silence. It was over in less than a minute. The Chief expected two packages, and he got two. He didn't realize that the bodies inside were not those that Consuelo had intended. Without a word, Tom climbed back into the car and drove out of the hospital complex.

No one would notice the disappearance of the guards for a few days. Their families were in distant provinces and they were living alone. People would assume they had gone to their province to vote. By the time anyone missed them Tom would be a long way away—and he wouldn't be coming back.

During their planning, the Senator and Tom agreed that it would be dangerous to deal with Paul on the Estate. It would be better if at least a couple of witnesses saw him leaving the Estate in good health.

Tony went back to keep Paul company. He was still watching the sports channel, but was beginning to doze now—the whiskey was taking its toll. Tony let him sleep through the afternoon. It suited their plan better for Paul to leave the Estate in darkness.

Paul opened his eyes a few hours later as Tony gently roused him.

"The Senator has gone to the casino and wants us to join him there. Are you up for it?"

Paul took a few moments to come round. What he really wanted was to go to sleep there on the couch, but he didn't want to offend the Senator, and maybe the Senator would talk to him about collecting his gold tomorrow. He nodded and slowly sat up.

"Are you ok to drive?"

Again, Paul nodded. He would never ever admit that he should not drive even if he was nearly incapable.

"I don't mind taking you, Paul, but perhaps you need to take your own car to get home afterwards."

This was Consuelo's idea. He wanted the guards to see Paul drive off on his own, clearly drunk and maybe not fit to drive.

Paul walked unsteadily towards his car; it was parked next to Tony's car. The guards saluted as they drove through the gates, Tony in the front car, and Paul following.

The gates to the casino were open and they drove straight in. The men at the gate showed little interest in them, which pleased Tony. He could hear the noise of the tires crushing the gravel as they proceeded past the guardhouse. They drove to the back part of the car park and picked a quiet area with large bushes shading the ground by the side fence. Tony found a spot with two spaces between other cars. It was perfect, the sun had set a while ago, and the growing darkness provided extra cover.

Tony swiftly got out of the car as soon as it came to a complete stop. He walked around the front, glancing around to ensure they were alone. He was no stranger to using a weapon and he never went anywhere without the Berretta pistol which was concealed in his shoulder holster.

Paul was taking quite a while to lock the door. He was having trouble finding the key hole in his inebriated state. He was still fumbling with the keys when he heard the click, the quiet but unmistakable sound of the cocking of a pistol. In less than a second, his training took over. He was lucky; his opposite side view mirror was bent at a helpful angle.

Through the front door window, Paul could see that the figure behind him was holding a gun and raising it up. He sharply stepped backwards and without turning his head brought his elbow hard into Tony's stomach. The startled man bent double from the blow. It took a second for him to recover. Paul grabbed the wrist that held the gun and twisted it around sharply until he heard the bone crack. The pistol fell to the ground between the two men. Tony's mouth was open in an attempt to scream, and he tried to straighten up. Paul covered it with his large hand before any sound could come out and slammed the man backwards hard against his car.

"What the fuck are you trying to do, Tony?" Paul snarled. "Your brother knows that if I disappear all the information about the murders will come out and he'll be ruined. What's he playing at?"

Despite the excruciating pain, Tony managed to talk.

"He got the packages, Paul. He got them back from the Post Office—they never went to Manila. You've got nothing on him."

This took Paul aback, but he quickly recovered.

"Do you really think I'm that stupid, Tony? You're lucky I need you to give your brother a message or I would kill you now. The packages I took into Benguet Post Office were dummies; I did that to fool the Senator. The real ones are already in Manila. Tell him to check the packages he has if he doesn't believe me. He'll find they are stuffed with blank paper."

"Ok, ok, Paul. I'll tell him. I'll go and tell him straight away," Tony said, anxious to escape without more injury.

"Oh, you can tell him alright Tony, but not tonight. I need some time to think now."

Paul moved too fast for the dazed Tony to react. In an instant Paul's closed fist connected with his chin and jolted his head sideways.

Tony fell to the ground like a sack of potatoes. Paul opened the back seat of Tony's car and with another glance around just to make sure he was still alone, poured the limp figure inside and quietly closed the door. Tony was still breathing; but he would be unconscious for a few hours.

So, the Senator doesn't intend to honor the bargain, Paul thought. He was sobering up very quickly. He needed time to think, and a safe place to do it.

The casino was open all night and there would be many cars left there while their well-to-do owners were inside the casino enjoying themselves so time was on his side, but where could he go. He certainly could not go home.

He tried to ring Lucy to warn her to get out of the house. There was no reply from the home phone or her cell phone. Although he didn't know it, her cell phone was off, and it was in her pants pocket. She was well on the way to Manila. He headed for the only place he could think of where he could be sure to be safe and lie low for a while.

Tom was pleased with himself. His plan was going well so far. Lucy and Dennis were safely on their way to Manila now, no one suspected anything. The Senator would never find out the truth—they'd live quietly abroad and keep their heads down. He had enough money to take care of them all for the rest of their lives. It was nearly midnight, and he decided not to return to the estate in the middle of the night. He felt like celebrating and the City Centre was close.

He drove into Benguet City Centre and parked up in front of a small hotel. It was well away from the area where he usually met Lucy. After checking in he had a bath and refreshed himself before walking out into the historic cobbled street.

He was a fit and quite well dressed guy and was soon approached by several young girls offering him a massage. He took his time making his selection. He would be on his way to join Lucy soon, so this may be his last chance for a bit of fun for a while.

As usual, he sat in the nearby pavement cafe to watch the 'fashion parade' of girls and boys looking for trade. The third one to approach him had a nice smile and long silky hair, she was probably a student. Taller than most of the girls, but thin and attractive and she was wearing the shortest skirt he had ever seen. After the events of the day, he needed relaxation.

He genuinely loved Lucy and promised himself that when they were really and properly together he would change his ways, but his twenty years in military jobs and situations all over the world had taught him to take his pleasure when he could for who knew what tomorrow would bring—it was a hard habit to break. He decided that tonight would be his last fling. He would soon be settled down with his new family.

He and the young girl laughed together as they strolled back to his hotel with her hanging on his arm and struggling to keep up. She said she was eighteen but was probably a bit younger. They undressed quickly and showered. No matter what her real age was, once they were naked in bed Tom became aware that she was no novice. He lay back on the bed first and admired her pale body as she walked towards him. Her breasts were small, but that had never bothered him.

She was clean shaven, he liked that.

CHAPTER SEVEN

The Senator rose early, as usual. It was the day before Polling Day and he was feeling in good spirits. As he walked through the glass doors onto the patio, the noise of the children laughing and running between the bushes came to his ears.

"The kids seem to be having fun." He smiled at Chloe, and rested his hand on her shoulder as she leaned in to him.

"They love to play in the garden, sweetheart. What are you doing today?"

"I'm sorry, Chloe. I have to leave right after breakfast. A quick stop at a polling station for lunch then off to Manila."

"I thought you could spend more time with us today."

"Just a few more days, darling, and the election will be over. Anyway, you'll be joining me in Manila tomorrow morning."

She glanced at him and gave him a withering look.

"I know, but we both know that we're going to see less of each other when you're President."

The Senator tried to console her

"I'm sure we'll all enjoy our new life. I think you'll soon get used to it."

He leaned in and kissed her. She was a real beauty. She was also intelligent and honest, and devoted to her man.

Simon, Brian and Tom were also at the table finishing their breakfast. There would be a final briefing before the Senator set off.

Consuelo was drinking orange juice when his phone rang. Simon reached over to take it.

"Hello, this is Senator Consuelo's office, can I help you?"

The Senator had long ago taught him to be less abrupt and friendlier when answering his phone.

As Simon listened to the croaky voice on the other end of the phone, his face fell. After about ten seconds, he passed it to the Senator.

"It's Tony, your brother. He's hurt. Paul got away," he whispered. He didn't want Chloe to hear.

The Senator rose from the table abruptly and walked just far enough away, out of earshot of his wife.

"Tony, are you ok? What happened?"

"Sorry, brother, I'm so sorry. He got the better of me. He's much sharper than he looks. He knocked me out and dumped me in the back of the car. A security guard just woke me."

"Don't worry, Tony. It's ok. Don't you remember? I got the packages and the originals from his house. There is nothing he can do now,"

"No, no, brother. Paul says the packages you took were decoys and the real ones are in Manila already."

Consuelo's face fell and he ran into his office. He opened the cupboards and threw the sack with the letters onto the floor. He grabbed one and tore it open—blank pages greeted him. His face went ashen and his eyed were wide with panic. He opened them all—they were all full of blank pages. He stared down at piles of white paper on the floor; he had certainly underestimated the man. He lifted the phone to his ear again.

"Are you still there, Tony?"

"Yes, I'm still here, brother,"

"Get back here as quick as you can. I'll decide what to do. Don't worry, we can fix this somehow."

He sat on the floor just thinking for a few minutes. After he composed himself he walked back to Chloe. She didn't realize anything was wrong.

"Sorry, sweetheart. Urgent business beckons."

Without waiting for a reply he turned to the other men.
"My office!"

He strode off with Brian, Simon and Tom close behind.

"He knocked out my brother and left him in the back of his car. These packages are fake. The real packages are already in Manila—the bastard's got us."

They all stood around the papers strewn on the floor. Simon spoke up first.

"What are we going to do? We know Paul isn't stupid and he's a highly trained soldier. He wouldn't be so foolish as to go back to his house, and he has no family around here. My guess is he'll take to the hills or try to leave the area. He'll know we'll be after him."

"I'll get the Police to put up road blocks," Brian said.

"No point," said Simon. "Paul left here with Tony about fourteen hours ago. Paul must have knocked him out as soon as they arrived at the Casino, more than thirteen hours ago. If he was going to leave the province he will have done so by now."

The Senator reflected for a couple of seconds.

"Do it anyway. We have nothing to lose, and he might make a mistake."

Then suddenly he had an idea.

"Wait, we've still got him. I know what to do."

He took out his cell phone; Paul's number was stored, he pressed it.

Paul drove a long way out of Benguet and up into the hills, until he found a quiet spot on a deserted road. Taking no chances, he pulled a long way off the road where he couldn't be seen by any passing traffic, and covered the car with branches just in case.

He spent the night on the back seat. He was not going anywhere until he knew Lucy was safe, and he needed a few hours sleep anyway to recover from the effects of the alcohol and the tiredness that was now overwhelming him.

A few hours after dawn, he woke to his phone ringing incessantly.

He thought it must be Lucy.

"Hello, Paul," said the familiar deep voice. "I hope you haven't done anything silly yet."

Paul said nothing. He'd just woken up, and hadn't come to his senses yet. The last thing he expected was a call from the Senator.

Consuelo continued. "I'm sorry about last night. I didn't know Tony was going to do that. He acted without my authority; we can still work something out, Paul."

Paul was recovering fast.

"Well, it's a bit late now, Senator. You had your chance. My next call will be to my colleagues in Manila and then you are done, finished."

The Senator breathed a sigh of relief. Paul hadn't contacted anyone yet.

"Of course you must do what you see fit, Paul, but I did think you might show more concern for your wife Lucy, and your son Dennis. They became my "guests" last night," he lied.

The Senator knew that Paul would have tried to contact them but would not have been able to and, as far as the Senator knew, they were dead.

Paul froze. He remembered he tried to ring them last night and couldn't get through. He could feel anger building inside, but he knew this was no time for rage, or threats. After a few seconds silence he spoke.

"What do you want?" he asked simply and quietly and waited for the response.

"Paul, my friend, all I've ever wanted is a peaceful life, and you know I'm a reasonable man."

Paul stayed silent while Consuelo continued.

"Let's be brutally frank, shall we? If you go to anyone with your story your family will die in a painful way, and don't forget that I have the power and influence to hunt you down as well."

He paused for his words to sink in.

"The death of a foreigner and his family could cause some...inconvenience...and I would avoid it if I can, you know I would."

Paul still couldn't yet think straight, but he wanted to know where the Senator was going with this. He knew he had to be careful. They had his family.

"What would you suggest?"

The Senator was already thinking on his feet.

"Well, how about this. First, you have to get all the envelopes back. I'll fly you and your family out of the country as soon as I have them. Of course, you'll have to sign a letter saying that all your accusations were false, and that you were just trying to make money off of me and the photos were all staged—just in case any of the these reports of yours come to light.

"I'll give you a little money to get started abroad and we can all be happy. You can bring some trusted friends with you to make sure I keep my side of the bargain. You know that I wouldn't want any shadow over the start of my Presidency. Your family will be fine Paul; do you think I am the kind of man who can kill women and children?"

Paul was still not awake; part of his brain knew the senator was lying, but right now he would go along with it. At this point, what other choice did he have?

"What do I have to do now?" Paul asked.

The Senator smiled. *How things can change in a few short hours,* he thought to himself.

"Go and get the letters and bring them to me. In a few days I'll come back to Benguet, as President. That gives us both time to sort out what we have to do."

"Just make sure you keep your word."

"Of course I will. I have too much to lose not to. Just contact me when you have the letters and we can arrange to meet,"

"Ok, but you better take good care of my family. I won't fall for any more tricks."

"Paul, you know I will. You can be with them again very soon."

Paul didn't believe or trust Consuelo. He had to formulate a plan.

"D'you think he fell for it?" asked Brian.

"I doubt it. He's not stupid. When he gets his wits together, he'll realize that we can't let him get off like that. The question is what he will do then. Anyway, I think we have a little time." The others nodded.

Tom was the first to speak.

"I don't think that he'll go to Manila and get the envelopes. He'll try to rescue his family. What else could he do? He is not the sort of man to run away and leave his family to their fate."

"I agree, and we mustn't underestimate him again," said the Senator.

"Organize a manhunt for him. We have no idea where he is, but start with the Estate and move outwards. If he finds out what we are doing then he will know we were bluffing. Simon, we have to go to Manila. We're late already."

He turned to the other two men.

"Brian and Tom, start spreading the rumor that we're holding a woman and her son here somewhere. Paul will ask around. It would be good for him to hear that, and in the meantime strengthen the security and start night patrols. He just might try something. If he does appear, he must be killed straight away, of course. Tell the security guards there will be a reward for the man that kills him."

The Senator rose from the table indicating the meeting was over.

There was some electioneering to do before he left the province for Manila. There should be plenty of photos in tomorrow mornings editions. What could be better?

At eleven thirty, he was walking towards the helicopter pad. Simon was on his phone arranging the press conference for the lunchtime meeting. A sleek black helicopter sat on the concrete forecourt, with its engines running. They all ducked to avoid the rotating blades as they carefully climbed aboard. A small security team had joined them as usual. The Senator was now in better spirits and was laughing and joking with his men as the twelve-seater machine rose into the sky.

An hour later he was landing in a school field. The school was preparing for the next day when it would be closed for polling, but the school staff and a few loyal parents had turned out to welcome him.

He bounded off the helicopter and greeted them warmly. The Mayor, the Returning Officer and the Senator made their way through the small crowd of supporters and retired to a private office.

"Well, how are you, Pedro? I hope you are doing your usual excellent work. I'm expecting great things from your town. I'm sure you're doing a great job. Where would I be without your help?"

Pedro beamed back at the Senator.

"I trust that all is prepared for tomorrow? I always know I can rely on you, Pedro."

"Of course, sir. Everything will be fine. We know we have ninety percent of the votes here—we always do—and the people are so grateful to you for your generosity, sir."

"What about the tellers, counters and checkers. Have they all been looked after?"

"Yes sir, they have, and they've done a fine job already."

The Returning Officer opened a tall cupboard and brought out a cardboard box. He reached in and passed to the Senator some of the paper he pulled out.

Smiling, he fully opened the cupboard to reveal many more similar boxes. They were all stuffed with voting papers already completed, with the votes cast for the Senator.

"I always tell people to vote early," the senator said, looking at the completed ballots.

The others laughed dutifully at his joke.

Consuelo opened his case and took a small package from it.

"I know life's a struggle for you and your family Pedro."

He passed a brown envelope to his grateful Returning Officer and said that he must now be on his way.

One of the attendees at the lunch was Edelweiss, a very pretty girl of nineteen who first caught the Senator's eye when she attended a party at his Estate more than a year ago. The well-developed body and smile had drawn the Senator's attention. She came with her mother, who was a Town Councilwoman. Instead of returning home with her mother that night, she'd arrived back in the village three days later and fifty thousand pesos richer.

Her mother, far from being upset, was pleased. She encouraged the 'friendship' for the benefits it would bring to their family. Edelweiss had since spent a lot of time at the Estate, sometimes as a 'guest' of the Senator and sometimes as company for one of his influential friends. In her short adult life she had shared the bed of Senators, Congressmen, Generals and foreign Royalty.

To the press and public she was his 'niece,' although the reality was more or less an open secret to those around him. He chose her to accompany him to Manila today 'to assist him with his preparations' for the acceptance, the day after tomorrow. She was eminently qualified for the position—she could be guaranteed to be discreet.

They were soon taking off again, bound for the final stop in the province, the Town Hall in the Capital City of Benguet, with the Senator's new assistant on board. His most powerful and influential Provincial allies would be there. The concrete car park at the side of the impressive Capital building was cleared so that his helicopter could land.

As he stepped down from the helicopter, his brother-in-law Rupert, the Mayor of Benguet, was waiting. He was about forty but looked much older due to his thinning hair and large stomach. This was the Senator's home town, little manipulation on the polling was needed here, but the usual wheels of vote rigging would still turn. Consuelo's heart skipped a beat as he walked through the door. His wife, Chloe, had decided to join him unexpectedly. She stood waiting for him in the ornate function room as the party made their way inside. Edelweiss spotted Chloe before the Senator did and discreetly ducked to one side, slipping past the entranceway into the servant's area.

Chloe knew about Edelweiss but the subject was very rarely raised between them. However, she insisted that Edelweiss should never be seen with the Senator in public. Consuelo, seeing Chloe, glanced around and was relieved to see that Edelweiss was no longer with them.

Edelweiss already knew some of the staff in the building. She'd occasionally been there in the company of the Senator and others. She settled herself into the kitchen, where she took up conversation with a young lad, Elmer, a driver for the Mayor. He was from her village and she knew him quite well.

After a while he smiled and went out. He soon returned with two glasses of champagne and sandwiches that he had managed to sneak away from the reception.

After they'd eaten, he offered to show her the garage and the Mayor's limousine. There was no one in the spacious garage and the chauffeur locked the only entrance behind them. She smiled as the lad pushed her up against the side of the car, then opened her mouth wide and eagerly accepted his tongue.

The very short red dress she wore for the enjoyment of the Senator was riding up over her thighs. She was quite pleased to give this slim young lad the benefit of it for a while. She raised her arms and put them around his neck to pull him closer. As her arms stretched, her dress rode up to show her tiny red thong that did little to cover anything. Her legs parted slightly as the eager hand moved between them and started its work. The effect of the alcohol heightened her senses and she gasped as she felt two fingers slip inside her. She was already wet in anticipation. After a minute or so, he pulled away and unlocked the car.

He opened the back door and gently eased her into the back seat with their mouths still locked together and her legs clamped around his hand.

"Don't stop," she said breathlessly.

His fingers felt so good.

She used both hands to open his pants and pull them down. His young cock stood proud, she was not disappointed and pulled him into her mouth. For a few moments he sighed as she went down on him.

"Wait. I want to come inside you," he said.

She helped him to reposition himself, he slipped easily into her. He slammed her hard and energetically.

The springs under the leather backseat of the Mayor's Bentley were soon creaking as two enjoined bodies sank into the upholstery and bounced vigorously. Their legs were sticking out of the still open door.

They made their way back to the kitchen after about thirty minutes.

"That was nice," Elmer said. "I hope we can do it again sometime."

"Of course we can. You have a nice cock, Elmer. I hope your wife, Maria appreciates it."

They both laughed, then parted after a last kiss. The driver had duties to attend to.

For the rest of the afternoon Edelweiss sat in the kitchen, bored. The junior secretary eventually collected her when the Senator was already aboard the 'copter. Chloe was now on the way back to the Estate.

The journey to Manila took two hours, Edelweiss could flirt with him all she wanted to, and she did want to. The happier he was with her, the bigger her 'pocket money' was when they parted. The helicopter would take her back to the province early in the morning; he was going to meet Chloe for breakfast. This was fine with her. The Senator was fit and energetic. It was likely that she would return home tired and a bit sore but probably fifty thousand pesos richer.

They landed on the roof of the Hotel early in the evening. Until they were inside the room, Edelweiss kept a discrete distance in case of surprise encounters with journalists or photographers

The Senator poured himself a whiskey while two of his men searched the rooms and swept them for electronic bugs. As they were finishing, Edelweiss crept in almost unobserved. She smiled and nodded at the two men as they left. They each took a chair and stationed themselves outside the door. They were prepared for a long night, as was Edelweiss.

The bus from Benguet sped along the deserted roads. Lucy dozed with Dennis resting against her. They were more than halfway to Manila. All she and Dennis had with them was their passports, not even a change of clothes. She was not concerned; in her pocket was more money than she had ever had before. She was looking forward to her new life with Tom.

It seemed to her that recent events were a dream. She was still too dazed to think clearly, but she would follow the instructions of her lover and trust him. It was too late to go back now, even if she wanted to—which she didn't. The bus was half-empty. She was comfortable and began to doze again.

The bright early morning sky and the noisy traffic woke her up. She could feel the bus moving more slowly now along EDSA (the main roadway snaking through the Capital). It would reach the bus terminal in perhaps twenty minutes. They took breakfast in McDonald's at Dennis' insistence. He was waking up now and asking questions. She told him that they were going shopping; his father had given her a generous allowance for new clothes.

He brightened up at the news and started thinking about what he would buy.

The shops were very busy as they were going to be closed the next day for polling. The familiar electronic sounds of a gaming arcade caught Dennis' ear. He dragged his mother in, and she was happy to leave him there for an hour or so.

Dennis became engrossed with his game, so Lucy set off to find a travel agent. It didn't take her long. After texting Tom, she left the shop with two first class tickets to Singapore on the eight p.m. flight. There had been a change of plan. Tom would now join them at the Intercontinental Hotel the day after tomorrow. He had an important delivery to make but assured her that all was fine. She should enjoy herself and not worry. She took him at his word.

Years ago, Tom worked in Singapore. He had a chalet home on the beach not far from the airport. One of his retired army friends was glad to act as caretaker for the place until Tom needed it. Even while Lucy was at the travel agents in Manila, far away in Singapore her new home was being prepared.

While Dennis was happily playing, Lucy had one difficult job to do. She took a deep breath as she pressed the speed dial.

"Hello, Paul."

He answered the phone after just two rings. There was silence at the other end. Lucy's was the last voice he expected to hear. Paul found his voice at last. "Lucy? Are you ok? Where are you?"

"I'm sorry, Paul. I'm not coming back. I've left you, it's over."

Paul was confused.

"What do you mean? Where are you? Is Dennis with you?"

"Paul, I'm fine, we're fine. Dennis is here. We're making a new life. Were already in Manila now. Don't try to find me"

Paul was trying hard to make sense of what he was hearing.

"Is someone with you? Is someone making you say these things?"

It was Lucy's turn to be confused.

"No, Paul. We're fine, we're ok. But we're not coming back home. I want a new start, away from you. I've been unhappy for a long time. I'm sorry."

She saw no point in telling him about Tom now, he would find out in time.

Paul was beginning to realize that Consuelo had lied to him. He asked her again, "Are you sure you're ok, and Dennis is ok?"

"Yes, yes, we really are fine, but I can't live with you anymore. We're starting a new life. Don't try to find us. I'll let you know about Dennis later. I won't stop you from seeing him. Good luck with your life, Paul."

The phone clicked off. Paul tried to ring back—Lucy had turned her phone off.

Paul was a usually a decisive man, it was unusual for him to feel confused or uncertain and he didn't like what he was feeling at the moment. He was out of his depth in a dangerous situation of his own creation. He tried to think straight. Soon his survival instincts began to take over. Never mind about Lucy for now. The Senator had tried to fool him again. Consuelo would definitely want him dead now. He looked at his watch. He hadn't called the lawyer's offices today, he didn't need to. He wanted things to run their course now. The lawyers would soon be taking the packages to their final destinations; the Senator was finished.

Paul knew things wouldn't happen quickly – he wouldn't be safe until the Consuelo was exposed and arrested. What should he do 'till then? After a couple of minutes he made up his mind. His car pulled out onto the highway and he started on the long journey to Manila.

When Lucy collected a reluctant Dennis, she told him they were going to Singapore for a surprise holiday and that his father would join them later. There would be plenty of time for explanations when they were safe in Singapore. No one in the Philippines knew that Tom owned property in Singapore except his mother, not even Lucy. He was a careful man.

As international airports go, Manila was the pits, however by late afternoon they were relaxing in the Singapore Airlines smart and nearly deserted First Class Lounge area enjoying free snacks and drinks. Lucy rang Tom for the last time before they boarded the flight. When the overhead speakers blasted out a garbled message that their flight was boarding, they made their way through the airport to the boarding gate.

A few hours later as dawn was breaking, Senator Consuelo woke up in a good mood. He'd enjoyed a good night's sleep after an enjoyable couple of hours with Edelweiss. She woke him as she got out of bed—she knew the drill, she had to be gone well before Chloe got there.

Consuelo dozed, but couldn't sleep after Edelweiss left. He turned on the television and was pleased to see the news commentator predicting an election win for him with a margin of about five percent. Chloe rang him at seven to say she was on her way from the airport; he would be pleased to see her.

Despite the age difference they made a good-looking couple and they were happy together. On the campaign trail, she was at his side whenever he needed her, and she did her bit to court support for her husband.

Jake, the hairdresser, came with her from the Estate. He would wait downstairs until he was called up.

She arrived about five minutes after the breakfast was delivered. The journey from the province made her hungry so she was glad to see the food. They kissed passionately when she entered, but she knew that was as far as it would go until this evening. They both had to relax and get ready for a busy day of media events.

Edelweiss boarded the private helicopter Consuelo had arranged for her; she was in and dozing before they took off. Monsoon winds delayed them for short while, but she landed at Benguet a couple of hours later and boarded the waiting jeep for the two-hour ride to her village.

She was fully awake now, thinking about her future. She greeted her mom and dad with a big hug and gave them each a share of her earnings. There'd been no time for breakfast in Manila and she was hungry. Her mother prepared pancit for her while she took a shower.

The food was her favorite, the smell was reassuring to her. Edelweiss enjoyed her food, but her mind was troubled. "Mom, sit down with me please, and you dad. I have something to tell you."

Back in Manila, Consuelo and Chloe sat down to a quiet meal. They didn't discuss the election. She knew he liked to take a break from it when he was with her. They discussed family matters; Consuelo really missed his kids when he was away. They talked about taking a short holiday in two or three months. She doubted if it would happen, but it was nice to talk about it.

The Senator settled down at the desk with his first coffee of the day and started on his phone calls. There were about twenty calls he must make before he headed out, but they would all be short. The polls had been open for an hour already and he wanted to make sure his people were in place and doing their duty.

His phone rang at nine a.m., it was Alexi.

"Hello, Enrique. How goes the election?"

"It's in the bag, Alexi. After tomorrow I'll be running the country." They both laughed.

"My friend, can you get the gold to me tomorrow? I have a plane coming in and I can take it out of the country myself. There'll be no one around to ask any questions."

"Sure, no problem. I'll have it brought down by truck. It won't attract attention that way. They'll probably get there by lunchtime tomorrow. Is that ok?"

"I'll have the money ready. It'll be good to see you again."

"Oh, I won't be coming. I'll be a little bit busy tomorrow being made President. I'll get Tom to do it. You can give the money to him, we can trust him."

"Ok, I'll be waiting. Good luck for tomorrow, Mr. President,"

"Thank you. But I won't need it. Let's get together again soon."

Consuelo sat back and took a sip of his coffee, after a couple of minutes in thought he looked at his watch, then he picked up his phone again and pressed a speed dial number.

"Hello, sir," Tom said. "What can I do for you?"

"I need you to bring the gold to Manila like we planned. You need to get it to the embassy by about noon tomorrow."

"Ok, sir. That's fine,"

This couldn't be better; it fit in exactly with his plans.

"I'll get some sleep today and set off at midnight. I'll get Marcos to come with me. He's been driving for years and we know he's loyal."

"Ok. When you have the money, ring me. We'll arrange to meet up in Manila."

"Yes, sir, no problem. See you tomorrow."

He walked down to find Marcos. The old man was weeding the rose beds. He straightened up as Tom approached.

"Hi Tom, what's up?" asked Marcos. "It's not often we see you down here."

"I need you to do a bit of driving for me. You ok with that?"

"I guess so. Is there extra pay?"

"Yes, sure Marcos—we're going to Manila—double pay for a day, and a cash bonus."

The old man smiled. "That'll be fine."

He bent down to start weeding again.

"That's settled then. We leave at midnight. Get some sleep."

Tom had his own plans once the delivery was made. He was planning to leave the Estate that night anyway, now he could do so without any questions. He could pass the money from the gold over to the Senator, and then disappear; it was a stroke of good luck. Anyway, he thought, who would come looking for them, apart from Paul, and Tom could easily deal with Paul. He smiled, relishing the thought.

The Senator looked up as she walked in; she'd taken her gown off but was still in her bra and panties. She was carrying the new suit she brought with her, made especially for his acceptance speech. He smiled at her.

"You really are very thoughtful, sweetheart, and very beautiful, too."

He looked her up and down as she sidled over to him and put her arms around his neck. He kissed her gently, not wanting to disturb her make-up.

"I'm so proud of you, sweetheart. I want you to look your best tomorrow," she said as she nuzzled into his neck.

He hugged her tightly for a few moments, and then released her.

"Let's go and face the world, today's the last day. You can enjoy yourself in the shops, apart from the TV interview where they want both of us. There is only one we have to do together—here is the time and place; try not to be late."

Chloe took the paper from him and stuffed it in her handbag without looking at it.

"You know I am always on time for anything important," she said with a pout, but she was only playing.

They made their way downstairs, confident and ready for the day. The modest hotel car with tinted windows was waiting for them when they stepped out into the bright Manila sun at about ten minutes to eleven. There were no press agents or followers there. They'd been lucky so far. Their stay had thankfully remained secret—the Senator hoped it would remain so. He didn't like the idea of being mobbed when they returned that evening.

The Senator gave Chloe money to amuse herself in the shops until she was needed. They were both happy today doing what they liked best.

After spending twenty minutes in the dense Manila traffic, Consuelo told the driver to pull over. They were outside Power Plant mall, one of Chloe's favourite shopping haunts. She quickly kissed him on the cheek and slid out of the car. In a few seconds, she'd disappeared into the crowds. He lay back and sighed. He could get on with the business at hand now.

"Take me to Traders," he barked at the driver who nodded smartly as he pulled away.

His phone rang.

"I'm on my way now. I'll probably be about an hour."

"Ok," said the caller. "See you soon. I'm in room 508."

They stopped by the double gates at the back of the hotel, the goods entrance. The Senator got out, telling the driver to park and wait for him. He knew his way into the back of the hotel and was ignored by the porters and cleaning staff as he made his way to the elevator.

The door opened a few seconds after he knocked.

"How are you, sir?"

"It's been a long time, Enrique," said the Chief Justice. "I expected that I'd see you well before now."

The Senator looked contrite, and tried to make light of the remark.

"I've seen how busy you are, fighting all the allegations against the Government. I thought I should leave you in peace."

A faint smile crossed the Chief Justice's lips.

"It's ok, I know you've been busy, but it looks as if all of your hard work has paid off. I'm very pleased for you."

"Thank you, I hope we will all benefit from the change,"

Consuelo moved towards the mini-bar as the old man sat down.

"Whiskey?"

The room was spacious with a lounge area set apart from the bedroom space. Two large winged armchairs gave it a club atmosphere.

"You know, I don't think you have ever told me what you want to do after the election."

The older man sighed.

"Enrique, I'm not getting any younger, I'll be quite happy with a quieter life. There's a problem though," he sighed.

"I'll probably have to return to private practice. I haven't lined my pockets like all the rest of them. I can't afford to retire yet."

The Senator grinned. When the Chief Justice requested a meeting with him on Polling Day he knew what it would be about. He was surprised he had not been approached earlier. He had been ahead in the polls for months now. The Chief Justice wasn't known for astute political timing.

"It can't be that bad, my friend," the Senator said in a comforting sort of way. "You've supported the President through thick and thin and stuck your neck out many times. I'm sure you've been well rewarded."

The Chief Justice glanced sideways at him. He was uncomfortable at the insinuation, but he realized he was the one here with the begging bowl. He said nothing.

"Maybe I can help," said Consuelo. "I must be frank with you. You must realize that I will be elected tomorrow, but I have concerns that some parties, many parties in fact, will try to cause problems, maybe they could allege electoral fraud or try other legal moves to have the result declared invalid."

The old man stared at him.

"Of course, there always is. It's how our country works."

"You've been around a long time, my friend. You deserve a peaceful break. Help me out and we'll both benefit."

The two men were eyeing each other now.

"I heard you had my replacement lined up weeks ago."

"As a famous British Prime Minister once said, 'A week is a long time in Politics'."

"Well, you're right, I suppose. So you may have need of my services after the election?"

The Senator put his glass down on the side table.

"Sir, we haven't seen eye to eye for a while, since I stopped supporting the President, but you've never tried to do me any harm or badmouth me. I respect you immensely for that. If you want to stay on as Chief Justice, I won't replace you."

The Chief Justice raised his eyebrows in surprise.

"At least not for the first year and by then you'll be at retirement age and you can go with dignity and a good pension."

"I'm sure you'll want something in return," the old man said without looking at Consuelo.

"Not much," the Senator said hurriedly. "As I said earlier, there may be 'elements' who may try to disrupt a smooth transition. False allegations may be made. Public demonstrations could happen...that sort of thing. It wouldn't be in the public interest for there to be uncertainty or disruption at this time."

"You want me to jump on any public disquiet to give you an easy time, and in return I can keep my job." He could live with this. He held his hand out to the Senator. "Ok. We have a deal."

"Excellent. I knew we could see eye to eye."

The Chief Justice looked at his watch then. "It's time I was going. There are still many things I have to do."

"Will I see you at the celebration party tomorrow night then?"

"I'll come if I can."

The Senator slipped a thick white envelope into his hand as he made his way to the door.

"What's this for?"

"Taxi fare back to your office."

The hotel car driver was waiting as arranged, and opened the back door as the Senator approached.

"Where to now, sir?"

"GMA television station."

They were soon in the thick of the Manila traffic again.

Bruce Aquino was in charge of the largest media empire in the Philippines. He had three television stations, five radio stations, one national, and seven regional newspapers.

Bruce was a celebrated political interviewer until his business successes propelled him into management. He planned to interview the couple himself. It would make good afternoon TV with plenty of re-runs on the evening news. Consuelo saw it as the first interview of his Presidency although he kept reminding himself it might pay to be a little humble and thankful.

Bruce had a private bar adjacent to his office. He decided to wait there for the Senator with a large brandy. He wasn't yet forty, but he had the liver of a sixty-year-old man—he would certainly die young.

"Welcome, my dear friend."

The practiced smile adorned his face as he thrust out his hand. The Senator returned the smile and clasped the hand warmly.

"Where's Chloe? I thought she would be joining us."

As if it were timed, Chloe swept into the room and hugged Bruce theatrically, then as an afterthought hugged her husband before sitting down on the chaise lounge. Bruce was prepared. He handed Chloe a glass of champagne, and the Senator a brandy. He hadn't forgotten how to interview, and having your guests relaxed was all part of the game. Today however, there would be no hatchet job. Bruce would help to portray the Senator in the best possible light. He passed a sheet of paper to Consuelo.

"These are the questions I propose to ask. Is there anything you want to add or change?"

The Senator looked through the list.

"No, they're fine. Good questions, nothing overtly controversial. Well done."

Chloe piped up,

"What about me. Don't I get to say anything?" The Senator remembered that the glass of champagne in her hand was not her first one today.

Bruce put his hand on her shoulder,

"Don't worry, my dear. I am going to ask you lots about what it is like being the wife of such a distinguished man. Just remember to say lots of nice things."

She was a bright girl, but today the patronization was lost on her. She finished the champagne and put the glass on the table. Consuelo prayed inwardly that Bruce wouldn't offer her another. He needn't have worried; the door opened just then and a small man wearing headphones around his neck entered.

"It's time to get ready."

The men finished their drinks and the three of them made their way down to the studio. Bruce had wanted it to go out live but the Senator refused, just in case Chloe said something she shouldn't. After the formalities of light make-up they found themselves under warm and bright lighting, waiting for Bruce to make his entrance. They didn't wait long.

The show started with five minutes of mutual admiration and amusing anecdotes, and Chloe showing just the right amount of leg to hold male viewer attention. When it was over, there were more hugs. Consuelo left by the back entrance, kissing his wife goodbye on the way out. Chloe hailed a taxi at the front of the building. She was not that well known publicly so she could get away with that. She just had time for a couple more hours shopping before meeting up with Consuelo again at their favorite bar.

The little resto-bar was small, quiet and secluded. There were a group of young office girls sitting in one corner and giggling over a bucket of six San Miguel beers and a plate of peanuts. The other twenty or so seats were empty. It was a Wednesday night so it wouldn't get much busier. Quiet jazz music enhanced the rather dreary and neglected look of the place. The owner had known the Senator for a long time. Hopefully, he and Chloe would be undisturbed. Since yesterday, in another hotel not far away and in the province, things were happening which the Senator couldn't have imagined. A prominent city lawyer was stuck in traffic, cursing the election for making him late.

Alberto Del Rosario had been a lawyer for thirty-two years. He was at the top, and enjoyed the benefits of lawyering for the rich and famous.

Some of his friends introduced him to Paul many years ago and the clever attorney had cultivated his acquaintance—foreigners were always good for business. He was late getting to the office today. It was the day before Election Day and there was a lot of heavy traffic.

The package arrived a few days ago and was still sitting on his desk. For the last couple of mornings he received the regular reassuring call from Paul first thing, but not today. It was now ten thirty already and he hadn't yet received a call. It was time to follow his client's instructions.

It took him more than half an hour to track down Bishop Ong who was in Taguig visiting a parochial church, but the Senior Bishop agreed to meet him in an hour. The Bishop knew Paul, and he also knew Alberto by reputation and was intrigued.

They met at the Bishop's Palace in Quezon City just before noon. The Bishop had a light lunch sent in to the small office where he received Alberto. The clergyman was in his full regalia and looked impressive. He was a tall, white haired man, but he looked slim, fit and youthful. Without a word, Alberto passed him the thick brown envelope

"What is this, my son? I don't think it's a bomb or you wouldn't be standing in the room with me."

The Bishop waved Alberto towards the chair in front of the desk, and gestured that he should sit down. Putting on his reading glasses, the old man squinted at the sheaf of pages, and the small coin attached to the top page.

He despised the current President for her corruption and blatant self-interest, but even more, he despised the aspiring President, Senator Consuelo. Unlike many of his peers, he'd been unwilling to turn a blind eye to the public philandering, illegal gambling, drug interests and smuggling operations of many of the current politicians.

It took him twenty minutes to read and digest the papers. His face became more and more serious as he read. His mind raced as he slowly took in all that the lawyer had laid before him. What a day for him to be presented with this, the day before Election Day. What could he do?

The Bishop composed himself.

"We've got to get the others together. There's no time to be lost. As far as I'm aware many of them are not even in Manila right now so we'll have to act fast."

Alberto was surprised. The Bishop looked up from his papers and stared at the lawyer. He realized then that Alberto had no idea what was in the package. He sighed and sat back in his chair.

"You'd better read this, my son. I see no reason why this should be kept secret from you. Anyway, I'm going to need your help."

He passed the papers over.

"Take your time to read them. I'll have some coffee sent in."

The Bishop rose from his seat.

"I know this man, Paul. This is no joke," he said on his way out.

"Where are you going, sir?"

"To pray, my son, to pray," the Bishop said over his shoulder as he left the room.

After thirty minutes the old man returned.

"Attorney, I'm sure you must appreciate the gravity of what you've read. Do you think we can we trust these documents?"

"We both know the man, your Grace. I believe this is genuine. Paul's a meticulous man and has always impressed me with his truthfulness."

The Bishop set about making phone calls. It was now just past two p.m. and even if he could get hold of the other five people, they would surely take many hours to return to Manila. Some wouldn't make it until the next day. By early evening, and after many exasperating conversations, he could not get enough of them to come back to Manila in time for a meeting today, or even for an early meeting tomorrow. Eventually he set the meeting for five o'clock on the following afternoon, Election Day.

The Bishop invited the lawyer to stay for dinner but he declined, taking his leave and telling the Bishop he'd be back tomorrow afternoon. It was just as well, the Bishop had much work to do planning the meeting. The next call he made was to the manager of the Manila Peninsula Hotel. He was Irish and a devout Catholic. He knew the man well and he knew he could count on his discretion.

The Manila Peninsula Hotel on Makati Avenue was one of the oldest and most prestigious hotels in Manila. Located right in the heart of the City, it overlooks the landscaped gardens on Ayala Triangle. Famous people often stayed there, so their arrival shouldn't arouse too much interest.

"Hello, my son."

Connor recognized the Bishop's voice.

"Good afternoon, your Grace. It's a pleasure to talk to you. How can I help you?"

"Connor, I need your assistance. I need a large room tomorrow. I'll be meeting with some senior people, and it must be very confidential. It's crucial that it doesn't leak out to the public. Can you help me?"

"Of course I can, your Grace."

"Thank you. Please, can you handle all the arrangements personally?"

"Yes, your Grace. It'll be a pleasure."

"Thank you so much, Connor. It is indeed for a very worthy cause. I'll need four internet-ready computers with video-cams and four phone lines. Is that possible?"

The other man confirmed it was.

"Security really is of the greatest importance. Please can you give us just one of your staff to look after us—a long term employee who you can trust completely?"

The Bishop didn't want unknown house cleaners and serving staff in and out of the room.

"It's likely to be a very long meeting, my son, it could go on overnight. Can you organize regular tea, coffee and snacks?"

"That's no problem, your Grace. All of that will be done. Is there anything else I can do?"

"You've been very helpful. There's nothing further I need right now. Can you text me the number and floor of the room later? I want my guests to be able to come straight in without having to hang around or ask for directions."

"Of course, you'll have it within thirty minutes."

The two men agreed that the room would be ready by midafternoon.

There was nothing else to do today. The Bishop had done all he could. He retired to try to sleep—and to pray.

Soon after breakfast the phone rang, an agitated General was on the other end. General Aquino was third ranking in command of all the country's armed forces—only the President and General Aguinaldo, the Chief of the armed forces, outranked him.

"Thank God I've been able to get hold of you, your Grace. I just got this package late last night, it's a time bomb! What do you think?"

"General, I share your concern. We have to take action quickly."

"I've tried to speak to the others but you are the first person I have been able to get through to," the General said.

"Now that I 've spoken to you, I've spoken to everyone. General, I got my package just before lunch yesterday so I've had some time. I've called a meeting at the Manila Peninsular Hotel at five p.m. tonight. They're all coming except Senator de Vera. He'll come later."

The General was impressed.

"I didn't think your Grace would be such a man of action, well done."

The Bishop smiled and took his words as a compliment.

"Thank you, General. It was obvious what had to be done, and I was the only person in a position to do it. I'll see you later."

It was fortunate that the General stayed in Manila after the weekend.

Alberto and the Bishop walked into the meeting room. The rich smell of coffee was welcoming. They were pleased to see everything ready. Alberto made them both a coffee. General Aquino arrived thirty minutes later and entered briskly without knocking. He smiled at the other two men and strode towards them with his hand outstretched. For a military man he was quite small, a trim waist and a small-framed body matched his five foot eight inches of height. He already knew the Bishop, who introduced him to Alberto.

The General was glad they had a lawyer there. They were definitely going to need legal advice tonight. As Alberto served coffee to the General, he wondered what he was involved in. He hoped they would only need him as a waiter tonight, but he was beginning to fear that this wouldn't be the case.

He phoned his wife—he was sorry but something very serious had come up. He didn't know when he would be back. She was very understanding and knew better than to ask him detailed questions.

The General was one of the rising stars in the Philippine Army. Luckily, he was a bright and academic man. He was from a very famous family, and entered the Military Academy straight after his law degree. He had connections and loyalties everywhere. These connections were going to help him tonight. His family and the family of Senator Consuelo had been at odds with each other for two generations, so he had no qualms whatsoever about going after the Senator—if the graphic accusations they had all read turned out to be true.

"Your Grace, before the others come I wonder if we might consider our situation and what may happen," the General said reflectively.

The Bishop nodded and sat down beside him.

"Are you happy for me to take charge of running the meeting? We need clear and disciplined leadership, and with all respect, it is not appropriate a senior clergyman. Is that ok with you?"

"I had assumed you would General. You're certainly the most capable to do it. You'll have my full support."

"Thank you. Let's see where we are now, shall we? What are your initial thoughts, your Grace?"

Everyone knew of the rumored excesses of the Senator. He had been convicted of many serious offenses over the years, but a cash hungry judge had always overturned any convictions. There had been no serious legal actions against him for fifteen years. That was probably because it was also well known that bad things happened to those involved in any action against him.

"To be frank with you, I long ago concluded that Consuelo would make a bad President and would be a disaster for the country. He would suppress the poor and keep them poor. There'll be lots of problems if we are successful in our endeavors tonight, but in the long term good will come out of it."

After the Bishop finished outlining his thoughts, the General spoke.

"Don't worry, your Grace. I feel the same. Consuelo has few friends in Manila. Once you get to know a bit about him, you realize how rotten he is."

General Raganit was the other General who received

the package. He received his fourth star at the age of thirty-nine and was the youngest serving general in the Philippine army. He strode into the room at four forty-five and went straight over to the board where his superior was scribbling industriously.

The junior man saluted the elder, General Aquino returned it smartly. There were no greetings or small talk.

"What can I do to help, Sir?"

"At ease, son. This is going to be a long night. Everything's under control right now, but I'll need your help later. Get yourself some coffee, because we're in for a long night. When you've caught your breath take charge of security here—things could get hectic. Make sure no one gets in who shouldn't, and that no news of this meeting leaks out."

As Raganit walked off towards the coffee table, Aquino's phone rang. It was Senator de Vera.

"I'm on my way but I won't be in Manila until midnight."

"Don't worry, sir, everything's ok. The meeting will start soon."

"That's good to hear, General. Let me assure you that whatever you all decide to do, I'll support you. We can't allow him to get away with this."

"So far we are all agreed on that, sir. Thanks for your support. Have a safe flight."

Senator de Vera was also on the ballot for the Presidency. He was trailing Consuelo by about five percent. The other politician on the list was Senator Cruz; de Vera had called him as soon as he'd reviewed Paul's bundle.

Senator Cruz was an older and longer term Senator; he was standing down at this election. He'd been a Vice President earlier in his career and still exerted influence in the highest political circles. Even though he was standing down, he would be a Senator for the next few days until the inauguration of his replacement.

He was regarded as an elder statesman and was well liked among most political circles and the public. They talked for a long time earlier on the phone and prepared themselves for the events that were likely to unfold.

General Raganit phoned the hotel manager.

"We need to beef up the security a bit. I notice the room has three entrance doors. Please lock two of them. I just want one way in and out. Also, I see we have the only occupied room on this corridor. Please put one of your staff at each end of the corridor. We don't need guests wandering down here by mistake."

"No problem," Connor said. "I'll see to it straight away."

Next, the General summoned two senior trusted sergeants to act as inside door attendants and security. They would leave hotel staff at the ends of the corridor so as not to create too much interest.

Senator Cruz arrived at six thirty, just after they assumed their posts. He looked around at the activity in the room.

"I'm very impressed, General."

"Thank you sir," the General said. "Do I have your permission to run the meeting, sir?"

"Of course you do, General. This mustn't be seen to be run by a politician. You're just the man for the job."

"Thank you, sir," the General said and then went back to his planning on the wall.

By seven p.m. they were all there except for Senator de Vera. He would be there later in the evening. Senator Cruz mused that it was probably a good job that the younger Senator was not there for a large part of the proceedings. He was likely to benefit from the actions they would plan tonight, and by this time tomorrow he could be the next President.

The Senior General was walking up and down the twelve-foot length of the whiteboards reviewing and amending his plan. He phoned some trusted subordinates in preparation and put them on notice that their assistance may be needed, but he wouldn't go too far until he had the support and authority of the rest of the group. The Chief of Police walked through the door. The final man had arrived; the nights' work had begun.

The General started the proceedings.

"Gentlemen, we all know why we're here. I'm grateful to Senator Cruz for asking me to lead the proceedings. We must be quick and diligent in our work, we don't have much time."

He looked around— everyone was nodding in agreement..

"I'm sure we all realize the implications. Unfortunately, the timing isn't good. We know that, as things stand, it's very likely that Senator Consuelo will be proclaimed the new President by lunchtime tomorrow. It's my view that this should be prevented at all costs, and it looks like it'll be up to us to do it."

The room fell silent with all eyes still on him.

"If these allegations are proved, it would be disastrous for the country for a newly elected President to be removed from office within days, or even worse, maybe managing somehow to 'overcome' this obstacle with his new power and influence and carry on as President.

"It's in the best interests of the country if this matter can be dealt with and the proclamation prevented. Before I carry on I must be certain that you all agree with me—we must all be set on the same course and working together. Each and every one of you will play an active part tonight. Let me have a show of hands to confirm your agreement so far."

The five raised their hands in the air simultaneously. He nodded and carried on. He moved to the start of the white boards. The stages of the 'operation' were set out as headings with notes and arrows. He had a laser pointer and he fixed the bright red light on the area in the mountains where the cave was. He'd already marked it with a red sticker.

"The cave illustrated in the photos is situated ten miles from Benguet, the capital of Abra. We all know the Governor of Ilocos Sur and that he's no friend of Consuelo. I think we can rely on him to help us tonight. The Governor has the resources and power to send in investigators, with police and troops in support in case of trouble."

He looked over at the Chief of the Makati Police.

"Would you like to be the one to persuade him to support our actions? I know you know him personally."

The Police Chief had his phone out before the General had finished speaking.

"With Consuelo away in Manila his people won't resist much. The Governor would need perhaps twenty well-armed troops to back up the police, just in case."

There were nods of agreement all around. The General continued linking up the people and the places on the white board. He went on to explain the scenario if, as expected, the scene that greeted them when they reached the cave matched the photos and the story.

"We have to decide the actions we'll take when we've confirmed the facts. We know that the Senator will be in Manila tonight and tomorrow so we could have him arrested here, if we can find him, but we must have overwhelming evidence. The Governor's men must get to the Abra Estate first, find the gold and get confessions from these men; Brian, Tom and the others involved."

The General paused for the assembled dignitaries to take in his words.

They unanimously agreed that the Governor should get his people to the cave and they should be prepared for an immediate visit to Senator Consuelo's Estate afterwards. The Chief of Police and General Aquino were talking to the Governor on Skype. The group was sending a copy of

Paul's documents to him. Alberto was scanning the bundle as they were speaking.

The General and the Governor had worked together on several occasions. Ilocos Sur was a rural and sparsely populated mountainous province. Communist insurgents (the 'New People's Army') had camps in the remote hills. They frequently raided homes in the nearby villages as well as attacking police and military targets.

Every so often, the military came up from Manila and raided suspected camps and rebel-supporting villages. General Aquino had stayed with the Governor to supervise several of these raids.

Chief Alveira hooked up with the Governor on Skype again; the man's voice came through loud and clear after about half a minute. When the video picture came online, he saw that the Governor was flanked on either side by his local Chief of Police, Abet Costello, and an army officer, Colonel Vicente, who ran the local garrison.

The Governor wasn't well educated. He had a law degree that his father, the previous Governor, had paid for, but no real education to speak of. However, he was streetwise and was known as a man of action. He stared straight at the Police Chief.

"My men are ready to move, General (in the Philippines the Police Chiefs are Generals). The papers I've examined, together with the presence of such eminent men there with you, leaves me in no doubt that we have to do this."

Chief Alveira breathed a sigh of relief and nodded.

"Thank you for that confirmation, Governor. May I now have a conference call with your two chiefs of staff?"

The Governor nodded and left the screen. Ten seconds later the Chief was facing a split screen with the local police chief and the army colonel both facing him side by side.

"The Authority for this operation must come from the highest level to protect us all. After we've discussed and agreed what to do I will confirm it to you by way of emailing you an official order signed by all of us here."

The other two men expressed their agreement.

"As this is basically a criminal investigation, it should be run by the police."

"Don't worry, Chief. The Colonel and I have worked together on many occasions and we're close colleagues. We'll get the job done, guaranteed."

CHAPTER EIGHT

The Governor called Chief Costello and Colonel Vicente into his office. As befitting a Governor, the office was opulently decorated. He came out from behind his desk and indicated three chairs at the other side of the room with a coffee table in the middle.

"Sit down, gentlemen. This is how we'll proceed."

He addressed the Police Chief.

"Abet, you take twenty men to the cave—check out the facts—if it's what we think it is deal with the bodies then seal off the crime scene. I want you to have soldiers with you when you go to the Senators Estate."

He turned to Vicente.

"Take another twenty men, well-armed, just in case. You may have to support the police operation, and deal with any resistance."

"Understood."

The Police Chief had his team together in less than fifteen minutes and was on the way to the cave. Colonel Vicente assembled a team of soldiers who would meet up with the police team later, when they'd finished their investigation.

Within the hour, he and his men were also on the road, and by eleven thirty he was parked where Simon stopped many days before. There were three police vehicles already there in a neat row facing the road but set back under the trees. Chief Costello and his men had been at the cave for half an hour.

It took three of the Chief's strongest men a few minutes to open up the cave entrance. As soon as the men opened up the entrance, the smell hit them. They staggered back holding their hands over their faces. The Chief stepped forward with a cloth over his face and slid carefully through the narrow entrance, closely followed by his men.

Three minutes later, he came out again slowly with his cloth still over his mouth. About five meters outside of the cave, he removed the cloth, taking a deep breath of fresh air and sat down. Before he had recovered his breath he was making a call.

Back in the hotel, the Makati Police Chief walked away from the group to answer his phone.

"It's all true, sir. The boys are still there. The bodies are in a bad state. Everything is as we thought it would be."

"Thank you, Chief. Please carry on. You know what must be done now."

"Yes, of course, sir. Good luck, sir."

"We are all going to need a lot of luck tonight. Carry on."

The Makati Chief turned around to face the room. He walked to the board and stood next to General Aquino.

"Can I have your attention please, everybody? I've just heard from the men in Abra. It's confirmed. They've found the bodies of the boys."

The room fell silent. General Aquino took over.

"Ok, gentlemen. We're now certain what we're dealing with. We've got a lot to do now so let's get on with it."

Everyone got back to their activities. The General turned to the Police Chief.

"There's no going back now."

Colonel Vicente phoned Chief Costello to tell him the news, then he waited for the police to get there. His men were taking forensic evidence and samples where possible, although there were no surfaces that they could get any fingerprints from. They took photos and marked the areas of the bodies before putting the unfortunate boys into body bags. Puncture wounds from daggers were still visible on the decaying bodies; there could be no doubt that their deaths were not accidental.

They left four men to secure the cave and six others carried the bodies on stretchers to the vehicles at the roadside. The Chief accompanied the bodies to the waiting vehicles.

In Manila, Senator Cruz was making calls to the bewildered bosses of the telephone company, and the local cell phone providers. After he spoke to each one, he passed the phone to Chief Alveira who confirmed the request. He ordered the directors to suspend the phone and internet services in Abra at exactly midnight and until further notice. They contacted their regional engineers immediately. Service cuts for hours on end were common; no one would think anything of it for quite a while.

Senator De Vera arrived at the hotel a little earlier than expected. By midnight, General Aquino and Senator Cruz had briefed him on the developments of the night so far.

"You must go, Senator. You shouldn't be here now. If all goes according to plan, you may well become President tomorrow, not Consuelo. It would look better if you weren't involved in this."

The Senator nodded. They shook hands and wished each other good luck. Attorney Alberto requested five minutes in private with the Senator before he left. They spent a few moments discussing some papers on a corner table. After the Senator signed the papers, he shook the attorney's hand and made as if to leave.

As he walked towards the door, he took General Aquino's arm conspiratorially.

"I realize it is right that I should not be here tonight, but there is much I too have to do now. I won't be sleeping, so please call me any time you need to, and please get someone to update me hourly, maybe General Raganit?"

"Agreed."

General Aquino smiled as he walked back into the room. Senator de Vera was already acting like a Commander in Chief.

Bishop Ong and Alberto were discussing the constitutional situation in case it was not possible to arrest Senator Consuelo until after he was pronounced the winner of the Presidential election. There would be no immunity for him until the Chief Justice had sworn him in, so they did have a couple of days. Provided that there was enough physical evidence and support from the right people, they could legally arrest him. They both agreed it would be much better if it could happen before he was pronounced the winner. Then he would have no time to gather his support.

The military men and the police chief concerned themselves with the problems and logistics of the arrest. In this volatile country there could be a possible attempt at flight or armed resistance by the Senator's security men who were sure to be close by.

In Abra, the convoy of six vehicles proceeded at a steady pace along the mainly deserted roads that led to Benguet and the Senator's Estate.

Tom and Marcos were well on their way to Manila with the gold. Tom had many things on his mind as he left Abra, although he did think that the convoy of official vehicles going past him on the quiet road was a bit unusual.

General Aquino looked at his watch, and phoned the Colonel.

"Hello, sir,"

The Colonel put his finger in his other ear so he could hear the call better above the engine noise.

"It's difficult to hear you, sir."

The General spoke carefully and slowly.

"We have to ensure no news of our actions get through to Consuelo or his group for the next few hours. If he hears of this too early our efforts may be wasted, do you understand?"

"I understand, sir,"

"We've arranged for a phone and internet blackout until midday tomorrow just in Abra—it will start in a few minutes, just before you reach the Estate."

"Ok, sir. That's fine. How will we communicate with you?"

"You won't be able to until the morning, Colonel. You'll be on your own. As soon as you have sufficient evidence and if possible have secured the gold, you and the Police Chief must get to Candon as quickly as you can. There is a lawyer there waiting to assist you. I'm texting you the details now."

"Very good, sir. No problem. We'll talk to you at dawn."

"Yes, Colonel. Please try to be there by six a.m.—time is going to be very tight."

"You can rely on us, sir. We'll get it done. We all realize how important this is."

"Good luck, Colonel."

Cell phones would still work in Candon. They had to be able to talk to their Colonel and Police Chief colleagues when they got there from Abra in the early hours of the morning. The group decided to use a local lawyer in that town, one who Senator Cruz knew well.

Attorney Ricardo de Leon was a portly man of about forty-five. He had a good brain, but was too lazy to make much of himself. He managed somehow to make a living on the three or four hours a day which he put in. His loyal staff had carried him for years.

The phone rang at one a.m. in the pitch-black tiny bedroom. It was answered after seven or eight rings by a croaky voice.

"Hello, who is this?"

His voice had more than an edge of irritation.

"Ricardo, my friend, I'm sorry to bother you in the middle of the night like this."

The sound of Senator Cruz's voice was very sobering to the befuddled attorney.

"Senator Cruz, I'm sorry, I was asleep,"

The befuddled lawyer quickly apologized. He was surprised to receive the call but only too anxious to help.

"It's fine, Ricardo. I am sorry to bother you at this time. I would not ring you at this hour unless it was necessary."

The eager attorney was soon on the way to his office in Candon to prepare for the arrival of the Colonel and the others. The Officers needed fast document scanning and internet.

When the impressive military convoy arrived at the bottom of the drive leading up to the Governor's Estate they could see lights on at the top of the drive. The Colonel and the Police Chief, each with two men in support, drove the final three hundred yards to the guarded entrance gate. They left the rest of the convoy at the bottom of the hill, just out of the line of sight of the guards at the gate. They didn't want to look like an invasion force, yet.

The three young security guards, who were dozing, stared at the two men getting out of the vehicle and striding towards them. When the guards saw the rank of the men approaching them they stood and saluted smartly, although they were not military and didn't really need to. This was a good start thought the Colonel.

"Relax boys. Please contact your security head and have him come meet us. Please apologize to him, but tell him we must meet with him immediately on an urgent security matter."

The young guards knew Brian would be sleeping so they called Pedro, his deputy, who was on duty. They waited patiently for Pedro to walk the five hundred yards from the security huts.

"Gentlemen, what can I do for you. I am Pedro Alvarez, Deputy Chief of security."

He put out his hand. Costello and Vicente smiled but ignored it.

"Pedro, we need immediate access to the Estate, this is police business, please let us in. Where's your boss?"

Pedro was formerly in the Philippine Marine Corps, and he was not about to defy a Colonel.

"Open up, let them in. Hurry!"

The boys scurried to pull open the old metal gates. Once inside, Pedro guided them up to the series of security huts and put them in a waiting area.

"Our security Chief is Brian, he's a guilo. Shall I fetch him?"

"Yes. Apologize to him for the disturbance, but tell him we must see him now."

Pedro marched smartly off.

Brian was fast asleep and Pedro had to bang loudly on the locked door to rouse him.

"What the hell's the matter, Pedro?

When Brian opened the door, Pedro strode in without asking.

"Sir, there are police and military men here. They're demanding to see you. I put them in the waiting room."

Brian sighed. It was bound to be something petty, but he had better go and see. He showered and dressed quickly. He decided a little formality might be appropriate. He donned his service uniform.

He tried to call his boss. The mobile phone network was down again. He cursed after trying again to get through to the Senator or his staff several times. Pedro waited for him and they headed off together.

The two men strode into the room. The Colonel and the police Chief rose as they entered. Brian beckoned them to sit. The Colonel looked closely—he recognized the man from the photos that the Governor had shown them when they were planning the operation.

"You must be Brian."

Brian raised his eyebrows in surprise and took the other man's hand warily.

"Yes, I am. Have we met before?"

"Maybe, your face is familiar."

The Colonel maintained eye contact. Brian decided not to pursue that line for now.

"We're sorry for the disturbance but the matter is urgent. This is a murder investigation and we need to interview several of the staff, including you, and conduct a search."

The smile on Brian's face disappeared. Chief Costello continued, not giving Brian time to respond.

"What we need is full access to all staff and the Estate. I have investigators outside waiting to come in and start their work. Please, advise your gate security to let them in."

He made it sound like a request but to Brian it felt more like an order and he was now wary.

"I'm sure that the Senator would want me to work with you any way I can. Unfortunately, I can't get hold of him right now. Do you have a warrant to search the house? I'm sure that you're aware that this is almost certainly the home of the next President of the Philippines."

The emphasis was not lost on the Colonel and the Police Chief. All three men knew that a warrant wasn't normally necessary in the course of an ongoing investigation, but with the influential people involved, they'd come prepared.

He passed a faxed letter to Brian; it had the heading of Camp Crame, the national police headquarters. Brian read it carefully. It was addressed to his boss the Senator, to Tom and himself by name and to several other people. Brian knew some of the names but not all of them. "— assist in any way possible... murder investigation... do not impede...immediate arrest and imprisonment..."

This wasn't a warrant, it was much worse. His eyes widened when he saw the names of the signatories.

Where the hell was the Senator? Brian was out of his depth and unsure of himself. He sat back in his chair for a few seconds. The other men gave him some time. Resignedly, he sat forward, picked up the walkie-talkie on his desk, and barked orders to guards on all stations to allow the police to enter and to assist them.

Pedro paced up and down outside. He wasn't happy. He'd served the Senator for twenty years and had expected to be made chief a few years ago. He was upset that the foreigner got the job over him.

He knew his boss wouldn't be happy at what was going on, but he didn't know what he could do about it.

The Police Chief smiled. He was relieved that Brian didn't ask how many men were coming in. He was now in a position to implement his own security plan. He rose and asked Brian to excuse him. He strode outside and borrowed a walkie-talkie from one of his men stationed outside the main door. The Colonel remained in the room and passed the time by asking Brian to list down all the staff and their positions. He knew what the Police Chief would be doing outside. Everything was going according to plan.

"I need you to make sure that no one goes in or out of the Estate. Leave six men at the bottom of the hill and set up a roadblock there. I doubt if we'll get any problems in the middle of the night, but you can't be sure. If anyone asks any questions, tell them it's a security scare associated with the elections."

"Very good, Sir."

"If you have any problems contact me."

"Ok, sir. Right away."

The Captain barked out his order to his men immediately after the Chief had stopped speaking.

Chief Costello rejoined Brian and the Colonel who were now drinking coffee. He could sense that the atmosphere had changed. The Colonel looked at Brian. The blood, and the confidence, was draining from his face.

"What's the matter, Brian? Have you got something to hide?"

"Of course not," Brian said.

He could hear lots of comings and goings outside and the Colonel was not answering any of his questions directly. The Colonel wanted to keep things friendly as long as possible—at least until all the security measures were in place.

When Chief Costello re-entered the room he knew they were ready. Costello was offered another coffee and refused. It was time to get down to business

As Costello sat down again, Brian spoke. His impatience was beginning to show now.

"Tell me what this is about please? I've cooperated with you so far. I think I deserve some answers."

"We're investigating three suspicious deaths that occurred near here about two weeks ago and we know that people from here were involved."

Costello managed to keep a blank expression.

Outside, in the general office, Pedro was very concerned. The boss would never normally behave like this. He knocked on the door and opened it a fraction.

"Can I have a word outside please, sir?"

"No, not now. Just do your job," Brian snapped.

Pedro sighed resignedly, and went back outside to see else he could do. The two men had never liked each other—Pedro didn't trust him—but there was nothing he could do. He kept trying to ring the Senator.

The Inspector, of course, had his plan already prepared; he and the chief decided how this would proceed before they arrived. He would take over two large rooms—half of the Security block—as his operations center. Pedro was told to clear the desks and relocate the staff.

Pedro was taken aback but was not prepared to seek further instructions from his boss who was clearly in no mood to be interrupted. He strode off to carry out the request.

"Oh, and please find me four sets of plans of the entire Estate as soon as possible," the Inspector shouted after him.

Costello and Vicente were aware that Brian had a revolver in a holster on his waist, and that the flap was undone. They presumed that he would have several more weapons close by or about his person. Brian's hand moved slowly down towards the gun and rested on the holster.

Ok, thought Costello, now is the time. He strode to the door and summoned the two soldiers into the room. They stood in front of the desk. The Colonel casually unbuttoned his jacket. He was now ready to grab the pistol in his breast holster if necessary.

"We have evidence, Brian, that you and others here were involved in unlawful killings. Please carefully and slowly remove any weapons you have and place them on the table. You are now under arrest."

He nodded at the two soldiers. Without taking their eyes off Brian, they swung their rifles around into a ready position. The guns were not pointed directly at Brian, but certainly the warning was clear. He eyed the side door.

"There are four armed men outside that door, Brian. You wouldn't get five yards."

Brian considered his position for just a few seconds. He was a brave man but not a stupid one, he had nowhere to go. Very slowly he placed the pistol from the holster, together with a smaller one from his ankle and two daggers from inside his jacket on the table. At the Colonel's nod, one of the guards picked up the weapons then they both left the room.

The three men were again alone. The Colonel produced a folder containing Paul's letter and the photos. Brian, of course, had seen it and read it before and his heart sank as he saw what they had. After scanning the first page, he put it down and said nothing. He was still sensible enough to let the other men make the first move.

"Brian, my friend. You're in a lot of trouble."

The Police Chief smiled calmly,

"You're looking at life imprisonment here, or possibly the death penalty."

He took a breath to let his words sink in.

"Look, Brian, we're on a tight timescale here and if you help us we can offer you a better future than that."

"What are you offering?"

"That's not how it works, Brian. You're not in a position to bargain. You give us full cooperation right now, and we'll see. Firstly, we want to interview this man Tom." He pointed at the man's photo on the desk.

"I presume, like the rest of the Estate, he's still sleeping. Make sure he cooperates with us right from the start; that will be your opening gesture of assistance."

The six men approached Tom's bedroom with caution. The door was slightly ajar. As they crept in, they quickly realized it was empty. The bed was made and the room was tidy. It was clear that Tom hadn't slept there that night.

They radioed the Colonel who whispered the news into the ear of Costello, who nodded.

"It looks like your friend Tom has flown the coop."

"He was here earlier." Brian was genuinely surprised.

"Ok then, the position is this. We want to clear this up in hours, not days, and with your help, we can do so. Your cooperation will buy you a much reduced sentence. You may've been involved, but we know that you weren't the brains behind this. You'll soon be able to fly off and enjoy the rest of your life in luxury. What do you say?"

"Let's suppose I agree to help you. What do you want me to do?"

Costello sighed. In the absence of Tom, they had to lay their cards on the table.

"Well, for a start you can tell us where the gold is."

Brian looked puzzled for a moment and then the penny dropped. If he didn't help them, it would take them far too long to find the gold, which he thought was still in the remote barn. Maybe they didn't know how much they were looking for. Maybe he could get away with just giving up the money, and perhaps he could try to retrieve the gold later.

"You're not looking only for gold, my friends. Some of the treasure has already been converted into something else."

"Ok, what is it now and where is it?" Costello said.

"I can tell you that, but without my help you won't find it quickly, certainly not in time to prevent Consuelo becoming President today. I'm going to need a lot more than a word in the judge's ear to help you destroy the Senator."

Colonel Vicente and Costello looked at each other. They needed Brian's help right now. Time was ticking away; it was already two thirty a.m. There was no time for haggling.

"We're in a position to offer you immunity, and safe passage out of the country in return," Colonel Vicente replied.

"Neither of you has anything like the authority to do that."

"That's true, but the next President of the Philippines does."

Costello produced a letter from his attaché case; it was signed by Senator De Vera, and acknowledged by all the other dignitaries at the hotel in Manila. It granted authority for Costello and Vicente, acting jointly, to offer immunity to anyone who assisted them in their endeavors tonight. It was dated for tomorrow.

Attorney Alberto was bright. He had the forethought to have Senator de Vera sign it before he left. They had emailed it to Governor Gallenosa, who printed it out and dispatched it with a military courier. The motorcyclist caught up with the convoy just as they arrived at the Senator's Estate.

Brian examined the document carefully, it looked ok. All they had to do was fill in the blanks. He felt for the keychain in his pocket. The keys to the rooms in the deserted building on the hill were on the chain. Brian knew he had to help them quickly.

"Ok, let's do it."

He passed the document back to the Police Chief who had his pen ready; Brian signed it as soon as Costello handed it back to him. The Colonel left the room in search of a Xerox machine.

After a few moments the Colonel returned and handed Brian a signed copy. Brian put it in his pocket. He had to trust these men and hope for the best.

"Come on; let me take you to what you're looking for."

The Colonel opened the door to one of his military vehicles parked outside. Two of the Colonel's men climbed into the back seat and the Colonel, the Police Chief and Brian squeezed into the middle seat. Brian immediately gave directions to the driver and they set off for the tall, half-finished structure that they could see in the distance.

After unlocking the upper doors and descending to the basement, they finally entered the room where the attaché cases were stored.

"There should be about fifteen million American dollars in these. I can't open them, I don't have the combination."

"Never mind, we can figure that out later."

They picked up a case each and made their way back up the stairs and locked the cases in the trunk of the car.

The Police Chief looked at his watch—it was three a.m. They were behind schedule. He spoke briefly to the Colonel. They should be on their way to Candon by now. There wouldn't be much time to put their plans into effect; dawn would break in a couple of hours. Brian's future now depended on the Senator being in jail for a very long time. He would do all he could to ensure that would happen. The men didn't live on the Estate so the Chief dispatched men to find them, with orders to get the men's statements to Candon as soon as possible, by whatever means they could.

The Colonel drove the four by four at a breakneck speed along the narrow and winding roads. The Police Chief sat in the back with Brian putting together Brian's statement of admission. The Colonel's driving didn't help, but the Chief did the best he could. They arrived at Candon at five forty five, just as it was beginning to get lighter. He had nine pages of corroborating detail and admission, signed by Brian, which would be enough to start with.

As soon as they arrived, Brian asked where the toilet was and excused himself. In the secluded cubicle he took out his cell phone, which now had a strong signal and made a hurried phone call, he cursed as he got the 'cannot be reached' message. He sent a long text message instead.

Attorney De Leon's office was a single, large room on the second floor of a dismal and dilapidated shopping mall. Three desks and various phones, faxes, and other old and unidentifiable office equipment were dotted around the room in a random manner. Luckily, the room had a wide window overlooking the main road below making it light and airy. He was a one-man band lawyer, operating with just one legal assistant and a secretary.

As instructed, De Leon phoned the group in Manila as soon as he saw the car pull up outside. Attorney Alberto answered the phone after a single ring. As he entered the room, Chief Costello took the phone from his outstretched hand without a word.

"We have a full confession and complete cooperation from one of the foreigners in the photos. The other one seems to have disappeared but my men are searching for him."

"How far does the man go in his statement?" Alberto inquired.

"He's given us everything, more than enough to nail Consuelo, and he's told us where to get more. He knows best where to place his loyalties now."

Costello scribbled down a fax number that Alberto relayed to him and passed it to the assistant. As they continued to speak, she faxed the handwritten and signed pages over. Alberto thanked Costello for his help and asked him to pass the phone to Vicente. By the time Vicente spoke, General Aquino was on the other end.

"Good morning, sir,"

"Congratulations. You've done a good job, Colonel, but I'm afraid that your work isn't finished. We've decided we must maintain the cell phone and internet blackout in Abra for six more hours. We don't want Consuelo to get wind of what's going on. You have to go back to his estate and keep the place locked down until noon. Keep up the security scare story; it should last for a while more."

Within the hour, the three men started back for Abra. Chief Costello offered to drive; he remembered the drive down and thought that he was likely to bring up his breakfast if the Colonel drove back.

When they got back, each man took charge of his own men and coordinated the inquiries and the search. In reality all they were now searching for was Tom and the gold. Brian had no idea where Tom might be. He'd be surprised if he knew the truth.

Pedro had a bad feeling. Brian disappears for hours with the newcomers, and then they all come back, acting very friendly. There was something wrong.

"Why are we letting these people take over, sir? Does the boss know they're here?"

"It's none of your damn business, Pedro. While the boss is away I'm in charge, just get on with your job."

Pedro walked off, trying to contain his temper. Tom and Marcos arrived in the busy provincial town of Tarlac just before eight, in time for breakfast. They were just a couple of hours away from Manila now, and they were hungry. The Jollibee restaurant in the center of the town wasn't busy now, it was a weekday, and the breakfast rush was ending.

"Did you hear about the three boys disappearing from the mountains near Santa?" Marcos asked Tom casually. Before he could answer, Marcos continued.

"Nearly two weeks now they've been gone. Not much hope for 'em now, I reckon."

Exactly twelve days, thought Tom, but he just nodded. His part in the murders had been playing on his mind. He had been a soldier most of his life and was no stranger to cold-blooded killing, but this one upset him. He thought of Dennis—just a few years younger than the boys. For the first time in his life he wished he could undo something bad he had done.

"Do you know the families?"

"Oh, aye, they're my neighbors. The eldest of the boys, Darwin, he's an only child. His poor mom cries all the time, his dad's dead. The poor woman ain't got anybody now, 'cept her brother, the boy's uncle, and he ain't well."

Tom didn't raise his eyes from the table.

"It's a mystery, Tom. I saw 'em just before they disappeared. They came here looking for a job. I guess they went off looking in the forest for food after that. How could all of them be gone? It don't bear thinking about."

Marcos seemed to want to continue with this topic of conversation. He hadn't connected the disappearance of the boys with their meeting with the Senator. Tom listened sullenly, and with a heavy heart. Marcos just took it for sympathy.

"If only they knew what had happened. If they'd washed up in the river or something, at least the poor families would have bodies to bury, at least they would know."

They continued their meal in silence and were back on the road by nine. It was Marcos' turn to drive. Tom looked at his watch. Just three more hours now and they would be at the embassy.

CHAPTER NINE

The hotel room in Manila burst into life as soon as the call from Candon came through. Everyone assumed that the surprise visit to Consuelo's Estate would be successful and had started to plan accordingly. It was time to put that plan into action.

The Police Chief had his four most trusted senior officers in the room with him. They grouped around one of the conference tables with the two Generals. The National Police Chief, General Ramos, was responsible for security at Manila Town Hall. This was where the election results would be announced. He was a known supporter of Consuelo. Luckily, they found out that he wasn't going to attend the event; he would leave it to his deputy because they had no reason to believe there could be any trouble. They just had to make sure no word got to the Senator before the arrest.

The Makati Chief of Police would be there to make the arrest. They had loyal police and military in and around the building, just in case. There were three battalions of soldiers the Generals knew they could rely on. Once they were sure Consuelo was inside the building, they would make their way to the perimeters of the Hall and await instructions. This had to be organized at the very last minute and as discretely as possible. Everything was beginning to fall into place.

General Aquino spoke with the men in the province for fifteen minutes. He was confident his rural counterparts and their police partners were handling the situation well. He called General Raganit to one side.

"It's time to tell the President."

Raganit nodded.

"I need you to stay here, tell everyone that the President may call here just to check things out."

"Of course, sir. Things will be fine here, just keep in touch."

Aquino nodded. The two men faced each other and saluted.

"Good luck, sir,"

General Aquino strode off closely followed by the Chief of Police, Senator Cruz, and Bishop Ong.

A car was waiting at the side street entrance to the hotel. The few people who were around at that time took little notice as the four men slipped out of the hotel and into the limousine. The General thought it would be better to turn up at Malacanang, the Presidential Palace, in a civilian car rather than in a military or police vehicle.

A Presidential Aide was walking towards the car as they parked in the Presidential compound.

"The boss was not best pleased at being woken this morning. I hope that whatever you need to see her about is as important as you say it is. Otherwise, we're all going to be in trouble."

The Chief of Police put his arm on the younger man's shoulder and assured him that the President would praise him for his actions, not scold him.

President Bautista entered the room quietly and was nearly at the table before the others noticed her. The military and police snapped to attention as soon as they realized she was there, while the Senator and the Bishop discreetly bowed. She beckoned them to an office table in one corner and bade them sit down. A uniformed and polite waitress appeared bearing hot coffee and croissants.

"Madam President, we regret this intrusion at such an hour, but when you see what we've brought you I'm sure you'll understand."

As he was speaking, the General was unfolding the papers he'd brought in front of the President.

"Ma'am, please take a few minutes to read these papers. It's important that you know what has happened in the last couple of days and nights. It took her about fifteen minutes, then she addressed the Bishop

"Your Grace, please tell me what has happened since you received this."

"Madam President, many distinguished men have been working through the night to find out the truth. Please talk to the Governor of Ilocos Sur. He's been working with us. His men have checked the details and arrested one of the killers, a foreigner who's confessed to everything. We must act with great urgency, Ma'am . This will all come out now, it can't be stopped. We can't allow a murderer to become the President of our country."

She nodded as he spoke. She'd already made up her mind.

"What action do you propose we take?" she asked. General Aquino smiled slightly—she said 'we' meaning she was already with them.

General Aquino felt it was time he got involved in the conversation.

"If I may, Ma'am. We intend to arrest the Senator at lunchtime, preferably before he is proclaimed as the next President."

"I agree. Why can't you arrest him now?"

"We would if we could, Ma'am, but we can't find out where he is. All we know for certain is that he'll turn up for the announcement of the result. We're preparing to arrest him there. If we issued an arrest warrant, he may go into hiding. We have to keep things quiet for another few hours."

"All right, I accept all you say. What would you have me do? There may be some little ways I can assist from behind the scenes."

"Thank you, Ma'am."

Just then his phone rang. It was the younger General back at the hotel. Someone had noticed unusual activity during the night and there was now a young lady reporter at the front desk asking questions. General Aquino's eyes rolled.

"Get her name please and give her my name. Tell her that if she stays put for one hour and talks to no one I'll see her personally and give her an exclusive interview. Please have someone with her at all times. Don't let her contact anyone. Take her phone from her if you have to."

Within thirty minutes they were back at the hotel with their colleagues. After a few moments the General slipped away. He made his way to a small interview room next to the foyer and asked General Raganit to fetch the reporter.

He stood, smiled and shook her hand as she entered. He invited her to sit down and asked for two coffees to be brought in. She was nervous which was good. A seasoned, well-connected and well-known reporter could have caused trouble, but Aquino was confident that this one wouldn't be a problem.

"Thank you for seeing me, sir."

"You're welcome, my dear. What can I do for you?"

The girl seemed to gain a little confidence. She was relieved that the General didn't shout at her, in fact, he seemed nice.

"My name is Lisa, Lisa Carriega, sir."

"Well it's nice to meet you, Lisa."

"I am a junior reporter with the Philippine Star, sir."

"Congratulations, you've done well."

"Thank you, sir. They made me a junior staff reporter last year, after I finished my three year apprenticeship. Before that I got a degree in communications from Ateneo University, first class. My boyfriend works here in the hotel, sir, as a night porter. He rang me when he noticed some important people coming and going, to an area of the hotel which was kept guarded. He thought there might be a story in it for me."

She suddenly had a worrying thought.

"Please, sir, I can't tell you his name. I think he'd be in trouble for what he did. He meant no harm at all, sir. He just wanted to help me."

"Don't worry about your boyfriend. I won't say anything."

"Thank you, sir," she said, the relief obvious on her face.

"If you'll do exactly as I say, by this afternoon you'll have an exclusive story that'll make you a household name and your career will skyrocket."

Her eyes widened.

"Why would you do this for me?" she asked, fearing an ulterior motive. She was after all a pretty girl.

The General sat back and laughed.

"My dear, I have three choices in front of me. The first is to have you arrested on a trumped up charge and detain you for a few hours. By then the action will be all over. Or, I can tell you that nothing is going on here and then leave you to wander around the hotel asking questions and making a nuisance of yourself."

She was listening attentively and hanging on his every word, but he wanted to put her at her ease.

"Don't worry my dear. My third option is to give you some limited information about what is really going on and put you in the right place at the right time to capitalize on it, in return for your discretion and co-operation for the next few hours. I think I can trust you. I think you know I could make life very difficult for you if you let me down."

She considered his words.

"The truth is, I could do with a friendly reporter on board with what we're doing here. The situation's going to get confusing for a few hours. I need someone to get good information out to the public. Will you help me?"

"I'll be pleased to do what I can, sir."

"I really hope so. I'm not keen to lock you up and I don't want you to be nosing around here this morning."

Lisa looked at him intently. She was not sure what to make of him, but he was seemed kindly. She decided her best course of action would be to trust him, at least for now.

"The third option will be fine."

Time was tight now. He was anxious to get on with other things. He gave her a very brief summary of the events of the past twenty-four hours and advised her to wait for his call.

When Aquino re-entered the operations room, the younger General was arranging the supporting troops and discussing their positioning. The only time they could be certain that their police colleagues could arrest Consuelo would be when he was on stage for the proclamation of the winner. They were still trying to find out if he was in Manila and if so, where he was staying, but they had drawn a blank so far.

General Raganit was sure he was in Manila. He'd given a television interview yesterday, and had to be here this morning. He couldn't be far away and if he wasn't here yet, he would be soon.

Chief Alveira looked pleased as he approached the two generals.

"Good news! One of my staff has got hold of the detailed security plans for this morning."

The three men sat down at a nearby table. The Chief laid out the papers and plans.

"It seems the security is quite low key—they're not expecting any trouble. That helps us a lot."

The other two nodded.

"Five armed officers in the wings on either side of the stage as close security, and about thirty other men spaced out inside the building."

The Chief pointed to the positions with his finger.

"There are four entrances, here, here, here and here," he said as he moved his finger around the board.

"There are just two armed men on each."

The two military men sat back. They looked at each other as if to say 'This is going to be easier than we thought.'

"Thank you, Chief. That's very helpful. Now we can be certain what we'll be up against."

General Raganit took the Chief off to a quiet corner.

"You're the most senior policeman here. It should be you that makes the arrest. Our job will be to keep you and your men safe while you do it and make sure he doesn't get away."

"I think we should arrest him in the auditorium, while he's on the stage," Chief Alveira said.

The other two men looked astonished. He saw the look on their faces.

"I know, I know, it will be in the glare of all the cameras, but it's definitely the safest place to do it. He'll have two layers of our security to get through if there's any trouble, the entrances to the auditorium, and to the building itself."

"We have to make sure you don't have a problem," General Aquino said.

"It'll be up to us to let you know when the area is secure for an arrest."

The two Generals stood up.

"Thank you, Chief. We'll leave you to get on with your arrangements. Don't worry, you can be sure that we'll be ready our end."

General Raganit had secured the cooperation of two companies of loyal and discreet soldiers. A Captain who was his batch mate at the Philippine Military Academy headed one of them, and a Major who was a close friend of General Aquino ran the other. Raganit was getting worried. The net was spreading and word might leak out. They had to keep a lid on it for a few more hours.

A shorter, but sharp military man came into the room, walked straight up to General Aquino and saluted smartly. Major Mark Ceneza was in charge of a small but elite section of Special Forces men. General Aquino decided that his unit was ideal for the most sensitive job.

"Hello, Mark. How are you?" He greeted his longtime friend with a crisp handshake.

"I'm sorry, it's difficult circumstances which bring us to work together again, but I know we can rely on you."

"Of course you can, General. What do you need us to do?"

"There are about forty police inside the building—we need them covered. We want to make sure they won't interfere with our task."

"Do you have a plan?"

"Yes, we want you to go and get some sniffer dogs, as soon as you can. We'll get you into the building on the pretense of a last minute bomb threat. You'll go in and position yourselves to cover the existing security men and make sure we do not have a problem with them. It should go smoothly since we have the advantage of surprise. You won't have a problem getting in, we'll make sure of that."

"Ok, no problem," Major Ceneza said. "I'll go and get the dogs. I'll let you know as soon as we're ready to go in."

"Make it quick, Mark. Time isn't on our side today."

General Raganit was on the other side of the room, talking quietly into his phone.

"Ok, Fred, this is what I need. There are four entrances to the building. I need you to station a large wagon close to each one with ten men inside, well hidden but ready to jump out, rifles ready, if necessary. There are two policemen on each door. When they see your men they're unlikely to resist."

"Right you are, my friend. We'll be ready."

Another cell phone rang in the room.

"Hello?" said attorney Alberto; it was a number he didn't recognize.

"Did you act on my instructions?"

It was a foreigner and Alberto was trying to place the vaguely familiar voice, but he couldn't. Then the penny dropped.

"Paul? Is that you? I thought you were dead."

"You're not the only one, mate. What did you do about the package?"

"Paul, it's too late now, I followed your instructions. The Bishop got his packet, they all did."

"Don't worry, that's fine, that's what I wanted. So what are they all doing about it?"

Alberto thought for a moment and decided there would be no harm in telling Paul the truth.

"Paul, I haven't got time to tell you everything that has happened since you dropped your little bombshell, but I can tell you that the Senator will get his comeuppance today. He's going to be arrested at the City Hall at the announcement of the result."

"That's just what I wanted to hear," Paul said, clearly pleased.

"Where are you, Paul? I need to see you. We'll need you to be a witness for the prosecution."

Paul laughed.

"Not a chance, mate."

The phone went down.

Alberto wondered whether he should tell the others that Paul was alive, but he decided not to, for now. They needed no distractions at this time and Paul's being alive was irrelevant to their work. He'd save it for later.

Edelweiss was facing her own problems with her family in Abra. She sat at the kitchen table in the tiny, bamboo hut. Her eyes were red. She'd been crying for two hours.

"Why do you have to go?" said her mother. Edelweiss reached across the kitchen table and put her hand on her mother's arm.

"I know I can get money to help us for now, but what about the future? I'm just a toy to the rich guys, and one day soon they'll get fed up with me."

Her mother carried on crying.

"Come on, mom."

Edelweiss shook her mother's arm.

"It's not forever. He loves me. He's promised I can still help you and dad."

She put her arms around her mother.

"Please mom, give us your blessing."

"I haven't even met the man," her mother wailed.

"I've known him for a long time, please trust me. I know what I'm doing. I'll call or text you every day."

Her mother's sobbing quieted a little.

"That's better, mom."

Edelweiss put both arms around her father.

"Thanks, Dad, for everything."

She held him tight and started to cry again. Her father was a practical man.

"You'll be alright, darling daughter. Make sure you call us tonight and tell us where you are."

"I will."

A tricycle was waiting outside to take her down to the main road where she would catch the bus. She was going to McDonald's in Candon. Her mother was still crying as she waved goodbye to her youngest daughter.

The outgoing President was still busy. She spent twenty minutes with her advisors before phoning Senator de Vera. He was expecting her call, and within thirty minutes of talking to her he was walking through the entry gate of the

Palace.

"Hello, Senator. I think we have some urgent business to discuss."

They were political allies now, of sorts, but were not close. Unfortunately for de Vera, the endorsement of the President was a poisoned chalice. He'd distanced himself from her as much as he could without losing credibility or upsetting her, but the damage was done.

"You know, Senator, I've made a lot of enemies in my time here—all Presidents do. Everyone remembers your mistakes and errors of judgment, but no one remembers all the good things you did and the people who you've helped."

Her 'errors of judgment' had been very profitable for her and her family and a few close friends. He knew what she was leading to but waited for her to continue.

"My family and I have been considering life after political office. All we want is a quiet and dignified retirement. I hope that is not too much to ask for after a lifetime of political service. I had a visit earlier from General Aquino and some other distinguished gentlemen. I think you know why they came to me."

"Yes, Ma'am, I do."

"Let's get to the point, Senator. We both know what's been happening through the night and the likelihood that by this afternoon Senator Consuelo will be in jail. How this is handled could give the runner up, almost certainly you, a great start to the Presidency. Alternatively we could spend weeks or months arguing about what to do and maybe re-run the election. That wouldn't be good for the country, and certainly not good for you. Time is short so I won't beat about the bush. I'm prepared to immediately endorse you as the new President after his arrest, and I'll make sure that the Chief Justice will do the same." She paused briefly.

"I think you know if I wanted to, I could make the waters very muddy, or perhaps make mischief in many other ways, but you're a good friend and I am not inclined to do that. I want you to sign and pre-date a declaration of amnesty for me and my family. You can date it for a month's time then announce it at the proper time. It will go down well with most people as you will be in your honeymoon period and Filipinos like a forgiving politician. Most of the country will see it as a typical Filipino act of compassion."

The Senator was surprised. He thought this request would come after he was elected, not before. He would have a hard time riding the storm if he gave her a pardon, but it would pass. On balance, he felt that would be more favorable than the prospect of a new election, and having her as an enemy.

The President, supported by the Chief Justice, could force through legislation for a new election if they wanted to. He didn't take very long considering his options.

"That's fine, Ma'am. I am willing to do that. Will your legal people draft it?"

The President opened the folder in front of her. She produced four copies of a twelve-page document.

"My lawyers were working before you arrived. Did you know that two Presidents before me have been granted complete immunity? My people had good precedents to copy from."

He slowly opened the first copy and went straight to the back page and signed it. The President raised her eyebrows.

"I thought, at least, you'd read it first."

"No need, I trust you."

In fact, nothing could be further from the truth, but he knew that she expected him to read it, so she wouldn't include anything he couldn't accept. Time was too short for negotiations and amendments.

After the Senator was gone, she sent for the Chief Justice. She appointed him early in her term, he was her man. However, she didn't know he was hopeful of retaining his job with the incoming administration and had courted favor with Senator Consuelo. The President was unaware of their secret meeting, or the tacit agreement they'd come to.

He tried to hide his dismay when the President explained the situation. He was in a difficult position now. His career could take a serious nosedive if he didn't now support the current President and her immediate plans. He was going to have some serious fence mending to do with President de Vera.

The morning started in a much more relaxed way for Senator Consuelo and Chloe. Light came streaming in through the open curtains at dawn; the brightness and the warmth soon woke the sleeping Senator and his lady.

Across town at the Peninsula Hotel, the 'gang of five' were packing up. It was time to get to City Hall and get everything in place for the arrest.

The Senator's car pulled up outside the City Hall at exactly eleven twenty and a barrage of photographers and reporters immediately besieged the car. Many pairs of eyes were on him as he exited the limousine, closely followed by Chloe. He was all smiles, as was Chloe, as they held hands and slowly climbed the steps to the impressive and ornate entranceway. There were probably three hundred or so people assembled around the doorway, hoping to catch a glimpse of the rich and famous. Television cameras were relaying the events live to twenty five million Filipinos following the events at home.

Generals Raganit and Aquino also had their eyes glued to the Senator. They had an excellent view from the top of a low-rise commercial building opposite the City Hall. The security guards in the building showed no concern when the two Generals appeared and insisted on checking the building for security purposes. They easily found their way onto the roof. It was an excellent vantage point, and they could liaise with their troops and control the outside operations from there.

They peered through military-grade binoculars as the Senator's car pulled up, and watched as he and Chloe got out. As soon as they were inside the building, the men were on their phones.

"Ok, Mark," said Aquino. "Take your men in now. Let me know when they're in position."

At the same time, Raganit was talking to his friend.

"Right, Fred. Move your troops close to the entrances now. When I contact you again I'll want your men to secure the entrances and prevent anyone from leaving, especially Consuelo. Are we clear?"

"As a bell, sir."

A modest and low-key reception was laid on for the four candidates and their families while they waited. Consuelo and Chloe were ushered into the small private dining hall and handed a glass of orange juice. *I'm almost there*, thought Consuelo. He tried to relax and make small talk with the others. The exit polls gave him a small lead over De Vera; his own poll had given him a bigger margin. Either way, he'd won.

The two minor candidates weren't a problem to him, and he chatted happily with them. Senator de Vera entered the room just before eleven thirty. For the briefest of seconds Consuelo eyed him with caution, then broke into a broad grin and strode over to shake his hand, mindful that there were plenty of photographers and journalists around.

The election was not a friendly fight. The two men loathed each other. However, neither of them wanted to look churlish at this time. De Vera accepted his handshake.

At eleven thirty, Major Ceneza opened the narrow, concealed back entrance to the building and started to usher in fifty marines with dogs, ignoring the bemused young police stationed by the door.

189

"Last minute bomb check. There's been a bomb threat," he said to them over his shoulder as he rushed past.

This was also a surprise to the deputy chief of security who had come down to see what was happening. He was in charge at that moment and was straight away on the phone to his boss. He waited for a call back and frowned when he got it.

The President had ordered it, so there was nothing he could do. The 'dog handlers' were well briefed. Under the pretense of checking for incendiary devices, they could easily penetrate the whole building and closely shadow the security personnel already there. The trick was to stretch out their work so that they were still there during the ceremony, to be in the right place at the crucial time. These were the elite, their group leaders were in direct radio contact with General Aquino.

Chief Alveira had another job to do. He briefed six senior uniformed police officers for this crucial task. This was a three-point plan. Firstly, the Senator had to be on stage. Secondly, the tight security surrounding the stage had to be 'neutralized' and overwhelmed by the 'dog handlers'. Finally, the troops hidden outside in trucks must be ready for action, just in case.

Forces under his control outnumbered the regular security forces; he felt reassured. He didn't think there would be any trouble now. The Police Chief wouldn't make a move until the two Generals had reported to him that all was in place. His officers were discretely hanging around at the back of the hall, blending in with their 'colleagues'.

Senator Consuelo never enjoyed small talk, and today of all days he was impatient to get on with the proceedings. He looked at his watch; it was eleven thirty, not much longer now. He put his champagne glass down as his cell phone rang. The voice was very familiar; as he heard the words, the smile left his face.

"Hello, my friend. I hope you're enjoying yourself. I know Lucy's alive and well, and far away from you and your murdering thugs."

The Senator felt a sensation of panic.

"Paul, listen, there has obviously been a mistake. Let's work something out, let's meet."

Paul laughed.

"You never give up, do you, you bastard. I just want you to know that everyone will know about your murdering thievery very soon. Wheels are already in motion."

"Paul, please, there is plenty to share around. Don't do anything you can't take back. I can still make you very rich."

"You still don't get it do you, Consuelo? You're finished, done, it's over. I've already made sure you'll get what's coming to you, and soon."

Paul closed his phone. The Senator stood there stupefied for a few moments until the panic started to subside. He had to act quickly; he had to have a plan. He excused himself from the room and found a quiet corridor close by. He rang Simon.

"Where are you?"

Simon could tell straight away that something wasn't right.

"I'm at the hotel, why? What's the matter?"

"It's Paul, he's still alive, and he knows we don't have Lucy. He says he's released the information about the cave already."

"Do you believe him?"

"Yes I do. Why wouldn't he? He has nothing to lose now. He wouldn't be so stupid as to trust us again. It's in his interest to cause me problems now."

"What do you want me to do?"

"I need time to think. If I can make it through the announcement and become the declared winner, maybe I can lean on enough people to keep a lid on this, or at the very least try to discredit it, but if my opponents have known about this for a while we may not have much time. Get my security guards together. There should be four in the hotel. Tell them there's a threat to my life, and get here with them as soon as you can."

"Ok. I will."

At precisely twelve noon, the Presiding Officer came in and asked them to take their seats. The unsuspecting civil servant hadn't been taken into the confidence of the plotters as he was known to be a supporter of Consuelo. He was about to get the shock of his life.

They proceeded slowly along the short corridor and turned right through the double doors leading to the stage area. Consuelo looked around, hoping to see Simon. At that precise moment, Simon was negotiating with the men guarding one of the side entrances. Simon always carried authorizations and permits from the Senator, and many of the dignitaries here today had brought their own guards, so it wasn't too difficult to get past the security.

On a nearby rooftop, a tall figure remained hidden in the shadows. He saw the two Generals take their positions, then moved his position to the other side of a ventilation exhaust so he would not be spotted. He had a good view of the main entrance. He wanted to check the positions of the other entrances. After five minutes he made his way back down to the street. Paul didn't want to miss the fun.

The City Hall stage was decorated with flowers and the National flag. At the front of the stage was a dais. At exactly mid-day, the returning officer and his two assistants climbed the three short steps. Behind them was a row of chairs for the candidates and their wives, about twelve seats in all. In front of the stage was row of padded chairs, reserved for dignitaries. Brilliant fluorescent lights and dazzling spotlights bathed the stage and the auditorium from both sides.

The hall was at full capacity of about sixteen hundred people. As the officials mounted the dais, the candidates and officials climbed the few steps up to the back of the stage to take their seats. The Makati Police Chief was, of course, included as a dignitary and took his seat. A text message would bring six supporting officers to his side. He was positioned in front of the steps going up to the stage so that he could get to Consuelo quickly. The man would have no time to put up a fight.

A uniformed security man with a rifle was in place at each side of the stage. Several others could be seen along the sides of the auditorium. He saw his 'dog handlers' moving slowly around behind the curtains. If any security men made a move to protect Consuelo, they would be dealt with swiftly.

He was waiting for a signal from the two Generals before he made his move. They would send him a simple text, 'OK,' then he would move in to make the most famous arrest of his life.

The Returning Officer looked around to ensure everyone was seated, then began his welcome speech. Chatter in the hall subsided as he started to speak. He spent about five minutes thanking everybody before starting to declare the votes for each candidate. Results for the two lowest candidates were being announced and still the Chief still hadn't received any texts. The Returning Officer was still speaking when the first text came in.

"OK"

The 'dog handlers' were in place. The Returning Officer stood to announce the results for Senator de Vera to a round of applause and shouts. The shouts were dying down as the second 'OK' text came in from General Raganit. It was time. The Returning Officer was preparing to announce the votes for Consuelo.

All eyes were focused on the stage. No one noticed the police Chief rise to join the group of officers moving swiftly forward from the back. Senator Consuelo rose to his feet smiling and walked towards the dais.

As he moved forward, he saw the group of policemen coming up the steps towards the platform, the blood drained from his face. They were staring straight at him; there could be little doubt of their intention. Then, out of the corner of his eye, he saw people moving quickly at the side of the stage on his right.

"Senator, over here."

He heard the familiar voice from the side of the stage. Simon had just managed to get there; he too saw the uniformed police approaching.

"Quickly, we have a car outside."

The Senator changed direction and moved swiftly towards the side of the stage, pushing other candidates roughly out of the way. The Senator's guards tried to get to the Senator to help him but were blocked by the dog handlers; there was no way out. The Police Chief and his arrest team moved in. Consuelo felt strong hands clasp his arms on either side. There was no use struggling now.

"Senator Enrique Consuelo. I'm arresting you on multiple charges of murder. You do not have—" The words trailed away and Enrique heard no more. He couldn't believe what was happening to him. He stood still and speechless. An officer roughly pulled his hands behind his back and handcuffed him.

Behind him, and getting attention from the clicking cameras, was a hysterical Chloe who began screaming when she saw her husband being handcuffed. He turned and tried to go to her but was restrained. Two of the 'dog-handlers' stepped forward smartly to stop her reaching the Senator.

Chief Alveira faced him.

"It's over, Consuelo. Come quietly now. You don't have a choice."

He turned to his men.

"Get him out of here."

Simon realized with dismay that he was too late. There was nothing he could do for his boss now. It was time he looked after himself. He moved quickly for the side exit, shouting for his men to follow him, but Chief Alveira had spotted him and was shouting into his radio.

Simon made his way to the side entrance surrounded by his men. The side doors burst open and the group rushed out of the building past the bewildered guards and into the side street.

"They're coming your way, Major," the General barked into his walkie talkie.

Just as he finished, the Major saw them emerging from the building about a hundred yards away.

"Go, go, go!"

The Major's men jumped down from the truck and ran towards the men running out of the side door. They were about fifty yards away when the Senator's Ford Expedition sped up the road from the other end and screeched to a halt. Simon's men pulled the doors open and piled in. Simon saw the soldiers raising their rifles as he threw himself into the rear seat. The driver gunned the engine and the car started away again before the last door closed, it didn't get very far.

Inside the Hall there was uproar. Under the glare of the lights and the noise of the media, the meekly protesting Senator was escorted out of the front door and straight towards a waiting windowless van. This was the first time in his life the Senator was speechless and shell-shocked— he was shaking. As he stumbled down the steps to the van, he nearly fell. Uniformed policemen held his arms on either side.

The lights from the cameras crowding around him hurt his eyes. He squinted and turned away, but he was unable to shade his eyes with his hands. As his eyes grew accustomed to the light he paused briefly. He saw a tall, familiar figure at the side of the curb a few yards ahead.

Paul clicked away with his camera, catching every detail of his enemy's panic and distress. As the Senator looked up at him, he smiled and said 'watch the birdie', then laughed as he watched the murderer being roughly pushed away towards the police van.

General Aquino was watching the action in the side street from his vantage point. He saw Simon and the guards come running out of the side door and diving into the car. He lifted his radio and commanded, "Stop the car. Use any means you have to."

The Major gave his orders; three men at the front lifted their rifles. Seven crisp shots rang out, one after the other. The car, which had been accelerating, slowed down. The two front tires were flat and there were four bullet holes in the windscreen.

Ten men quickly surrounded the car, their rifles pointed at those inside. At that moment, Chief Alveira burst through the side door to behold the astonishing scene. All four doors of the car were wide open now and the driver was slumped over the wheel, dead. Two of the guards were still in the car, not daring to move. Simon was slumped on the back seat with blood seeping from two holes—one in his shoulder and one in his leg.

The commotion brought a crowd from the main street. Onlookers and photographers rushed round the corner then approached the scene cautiously. The photographers centered their attention on Simon; he was prone on the seat, bloody from the two bullet wounds.

"He's still alive," proclaimed a young soldier who was cautiously checking the bullet-riddled car.

General Raganit was straight on the radio calling for an ambulance. Chief Alveira arrived and called the two closest soldiers to him.

"Stay with him, ride in the ambulance to the hospital. Stay there until the police take over."

The men saluted smartly and then went to tend Simon. He had lost a lot of blood and was unconscious now.

A few moments earlier, a young girl made her way, unnoticed, out of the front of the City Hall in time to witness the Senator being bundled into the van. She ran straight to the police inspector in charge and spoke to him. After making a brief phone call he walked with her to the van and let her in the passenger door. She would ride with the Senator to the police station. General Aquino had kept his promise.

The Senator heard a door open and felt a hand pushing his head as he was propelled forward into the van. Reporters were shouting questions at him, but he ignored them.

He fell forward into the empty back seat and struggled to sit upright as he could feel an officer climbing in beside him.

After the door slammed shut, the noise of the shouting and the cameras became muffled. Officers cleared onlookers from around the front of the vehicle, after a couple of minutes the van pulled slowly away from the curb. They travelled through the busy Manila traffic at a snail's pace.

The reporters and photographers rushed to their cars and vans, only to find troops there. They were prevented from leaving for thirty minutes under the Chief's orders. The Senator's supporters could try to make trouble—it was better if his whereabouts weren't known for a while. They would assume that he was going to the nearby Makati Police Station, but the Police Chief had anticipated this. They took him to the larger and quieter station in nearby Quezon City.

Simon opened his eyes to bright lights and white walls. He sat up, or tried to, and fell back into the pillows in agony. As the pain began to subside, he could see that the wounds on his shoulder and his leg had been dressed. He couldn't move and felt faint. His head swirled whenever he lifted it. He must have lost a lot of blood. He lay there, immobilized and bewildered, drifting in and out of consciousness.

In his fitful sleep, his mind was filled with painful memories. He'd told no one in the Philippines of his past. His military experience and abilities were true, but there were things that he'd been involved in during his life that he never revealed to anyone. Memories of the painful events that resulted in him fleeing to Asia were slowly coming back. He remembered hearing the shots, and then the pain. He remembered the first aiders who tried to patch him up before the ambulance arrived.

Then he remembered the cameras. His eyes opened wide with shock and fear. As he was being put on a stretcher there were cameras everywhere—still cameras, video cameras, both local and international. So many clicks and blinding flashes. He remembered trying to cover his face but his arms wouldn't move.

He had to get out. The pain didn't matter now. The adrenaline helped him to sit up on the edge of the bed. It was agony, but it had to be done. The damage to his leg was a flesh wound. Luckily it hadn't affected the artery or any bones. With all the strength he could muster he stood up. He saw his wallet on the side table and managed to put it into his pajama pocket. If only he could get to a taxi he'd be ok.

Slowly swinging one leg after the other he made it to the door, leaving a trail of blood behind him—his leg wound had opened. With all the strength he could muster, he pushed the swing doors open, only to see two startled soldiers stationed outside his room staring at him. He felt his consciousness slipping away as he looked from one to the other.

"Oh, fuck," he muttered as he collapsed at their feet.

Consuelo arrived at the Police Station thirty minutes later. It was early afternoon and the usually quiet station was prepared for its new guest. The plan to confuse the media was working so far. The crestfallen Senator was ushered out of the car and pushed towards the imposing old stone building. Lisa was right behind him with her camera. Despite her gentle coaxing, he was quiet for the whole journey.

His minders hustled him inside and closed the front doors firmly to the expected reporters and cameramen. It wouldn't take the media long to ferret out where he was. His two minders propelled him towards the custody desk. He gazed around the room; it was empty, except for the five officers behind the duty desk in front of him.

General Aquino arranged for Lisa to interview Consuelo after he was processed. The Inspector in charge was told to make sure that Consuelo would agree. She was going to get twenty minutes with him. It was the first chance he would get to put his side to the press.

The interview room was sparse and warm; there was no air-conditioning. A small, noisy and ineffective fan struggled noisily in the corner. The sergeant finally agreed to Consuelo's request to have his handcuffs removed. His wrists were red and sore. He sat and rubbed them while he waited. A couple of minutes later a young officer escorted Lisa into the interview room. After offering the Senator her condolences, she switched her tape recorder on and allowed the Senator to protest his innocence to her and plead for justice. With his agreement now, she took several more photographs. She left, smiling, with enough material in her bag to send her career into the upper atmosphere.

As she left the room, the sergeant returned with a bundle of papers and slammed them down on the desk. On the top was a copy of the familiar package from Paul. Underneath the photographs were signed statements from Brian, and three of the workers who were involved.

He didn't need to study them, he knew what was there. Before he could collect his thoughts the Makati Police Chief burst through the door holding a mobile phone in one hand and a piece of paper in the other.

"The President wants to talk to you."

He handed the phone to the astonished Consuelo and slipped the piece of paper in front of him. Consuelo turned away and ignored the paper while he spoke to the President.

"Madam President?"

"Consuelo," she said briskly, all courtesy was dispensed with now.

"I don't have time to debate matters with you. You know you can't get out of this one—I've seen the mountain of evidence. This is the deal. I'm prepared to guarantee you a swift trial. Also, you have my word that when you're convicted you will be pardoned. This has already been arranged. I can guarantee it."

Even though his usual bright mind had left him, he had enough sense in him still to wonder how the President had learned of his predicament so quickly. She didn't allow him time to consider the matter further.

"Sign the paper in front of you Consuelo, sign it now. There's no way you'll ever become President, I'm sure you realize this. Sign the paper and I guarantee you I will keep my word."

The President had finished talking.

He looked at the paper closely. It wasn't a confession. It was a declaration that he was withdrawing from the race unconditionally. It also said that he was giving up all rights and claims to the Presidency, without admitting responsibility for his crimes.

He put his head in his hands and wept. As he rested his elbows on the table, he felt a pen being placed in his left hand. They even knew he was left-handed. His hand was shaking as he lifted it and looked for a place to sign.

Within two seconds of the paper being signed, the senior officer whisked it off the table and disappeared out of the door. A police motorcycle rider was waiting at a side entrance. Before the ink was dry on the paper it was on its way.

Back at the City Hall, the pandemonium had subsided

and there were few people remaining. The press was interviewing anyone who was left, and each other. There was little activity, but broadcasts were still going out live on all stations in the Republic and even on some overseas networks.

After the arrest, the Returning Officer sought guidance from the Palace and the Chief Justice. The President's Chief of Staff told him to wait there and not to leave the hall. He let this be known to the journalists. They were waiting there as well wondering what would happen next.

Chloe just found out where her husband was being detained and was on her way out of the door when the police courier rushed past her and delivered his envelope to the waiting Returning Officer. In anticipation, the Chief Justice joined him, and they read it together.

The two men huddled in a quiet corner for a while poring over the letter, then called Senator de Vera over. He'd put his considerable acting skills to use that morning, with convincing looks of astonishment recorded for the world to see by the eager press.

The Senator nodded in agreement as the two men quietly spoke with him, and then the Returning Officer and the Chief Justice walked back on to the stage and called for order. The room quieted down. Everyone wanted to make sure that they heard or recorded every word.

"Ladies and Gentlemen, the scenes you've witnessed here today are unprecedented in the history of our country. I can confirm that the Senator has been arrested on a triple count of murder. He's currently in police custody."

You could have heard a pin drop in the hall. There were still a couple of hundred people left in the building, mostly officials, police and press.

"I have discussed the legal position with the Chief Justice here and several senior Senators. The fact that Senator Consuelo is charged with murder doesn't preclude him from assuming the Presidency. However, under the circumstances, the Senator has withdrawn from the election voluntarily."

He waved the piece of paper signed by Consuelo in the air by way of verification.

"This being the case, I now declare that Senator de Vera has been duly elected the President of the Republic of the Philippines."

He looked around to see Senator de Vera waiting behind the stage area in anticipation and beckoned him to come up onto the stage. De Vera had a confident but somber expression; it was time to start acting in a Presidential manner. He firmly shook the hands of the Returning Officer and the Chief Justice, looking from left to right, for the benefit of the photographers.

"It's with sadness and humility that I am bound to accept the result of our election and the operation of our Sovereign Laws. Our great country is a democracy and we must show the world that we operate under the rule of law."

There was a little muted applause, which swiftly died away.

"I will do my duty to the people of the Philippines and serve them as their President. If it's later proved that Senator Consuelo is innocent of the charges made against him I'll resign and call for fresh elections."

There was more generous applause now as the Senator, now President Elect, made his way down from the stage.

At Consuelo's Estate in Abra, Brian was having lunch with Colonel Vicente and Chief Costello. The three men watched the news of Consuelo's arrest and 'abdication', and Simon's capture on the national news network with great interest. They were in good spirits now.

They searched the place but found no sign of Tom. He was undoubtedly far away by now. One of the trucks went missing last night, maybe Tom had taken that. As soon as the phone lines were restored, their boss, the Governor,

summoned Colonel Vicente and the Police Chief back to
Ilocos Sur. He told them to bring Brian with them. The
three men set off for Vigan soon after lunch. They used
one of the cars from Consuelo's Estate. They didn't think
he would mind now. Colonel Vicente made sure the
briefcases with the money were still in the trunk before
they set off.

The roads were quiet at that time in the afternoon and
they made it back in less than an hour.

Pedro watched the car disappear down the drive with
his boss and the two others inside. Brian had given him no
orders; he hadn't even spoken to him since he had
returned from his mysterious overnight trip. He still
couldn't get through the Senator, but he knew that
something was definitely not right.

He made his way to Brian's room. The door was
locked, but he knew there was a spare key in the security
lodge. Three minutes later he was standing in the room. It
was tidy, and empty, just like Tom's room. Pedro knew
then that his boss was not coming back.

Governor Gallenosa welcomed the men into his office
and shut the door; each of them was carrying one of the
black briefcases. Brian noticed that there were copies of
his statement and pardon on the Governor's desk.

His men gave a brief report of the events of the night.
Finally, the Governor picked up Brian's statement and
smiled.

"There's no mention of Consuelo's gold or money in
this report," the Governor said in mock surprise.

"It looks like Consuelo must have spent or otherwise
got rid of the gold or whatever he had it turned into."

The three men laughed.

"Yes it does. We couldn't find it anywhere."

The Colonel joined in the spirit of the joke.

The Governor opened a wooden cabinet behind him
and poured a generous whiskey for each of them. The

others stood up and the four men toasted their good fortune. The Governor raised his eyebrows at the Chief, who walked to the door and locked it with a quiet click.

There was a meeting table in one corner of the Governor's large office. The Colonel put the cases on the table. The Governor took a small crowbar from his desk drawer and levered them open—the locks broke quite easily—to reveal neat bundles of hundred dollar bills.

"It's such a shame that you never managed to find this."

The Governor stared at the mounds of money. All four men laughed again.

"As far as anyone will know, the Senator spent it all. No one must know about this money."

He glanced at the fortune on his table and at the other three men. They were all nodding solemnly.

"Ok, let's get it sorted out and then it'll really have disappeared."

The Governor was prepared. There were four cases in the corner of the room. He put them on the table and started to divide the money up, making four equal piles, under the watchful eyes of the other three.

After they packed the money into the four new cases their business was done. Brian earlier asked for a car and the Governor readily agreed. The value of a car was nothing, considering their good fortune. He said goodbye to the others, then threw his case into the back seat of the nearly new Pajero that was waiting for him. He drove off without looking back. It was only a short drive to Candon, but he hurried. He was late for his rendezvous.

Pedro stared intently at the computer screen in the reception area. He was sat at the one that Brian always used. Brian was sloppy with computer security, often forgetting to log himself out.

Pedro, on the other hand, had earned a degree in computer technology before entering the Officer Training Academy, and at that moment he was reading the details of

Brian's email inbox. "Got you, you bastard," he said triumphantly.

CHAPTER TEN

Chloe was recovering from the shock of the day's events, but it wasn't over yet. Right now, she had a husband in trouble and she had to help him somehow. She also had a family and a future to consider. She would have to be very careful.

When she arrived at the police station the young man on duty escorted her through to the high security prison attached to the station, and into the Governor's office. It had a faintly musty smell that she knew would make her nauseous if she had to endure it for long. He showed her to a faded couch that squeaked as she sat down on it. Then she waited.

After twenty minutes, the Governor came in. He was a thin, wiry man of about fifty. His clothes were worn and ill fitting.

He had risen through the ranks of the prison service slowly, and was without family influence or money. He deliberately didn't see her as soon as she arrived. The message was clear—I'm the boss, you have to wait until I'm ready.

Chloe sat behind a glass coffee table on the other side of the room from the Governor's rather grand desk.

Unexpectedly, he came over and sat beside her on the couch. She felt uncomfortable at his closeness.

"I'm sorry, my dear, this must be quite a trial for you. Is there anything I can do to help you at this time? Senator Consuelo is a great man. I'm sure he will work this out soon. Don't worry, my dear, I'll make sure he's well looked after while he's my guest."

Chloe composed herself; she was trying hard to tolerate his insipid manner. She asked if she could see her husband privately, and then meet with the Governor again later.

It was a dirty, dark and smelly place. She'd never been in any prison before, but she knew that the Manila prisons were among the worst and most overcrowded in the world. The experience of learning about them first hand was not something that she ever imagined she would have to do.

They passed along quiet echoing corridors with barred doors on either side. The inhabitants were quiet, probably sleeping or resting at that time. The smells dimmed and the light increased as they walked out and through an open quadrangle with flower borders and ornamental trees in the middle.

The new block, where the Senator was kept, was thankfully cleaner and lighter. Chloe was relieved. The musty smell was fading even more and she could now detect a faint hint of disinfectant. The Governor showed her into a pleasant interview room with clean white walls and two padded chairs with a table in between.

She was nervous, and she did not like being in this place. What could she say to her husband? How could she help him?

Throughout their relationship he'd been the strong one, always in control. She sensed that this had already changed.

It was another ten minutes before the Governor reappeared. This time Enrique was behind him. Two guards took up the rear and discreetly stood in the corner.

Consuelo looked clean and tidy although his new smart suit was now very crumpled.

She rushed to him and hugged him. He responded gratefully. After a few moments she let him go and they sat down on the couch together holding hands. The Governor stood away from the couple for a few moments, but now came over and told them quietly to take all the time they wanted. As he moved towards the door, as if to leave, the guards in the corner remained motionless.

Chloe pleaded gently with the Governor to let them be alone for a short while. He considered for a moment and then nodded in agreement. He left the room closely followed by the guards, who took up their positions outside.

"Oh, my darling, I'm so sorry. Be strong, please, I beg you. I can work this out."

The Senator smoothed her hair.

"Everything will be back to normal soon. I just need to get my people working on it."

It calmed her to hear the words although she knew things could not possibly be that simple.

As soon as the Governor was out of the room, the Senator passed a small piece of paper to Chloe. It had a phone number on it.

"Get hold of Dominic right away, make sure he calls me. Tell the Governor to let me have my phone back. Dominic will reward him tomorrow. We need to work on this quickly."

Chloe nodded and pocketed the paper, trying unsuccessfully to hide her tears.

Consuelo took her face in his hands

"My darling, I didn't do it. They have no proof, sweetheart. I wasn't there. My rivals have conspired against me, but I'll win out in the end."

He forced a smile and so did she. She still didn't believe him, but it didn't matter. She didn't care what he'd done; she just cared how much it could affect their lives.

Their parting was awkward, but mercifully brief. She promised to return soon. Chloe was anxious now to get back to the province to make sure their children were ok. She would be back in a couple of days. He nodded understandingly and released her from their embrace.

Once inside the Governor's office again, she sensed the atmosphere had changed. He sat behind his impressive desk and, although he rose and came around with his hand outstretched to greet her, his manner was now definitely more businesslike. He led her to the seat on the opposite side of his desk then resumed his seat.

"Thank you for taking good care of my husband."

She tried not to show her dislike of the man. It was important to get him on her side. Of course, she'd have to arrange a sum money for him, quietly, but it was still best not to antagonize him.

"I hope you can assist me with some simple requests, just to make life a little easier for him."

"Of course, my dear. Consider it done. In view of his position, we've already housed him in the 'V.I.P.' section of the jail. He has a clean and spacious cell with bathroom and toilet and is allowed visitors at any time."

She smiled and thanked him.

"Of course the extra attention and services come at a price, my dear."

She cringed inwardly again at the continued familiarity, but maintained her fixed smile.

"Don't worry. Tomorrow my husband's lawyer will visit. I will make sure that he sees you to work out all the financial arrangements."

The Governor nodded, satisfied. Dealing with lawyers was much easier than dealing with the inmates or their families. The lawyers would be generous to keep their clients happy since it wasn't their money. Chloe rose, her business here was done for now and she couldn't wait to get out of that terrible place.

The traffic got heavier as Tom and Marcos made their way towards the Afghan embassy. It was midday, and they were still probably half an hour away. Tom took a call and immediately recognized the crisp Persian accent of Alexi.

"Hello Tom, how are you? When do you think you'll arrive?"

"Traffic's bad today, we're probably about thirty minutes away."

"That's fine, my friend, don't worry. I'm having lunch with some people. Why don't you take a break, then come along at about two p.m.?"

"That sounds like a plan. I was getting hungry anyway."

"That's settled then. I'll see you this afternoon,"

"Come on, Marcos. Let's find somewhere nice to eat."

Marcos was uncomfortable in better class eateries. They found a quiet carinderia that sold food from their local province. The traffic had eased a little bit when they set off again.

The Afghan embassy was in a quiet side street in Makati, away from the busy business district. Just before they entered the road leading to the embassy, Tom asked Marcos to pull over.

"I won't need you anymore, my friend. I'll make my own way back. Why don't you enjoy yourself in Manila for a few days?"

Tom pressed twenty thousand pesos into Marcos' hand. This was more than two month's salary for the lowly gardener.

"Thank you very much, sir. God bless you, sir."

He stuffed the money into his back pocket as he slid down from the cab.

"I'll see you back at the Estate."

Tom didn't reply, but he returned the old man's wave and watched him saunter off down the road.

As Tom pulled up outside the high walled Embassy, the tall and heavy solid metal gates started to swing inwards, they were electronically controlled. A smiling Afghan security officer came towards the truck.

"Are you Mr. Tom?"

"Yes, I am" said Tom, reaching into his pocket for some identification.

The friendly guard stood smartly to attention and saluted as the truck slowly proceeded past the guardhouse and around the driveway. Twenty yards further along, two other younger guards directed the truck into a space at the back of the building under a covered canopy. It was a short walk to the side entrance of the imposing building.

Tom soon found himself in a wood paneled room, decorated in modern Arabic style, with a bronze coffee table centering two plush couches. Alexi sat down in the furthest one and indicated that Tom should take the nearer one. Alexi greeted him warmly, then leaned forward and poured two small cups of tea.

"Very impressive, Alexi," he said, gesturing at his surroundings.

The Pashtun smiled and slightly bowed his head.

"Thank you, Tom. I appreciate nice things, and luckily, I'm also one of those people who can afford them! Tom, the Senator must trust you very much. He's told me to let you have the money."

"I've worked for him for a long time, and he treats me well," said Tom.

"I've prepared the cash in four cases, as the Senator instructed. Do you want to count the money?"

"No, of course not. We've known you long enough, Alexi. I know it'll all be there."

"Thank you, my friend. I'll go and get it."

Alexi returned after a few moments; two guards carried the cases. Tom followed them through the house to the back yard. Alexi and the guards waited for Tom to unlock the tailgate so the men could unload the valuable cargo.

"Help yourself," he said, lowering the tailgate and revealing the stacked boxes.

Alexi barked something in Farsi to the guards. One of them opened the side door of the adjacent security van. The guards were stronger than they looked. They set up a relay taking the boxes one by one from the back of the truck and stacking them neatly into the security truck.

Alexi and Tom stood side by side watching the relay gang at work.

"I guess things will be different for you after today," Alexi commented.

"Yes, they most certainly will."

Alexi was referring to the anticipated election of Tom's boss as President of the Philippines. Tom was not.

"It's about time I was on my way. The Senator will be expecting me to meet him with the money now."

"Ok, my friend. Give my best regards to the President."

Alexi waited while Tom climbed into the cab. He arranged the four cases behind the front seats out of sight then set off, giving a wave to the waiting Alexi as he drove away. The security gate was already open, and the friendly guard saluted again as he drove out.

He was due at the Shangri-la hotel where he would meet with the Senator and Simon. Once he'd passed over the money, he could start following his own plans. No need to tell the Senator or Brian; they'd find out soon enough.

A local radio station played nearly non-stop country and western music, Tom's favorite. The announcer spoke Tagalog in between the music but Tom put up with that. However, every hour on the hour there was a brief news summary in English. As Tom turned the radio on, he heard the familiar beeps that signified an upcoming news broadcast. 'Three o'clock,' he thought. 'I'm making good time.'

The announcer's voice was loud and clear.

"In a dramatic scene today, Senator Enrique Consuelo has been arrested for multiple murders. One of his close accomplices was injured in the arrest, but the police are searching for several others."

Tom wasn't listening carefully at first, but when he heard the word Consuelo, he paid more attention. By the end of the sentence he was riveted and turned the volume up. The announcer continued to give the details of the events of just a couple of hours earlier as the blood drained from Tom's face.

He pulled up by the side of the road and concentrated on the broadcast. The announcer gave graphic details of the discovery of the boys' bodies in the province and the Senator's attempt to flee, followed by the dramatic and bloody arrests. Tom sat there rigid. What should he do? He knew he must be one of the wanted men. He was sitting in a truck in an up market street in Manila with enough money to buy the whole street ten times over, and a price on his head. The only thing he was certain of was that he couldn't stay there. Then he had an idea. He made a phone call and set off down the street.

The bus station at Cubao was always a busy place twenty-four hours a day, but late afternoon was probably its least busy time. Tom parked the truck in a street with good lighting, making sure the cases were not visible, and then carefully locked it. He walked to a nearby fruit vendor and, after selecting different vegetables, he ended up with four plastic bags. Just around the corner was a group of three beggars. One had lost a leg and one appeared to be blind. The third was pitifully thin but didn't seem to be missing anything. The tall American stood before them and emptied the vegetables on the ground in front of them.

"It's your lucky day, lads."

He smiled and walked away from the bewildered men who were now scrabbling for their share.

He scrambled back into the cab of his truck with the four dirty bags. After checking that there was no one around, he opened one of the cases, and took out several wedges of $100 bills and put them inside a bag, which he then put inside the others. He looked at his watch and dismounted the cab again with the carrier bags.

The bus station was just twenty yards further on and he planned to find a seat where he could keep an eye on the truck. He was lucky; a cluster of five or six seats was empty next to the ticket counter and adjacent to a wide panoramic window with a good view of the road and the truck. He sat back to relax and waited, he didn't wait long. The old man shuffled up and sat down next to him.

"Have you heard about the Guv'nor?"

Tom nodded.

"What we gonna do?" asked Marcos. "If he's banged up I reckon the lot of us will be out of a job sooner or later."

"Cheer up Marcos, you look so miserable."

He shook the old man by the shoulder.

"I didn't call you back here just to discuss the fate of our boss."

Marcos raised his head a bit and looked at him.

"Why did you get me here then? I could be on my way to Ilocos by now."

"I think you'll be glad you stayed."

He reached down, picked up the grubby bags, and put them down again closer to Marcos, and then he spoke to him in a very low voice.

"Take a look."

Marcos gave him a puzzled stare, and then he bent down and opened the bag cautiously, as if he were afraid something would jump out. His mouth dropped open as he saw the bundles. He reached a hand in. Tom quickly grabbed his hand before it came out of the bag.

"Don't take it out here."

Both men looked around and Marcos withdrew his empty hand quickly.

Tom took Marcos gently by the shoulders, stared into his eyes and whispered,

"There's enough in there for you and the families of the three missing boys to live well for the rest of your lives."

Marcos sat back, dumbfounded.

"Is it stolen?"

Tom sighed.

"It belonged to someone a long time ago, but not now. I can guarantee you that no one is going to come after you looking for it, as long as you don't go wild and draw attention to yourself. Don't change the money in the province, go to Baguio or come to Manila now and again, it's safer that way. You're not some kid, Marcos, make sure no one knows. Leave the families a small package from time to time, anonymously, you understand?"

Marcos nodded and looked up at Tom.

"Why are you doing this for us? Do you know something about the boys?"

"All I can tell you, Marcos, is that they won't be coming back."

Marcos felt it would be unwise to press the man further.

"Well, no matter why you're doing this, I thank you on their behalf and for me and my family too. God bless you!"

"I doubt He will ever do that, but you're welcome to it, my friend. It's only right. Let's leave it at that. Now, put that plastic bag safely away, and make sure you take good care of it."

Marcos nodded as he zipped up the bag. Tom waited until the old man's bus came and saw him safely off.

"See you back in Ilocos," Marcos said as he boarded the bus.

"Sure."

Tom smiled, knowing that he would never see the old man again.

Brian finally pulled into the only parking space outside McDonald's in Candon. It was six p.m. The pouting face of a young girl glared at him through the panoramic window. Edelweiss was not pleased that she had been kept waiting for so long. The battery on her game boy had run out a couple of hours ago and there was no charge left on her cell phone. Nevertheless, she ran towards him and kissed him as he walked into the busy restaurant.

"I thought you weren't coming, darling. I was so worried. I thought you left me."

"Well, I did try to call you, but your phone was dead."

"I know, I know, no battery."

"Well, I'm here now, and I'm not going anywhere without you."

The scheduled Philippine Airlines flight to Hong Kong left Laoag at midnight. He had already booked the tickets. Brian was going to take her to the best restaurant in Laoag to celebrate before they had to go to the airport.

He knew about Edelweiss and her activities, and didn't mind a bit. The spirited young girl had taken his interest about six months ago. They became lovers very quickly and he liked her more and more each time he met her. He was not a jealous man and enjoyed her tales. She had really done some outrageous things, and she wasn't yet twenty.

He finally asked her to go away with him two weeks ago. She was surprised at his offer, but when she realized that he was serious she considered it for a couple of days. Finally, she agreed. He decided that now was the time after he gave his statement to Chief Costello and when they hatched their plan for the sharing of the fortune. When he phoned her she was surprised, but the promise of a carefree comfortable life with a strong and caring man clinched the deal.

Paul was a happy man. He enjoyed seeing the Senator's face and watching him being bundled into the police van. He slept briefly at his hotel and awoke to the continual drone of the repeating newscast. He looked at his watch—five p.m.—he had slept for four hours. After he pulled himself around, he had to decide what to do, but first things first; he was hungry.

When he had showered, he made his way to the Woodman's Pub just down the road from his hotel. Paul was mixed up. He was pleased that Consuelo had been brought down, but he had time to think now. He'd treated his wife badly for years and now he'd lost her. The meal was hardly touched, but he finished his beer, and made a short phone call. The humid evening air hit him as he strolled out into the dusty street. A taxi pulled up hoping for a fare, and he got in.

When he arrived, he could see that at the top of the drive the door was open. He walked into the spacious hall and was pleased to see Ruth there with a big smile. She hugged him and pulled him into the drawing room.

"It's good to see you back. Are you ok? You didn't sound so good when you rang."

"Ruth, you're not going to believe what has happened to me since we last met."

"Well you can tell me tomorrow. I can see you're exhausted, come and get some rest."

She led him upstairs to the now familiar bed and took his shoes off as he lay down. Paul mumbled a thank you as he nestled into the pillow and began to doze. Ruth sat with him for a while and quietly left.

Chloe had one job to do before returning to the hotel. Carlos, the headwaiter at the Dusit Thani Hotel, was surprised to see her. There was no one in Manila who hadn't heard the news by now. He greeted her as an old friend and told her he couldn't believe what had happened to her husband today.

The well-appointed restaurant was nearly empty at that time of day and there was no one there who might recognize her. She asked him to sit with her for a while.

She hadn't eaten since breakfast and was very hungry. Carlos called to a nearby waitress who ran out to the kitchen to get some soup and a sandwich.

"Here's a list of the food he likes, nothing too rich or fatty—he has to watch his diet. Just make sure he gets a good meal three times a day. I can't bear the thought of him eating the awful prison food. I've made sure the guards will let your people in. There won't be any problems."

Carlos read through the items in a few seconds. "That's fine, Ma'am. You can leave it to me. I'll make sure he is well looked after. I'm sure he won't be there long."

"Thanks for your concern, Carlos. I hope you are right."

An hour later, Chloe was back in the Shangri–La Hotel. Consuelo's lawyer, Dominic, would arrive in a few hours. They would discuss things over dinner that evening, but she had some urgent calls to make and also needed a rest. After twenty minutes of phoning, she set her alarm for seven p.m., she knew she would sleep through otherwise.

Dominic was a bright lawyer who had caught the Senator's eye when he had successfully defended one of the Senator's friends six years ago. Since then, Consuelo regarded him more or less as his primary lawyer. Chloe had called him from the taxi when she was on her way to the hotel. She told him that the Senator needed his help and arranged a meeting with him for later that evening.

He got working straight after the call. One call in particular paid off. He left the office early that evening. The police Colonel, a man he had known for years, was waiting for him at their usual bar just a few blocks from the attorney's office. He'd changed into plain clothes for the meeting; they were just two friends out for a drink. He passed over to the lawyer the copies of everything to do with the case that he could get his hands on; he had managed to see off two beers while Dominic read it. It included a copy of Paul's package.

"We've got more than enough here to ensure that our would-be President will never come out of jail, and we've only just started. With the Senator behind bars, everyone's keen to spill the beans. We've been liaising with Police Chief Costello in Ilocos Sur who conducted the initial investigation last night—very thorough job I might add," he said admiringly.

"We have a team of officers from National Headquarters getting ready to go to the province. They will take over the investigation in the next day or two."

He took a sip of his third beer.

"From what this foreigner, Brian, has told us they'll be busy for a few days. The number of people who want to stick the knife in the Senator grows by the hour. Right now the best thing you could do for your client is to break him out of jail."

He laughed, but he glanced sideways at Dominic to see his reaction. They were quiet for a moment.

Dominic was quiet, but his friend wanted to follow the conversation through.

"It could be done you know, but the price would be very high."

Dominic forced a laugh, although he knew his friend was serious.

"I'll be meeting with him soon. I'll let you know what he says. Purely speculatively, how much would we be talking about? It would have to include safe passage out of the country for him and his family."

The Colonel nodded as if that were taken for granted. "Ten million pesos."

Dominic sighed.

"I really don't believe that things are that serious yet, but I'll run it past the Senator."

The Colonel leaned over and put his hand on Dominic's arm conspiratorially.

"I think you know that they are. Another thing you must tell your client is that we must know by tomorrow night and the 'event' must happen straight away—probably after breakfast the next day. The longer he's there and the more evidence mounts up the more difficult it'll be. The price goes up to twenty million after tomorrow."

Dominic said nothing. He wasn't surprised that an offer like this had come. He was just a little surprised that it had come so quickly, and via his friend, a middle ranking Colonel.

The two friends parted at seven-thirty promising to be in touch the next day. Dominic looked at his watch. He was in plenty of time for his meeting with Chloe, but he was glad he didn't tell his friend about his next appointment. He might have put more pressure on.

Tom was stuck in traffic. The truck was heavy and difficult to maneuver through some of the narrow and winding streets, and it was not the safest of places to leave anything valuable, even locked. Once he'd found a used car dealer, he parked it on the road in full view and just down the road the car lot. He made sure it was in his sight at all times. Before he locked it up, he took a bundle of dollars from the top case and covered them again so that they weren't in view.

The owner of the car lot was an elderly Chinese Filipino. He saw the tall American stroll into the lot and take an interest in some of the cheaper cars. He put out his cigar and emerged from his steel hut.

"Hi there," he called out cheerily as the American approached.

"I just need a cheap run-around."

Tom cast his eyes around the lot.

"Will you take US Dollars?"

"I sure will. What's your budget, son?"

"Oh, let's say around $3,000."

"Ok, we can find you a nice little runner for that. How about this one?"

He led Tom over to a white Toyota, it looked old, but in good condition.

Tom glanced up the road at the truck. The road was quiet, there were few people around, and there was no sign of anyone near the truck. The old man opened the driver's door for him and he sat behind the wheel. Tom felt his way around the controls and adjusted the seat.

"This is a good runner," said the old man.

"Had a new engine just a couple of years ago. It'll last you for years. Do you want to take it for a spin?"

Tom looked at his watch; he had to get a move on. "I'll tell you what, I'll give you the $3,000, you give me the papers, and I'll drive it away. If I don't like it I'll bring it back. What do you say?"

The old man beamed.

"You're the boss. Whatever you want, sir. It's got a couple of liters of gas in the tank."

Five minutes later Tom was pulling out onto the deserted road. He drove the car around the block; he didn't want the old man to notice him pull up behind the old truck a couple of hundred yards down the road.

He swiftly transferred the cases to the trunk of the car. He locked the empty truck and, after checking again that there was no one around, threw the keys into a nearby drain. He made a phone call as he pulled away from the curb.

"I'm on my way."

He reached the tree-lined and well-kept avenues of Dasmarinas Village after about an hour of heavy traffic. As he approached a small two–story house on the right he slowed down and pulled off the road. The gates were open—he was expected.

A tall and elegant woman appeared at the door after one ring. She smiled at him and kissed him on the cheek. Although she was in her late sixties, she looked fit and alert. He was pleased to see how good she still looked for her age. Tom was an only child and his father died many years ago and he loved his mother very much. He returned her greeting with a warm smile and a hug. They hadn't seen each other for about three months.

"So you've finally done it then, dear. You're taking her away from that monster. I'm so glad—for both of you."

She knew about his relationship with Lucy and his feelings for her almost from the beginning. They had met on several occasions. She liked Lucy and had always hoped that one day she would leave her brutish husband and start a life with her son.

"It was only a matter of waiting for the right moment, mum."

"Well, it's about time. I can't tell you how pleased I am. What will you do?

"Well, I don't need to worry about money now. We'll live in Singapore for a while. Then we'll see what happens."

His mum nodded.

"That's nice, son. I know you're going to be happy."

Tom felt it was time to change the subject.

"Mum, I want you to look after something for me."

"Yes, of course, dear, what is it? Have you robbed a bank?"

She saw from the look on his face that he was serious.

"Are you in trouble, son?" she asked, looking a little concerned.

He sighed and looked away from her.

"Mum, I am sure you've seen all the news today, about Senator Consuelo."

"Of course, everybody's talking about it. Are you involved with that?"

Tom nodded.

"Oh, my dear. What can I do to help?"

"It's ok. Mum, I just want you to look after some money for me, it's to do with my job, but I don't want to carry it with me."

She trusted her son.

"Put it somewhere safe, but don't put it in the bank. They'll want to know where it came from. I don't need it right now mum, use some of it for whatever you want."

His mum knew him very well; she could sense he was troubled. She moved closer to him.

"Is there something wrong, son? Is there something you want to tell me?"

He sighed, but said nothing. She wanted to ask more questions, but she sensed that it was probably not the right time to push him.

"Whatever you want, son. If that will make you happy, then of course I will."

"Thanks, mum. Yes, that will make me very happy."

"Is there anything else I can do for you?"

"You can give me a warm bed for the night and a lift to the airport tomorrow."

Dominic rose from the lounge chair as he saw her come out of the elevator. She felt better after her nap—refreshed and stronger. He chose a small table in the corner, it was as far away from other diners as he could find. No one paid them any attention. They had met many times over the years; he greeted her with a sympathetic smile and a brief hug.

"Ok, Dominic, first things first. Who do we have to pay off, and how much is it going to cost to get him out of there?"

He was surprised at her directness; this meeting wasn't going to be easy.

"Chloe, I'm sorry but it's not that simple this time. I've made many phone calls today and there's a mass of evidence against him. More importantly, his rival has just been proclaimed the next President and the current President has let it be known that she won't assist Enrique.

He's losing friends fast. I don't think we can get him out on bail at least until after he's been arraigned in a week's time."

The news wasn't a surprise to Chloe. Deep down she knew that he was capable of anything to protect himself, and with no one important to help him he was unlikely to get out of jail, no matter what the price.

"Well, what can we do for him, then?"

"We'll set about working out his defense immediately," Dominick replied swiftly, slipping into his lawyer mode.

"We need supportive statements from you and from others putting him somewhere else at all the relevant times. The best thing you can do for now is to get back to the province and try to stop things falling apart there."

"The Senator's accused, among other things, of being the mastermind behind the murder of three young boys. You need to visit their families as soon as possible and buy them off. I'm sure they're poor and despite the loss of their sons, they'll accept 'compensation' from you not to proceed with charges."

"How much should I offer them?"

Dominic gave her a figure but then advised her that they may have to go much higher if the family or witnesses were greedy and good negotiators. They knew the Senator was a very rich man.

"What do you know about the gold, Chloe?"

"Honestly, Dominic, I know nothing about it. The first I heard of it was on the television news. I don't know whether it's made up or true. If it's true, Enrique never told me anything about it."

Clearly now was not the time to push her. Dominic was inclined to believe her anyway so he nodded and let the matter drop. Over the next couple of hours Chloe learned about everything; the picture didn't look good.

Dominic knew that over the past couple of years the Senator had hidden a lot of money and assets in Chloe's name—both in the Philippines and abroad. Dominic advised her to make them as difficult to trace as possible and get them as far away from the Philippines as she could.

"Do it quickly, Chloe. You only have a day or two before investigators will be crawling all over the Estate. If things go badly for him, the courts may seek to get it back from you."

Chloe nodded glumly.

"Also you should steel yourself for other law suits to be filed. The Senator has made enemies over the years and many will now pile in to try to collect what they consider as their due. They'll see him as vulnerable now."

Later in the evening, when they were both a little more forthcoming, thanks to the wine (two empty bottles sat on the table), he confessed he didn't think the Senator could buy himself out of this very easily. He warned Chloe that she could get herself into trouble by trying to buy people off. She should be very careful and use third parties for the negotiations. There was greater danger for her if she became directly involved.

"You don't want to end up in there with him, do you?"

After Dominic left, she made her way back up to her room. She was planning what she should do tomorrow and somehow she didn't think she would be visiting the parents of the dead boys. The anesthesia of the alcohol was beginning to work. She couldn't truly comprehend the ramifications of what she'd learned tonight and resolved not to think about things any more until the morning After a couple of tries, her electronic key worked and she was in her room. She fell asleep immediately.

Senator Consuelo now lay on his mattress, exhausted. He was in the best V.I.P. room on the block, but it was like a cheap motel room in the provinces. It had a clean, if old, bathroom with a hot shower area, and there was a chair and a small writing desk in the corner. A worn carpet with frayed edges covered most of the floor, and a noisy air conditioner vibrated inside the wall. There was no wall at the front, it was all iron bars. A small window high up on the back wall was the only natural light. The small electric light dangling by a cord in the center was very dim. The accommodation was sparse, but it was comfortable.

Dinner arrived at six p.m. For the first time since his arrest, he smiled in surprise as the waiter from the hotel laid out in front of him a gourmet meal of lobster tail with sautéed potatoes—one of his favorites. He thought of Chloe and mentally thanked her for this thoughtfulness.

The wine mellowed him and he felt at ease. If there were anything he needed one of the guards would fetch it and get a generous tip for his services. The only thing the Senator had asked for so far was a writing pad, pencils, pens, and envelopes. He was an organized man and had started to list his jobs for tomorrow. Finally, before he settled down to sleep, he set the alarm on his cell phone for six.

Laoag airport was nominally an International Airport because it flew to Hong Kong as well as a few domestic routes, but the rambling shacks and draughty halls which comprised the tiny complex resembled a farm more than an airport.

Luggage was loaded and unloaded by carts. Arriving passengers were often surprised to see their bags being dumped in a heap in the middle of the floor for them to sort through.

It was ten thirty in the evening, the passengers for the next departure, the midnight flight to Hong Kong, would start to arrive soon. The old green army jeep, its flaky paint still showing the camouflage colors of its past, drove slowly into the nearly empty car park.

Pedro was unaware of the events of the day. He was not a man who read newspapers or watched TV, except for sports, and he left the estate early in the afternoon, before the arrest hit the headlines.

He made his way to the observation platform on the third floor. He had put on his AFP lieutenant uniform, and the security guards waved him through.

The viewing area spanned the width of the airport. From the panoramic window on one side you could watch the arriving cars, buses and taxis pull up and disgorge their passengers before parking or disappearing back down the unfinished approach road.

Brian and Edelweiss left the restaurant and picked up their bags from the hotel. They arrived at the entrance to departures about eleven p.m.—they were in plenty of time.

Pedro had his high powered binoculars. He didn't want to make a mistake. He slipped into the toilets. His briefcase contained a high powered rifle, in two parts. He hadn't used it since his army days except for his regular practice however, he was still a crack shot. He carefully fitted the two pieces together; it took only a few seconds, he was very practiced at it.

There was a small window at the top of the toilet cubicle which looked out directly over the boarding area. Luckily, he was very tall. When he stood on the toilet bowl he had a clear view of people leaving the terminal—right up to the steps of the plane. The passengers had to walk from the departure building over the concrete to the steps of the aircraft. Pedro estimated he would have about thirty seconds to get his shot in.

There was no cafe or restaurant within the airport building, just a tiny gift cubicle and a drinks vending machine. Brian came back to the waiting area where Edelweiss sat not-too patiently with two cans of coke.

"Is that all they've got? I'm hungry. Don't they have any chips?"

"Sorry sweetheart. It's only a couple of hours. You can have whatever you want when we get to Hong Kong. There are some great restaurants right there in the airport."

She brightened a little.

"Do they have Filipino food?"

"Yes, sweetheart, they do."

He hoped her mood would improve by the time they got there and discovered there was no Filipino food at the airport.

People were lining up now, but Brian saw no point in standing when he could be sitting. He would wait until the last stragglers were going through.

The toilet window was hinged at the top and swung upwards easily. There was just room to poke the gun through and focus through the crosshairs of the zoom sight. He was uncomfortable, but he could put up with it for a while. The door was locked, in any case there was no one else using the toilet area.

There was a small rock on the runway half way between the departure door of the airport and the plane steps. Pedro focused on it, knowing it was near enough the route that Brian must take to the plane.

The thirty minutes that he waited seemed like thirty hours. His back was hurting and his legs ached but he forgot that when he saw the passengers start to come into sight. He could narrow down his target field now.

Ten minutes later Brian still had not come through and there were just stragglers now. Suddenly he came into view with a young girl on his arm. Pedro thought he knew her but could not be sure with just a back view.

It took just ten seconds to perfect the focus and the aim. A quiet pop somewhat understated the deed.

Brian first felt the pressure, like someone had pushed him from behind. Then the blinding pain hit him as his shattered spine and torn heart muscles cried desperately for help.

He just started to wonder what had happened to him as his legs gave way and he sank to his knees. That was the time when Edelweiss realized something was wrong. She thought he'd stumbled, grabbed his arm to steady him, then let him go with a yelp as she saw his white face with blood trickling out of the corner of his mouth. He looked at her but couldn't say anything.

He stayed in that position for maybe three or four seconds, like a chopped tree waiting to fall, then he slowly toppled forward. The growing red patch on his back was visible now. Edelweiss screamed and screamed.

Brian crumpled noiselessly onto the ground. The wound was dead center and six inches below the shoulder blade—a perfect shot.

Other passengers were screaming, and running for the plane to take shelter—no one came to her aid.

"Help me, please!"

Edelweiss looked around frantically. She was on her own on the tarmac with the body of her lover. She burst into tears and sat holding him. Nobody dared to help her. She knew it was too late anyway. Eventually a tall uniformed figure approached her.

"It's ok, sweetheart. He's gone. I saw the shooters ride off quickly on a motorcycle. There were two of them, but there's no danger now."

The tall, familiar, military man knelt down and put an arm around her shoulder. She leaned into him, still sobbing.

The airport security knew Pedro, they were happy he seemed to be taking charge.

"I'm going to get this poor girl away from here. Tell the police to call me. I'll give them a report. I hope they find the bastards."

Pedro guided the grieving girl away from the scene, stopping only to retrieve Brian's case which lay on the ground at his feet.

He suddenly realized who the girl was.

"It's Edelweiss isn't it?"

She nodded through her tears.

He sat her down in the open air canteen just down from the airport and brought her a glass of water.

"What were you doing with Brian?"

"He was my boyfriend, we kept it quiet. I don't know what I'll do now."

"I'll take you home to your family. That's the best thing for now."

"No, thank you. I don't want to face them yet. Please, can you drop me in Benguet? I have a friend there. I'll stay with her for a while"

She was a lot more composed by the time they reached the City Center. Pedro dropped her by KFC. It was one of the few places open at that time in the morning. He gave her a few thousand pesos, he'd managed to look in Brian's case—he could afford to.

She sat quietly in a corner with hot chocolate and lifted her phone to call her friend when she was distracted. There was a group of young Americans laughing in the corner. They had the munchies after a night out in Benguet's clubs and bars.

"Hi, Sweetie."

He was not that old, maybe thirty—quite attractive, he looked like a tourist.

"Care to join us?"

She returned his smile and stood up. The whistles that she got as she walked over to the table made her feel good.

Chloe knocked the alarm clock off the side table by her bed. Its shrill buzzing pulled her out of her deep sleep soon after dawn. She was a morning person; it didn't take her long to come round. After a quick shower, she made the plane with time to spare.

News of the Senators arrest filled the first five pages of the newspaper the flight attendant handed her as she boarded. The front-page story described the activities of the night before, the urgent investigations and the night-time raid in Abra. It was a concise and accurate piece of reporting. The by-line was 'by Lisa Carriega, senior political correspondent.'

Chloe soon arrived in the province, refreshed and prepared for the difficult day ahead. A long-serving guard (one of the few who could drive) had been sent to meet her. Brian hadn't been seen since yesterday afternoon and his deputy, Pedro, had not been there since last night.

The children knew their mom was on the way home, and they were excited. They ran down the stairs, giggling. The Estate was a fun place to grow up. They were well taken care of, but missed their mom when she was away. Her car turned the corner and started up the drive towards the house. Waving and shouting excitedly, they ran towards their mom. Chloe got out of the car just after it went through the first gate and hugged her children.

In Manila, Paul and Ruth were taking a mid-morning 'brunch' on the patio behind her house. The open wooden floor area was an extension to the house and overlooked a small enclosed but very tidy garden, with mature mango trees shading the lawn area at the bottom.

Ruth tried to make conversation, but Paul was mostly lost in thought so she didn't push. He would tell her what he wanted her to know in his own good time.

She watched him as he chewed on his bacon sandwich.

"Is there anything else I can get you?" She put her hand on his arm, he tried to smile.

"Thank you Ruth, but there's nothing I want right now. I'm sorry to dump myself on you at short notice, I just didn't know who else to turn to."

"It's alright my dear, don't be silly. I'm always here, any time you need me."

Tears were welling in his eyes.

"I've been stupid, again, Ruth. I thought I was clever. I thought I could outsmart Consuelo. I should've known better."

He held his head in his hands.

"Ruth, I was so stupid, and I was greedy…and now I've lost everything. I've neglected Lucy for a long time now and I was so preoccupied with trying to screw money out of Consuelo."

"Paul, have you got anything to do with what's been going on today? The arrest that's been all over the news."

"Ruth, I've got everything to do with it. I discovered what he did, and he tried to kill me rather than pay me off so I made sure he would get his comeuppance."

Ruth stroked his hair,

"Well, he can't hurt you now, dear, and you never know what's in the future. Lucy might come back."

"She's not coming back. I could tell by the way she spoke. She was different, strong, and she won't be back." He sobbed quietly. Ruth held him gently, saying nothing.

"Can I stay with you, Ruth?"

He looked up at her with the expression of a lost little boy.

"Of course you can, my dear, of course you can. Stay as long as you like."

On the Police Chief's orders, the hospital kept Simon sedated. He slept the rest of the day and through the night. It was nearly noon on the following day when the drugs began to wear off and he started to wake. He was closing his eyes again when he heard voices outside the room. Someone was arguing with the two guards.

"Why can't I see him?"

Simon heard a high-pitched voice that he instantly recognized.

"He's not going anywhere is he? It's not like I can help him to escape, can I?"

After a few moments the door opened and a slim figure slipped into the room and closed the door.

"Hello, flower," said Simon sleepily.

"Hello, gorgeous," said Jake, trying to hide his surprise at the state his lover was in.

"Oh, sweetheart, what have they done to you?" The effeminate hairdresser was trying not to cry. He pulled up a chair next to Simon's bed and took his hand.

"How bad is it?"

"It's nothing. I have much bigger problems than a wounded leg and shoulder. I have to get out of here. I need your help, Jake."

"Of course, anything. What shall I do?"

"The bastards took my phone. I can't contact anyone. As soon as I'm well enough, they will move me to jail, then I'll never be able to get out."

He spoke quietly now, in case the guards were listening.

"There should be four of the Senator's guards still in Manila. We left two at the hotel and there were two following the Senator's car when we arrived at the City Hall. Can you find them? If they turn up in force here the two fools outside my door won't stand a chance. They can get me out, but we have to do it quickly."

"Ok, I'll try; I'll go back to the hotel now. If I can find them, we'll be back soon."

Jake stood up to leave.

"Here's the key to my room at the hotel. You'll find some money, a lot of money. It's in the inside pockets of one of my jackets. I was looking after it for the Senator, but he's not going to need it. If we give the lads outside the door a few dollars, things will go easier."

Jake kissed him on the cheek.

"I'll be back as soon as I can."

Jake went straight back to the hotel, and to Simon's room. There were five jackets among the clothes neatly hanging in the wardrobe. The inside breast pocket of the nearest one was bulging. He pulled out a thick envelope. Inside were bundles of $100 bills. He put them in the side pocket of his bag and zipped it up.

Two of the guards were in the bar, drinking beer and wondering what to do.

"Simon needs your help," Jake said as he sat down beside the surprised pair.

"He's in the hospital, and he wants you to get him out before they take him to jail. There are a couple of young guys guarding his door but that's all. If the four of you came, and gave them some money to look the other way it would be simple. This should do it."

Jake gave them a few $100 bills.

The men looked at each other.

"Come on then, what are we waiting for? Let's go and get the boss."

Their bravado came from the beer, but they were still capable of this easy job, especially if there were four of them.

"Where did the others go? We've got to find them," said Jake.

Police Chief Alveira sat in his office surrounded by papers. The clock on the wall told him his guests were ten minutes late, then the sharp knock on the door told him they had arrived. Inspector Renee Bernarde was a short clean-shaven man of about forty, with a thin moustache. His companion, Sergeant Franke, was younger, taller and thinner. Neither of them smiled.

"Thank you for seeing me, sir."

Bernarde shook the Chief's' proffered hand firmly.

"It's a pleasure, my friend. Please sit down. We should all work together, shouldn't we? Anyway, I was intrigued by your request. What's this all about?"

Bernarde took a file from his slim attaché case and put two pictures onto the table. They were of Simon lying in the back seat of the Senator's car. Chief Alveira picked them up.

"This man worked for Consuelo. He was wounded when we arrested the Senator yesterday. His name's Simon, I think," offered the Chief.

The Inspector nodded.

"I recognized him when I saw the television footage of the capture. He lived in Belgium for a while under the name of Nick, Nick Barker. He fled the country just before we could arrest him."

The Chief raised his eyebrows. As if to answer his unspoken questions, Bernarde continued. "We know it's the same man. We've compared the many photos of him in the news yesterday with our records, and done biometric tests. It's definitely, without question, him. We jumped on the next plane as soon as we could be sure."

"He must be important, for you to come all this way so quickly."

"I've been on the case for a long time, sir. He worked in Belgium as an English teacher. While he was there he started molesting young boys. We have seventeen complaints on file. We were about to arrest him, but he got out just before we did."

"I see. And you're sure it's the same man?" Alveira asked. "We'll be charging him with murder here in the Philippines and probably other things as well, and I'm sure you know there's no extradition treaty between our countries, and we would certainly delay any requests, under the circumstances."

"Yes, I understand. It's definitely him, sir. I'll just be happy to see him locked up somewhere. It may as well be here. I've heard stories about the prisons here. It would serve him right to be locked up here. Maybe we can get our hands on him in the future."

Chief Alveira smiled and nodded,

"Thank you for your understanding."

"I just have one request, sir," said the Inspector. "I interviewed him several times before he escaped. Just for formalities sake, can I meet him and arrest him. At least I can say I've done my job then. I can then go home and tell the press we have found our man, even if we can't get him back home to face trial."

Chief Alveira laughed.

"Ok, my friend, if it'll make you happy. I must admit, I'll enjoy seeing the look on his face. Let's go."

The three men entered the hospital room without knocking. The noise roused Simon from his light sleep. He knew Alveira of course, but who were these other two? He thought he knew the older man but could not quite place where from—then he remembered..

"How the hell...?"

"Are you pleased to see me, Simon? Or should I call you Nick?"

Simon lay back in despair. Back at the City Hall, when he realized they were taking his picture, he knew it would be in the international papers, and he would probably be found out. Was he better off in a Belgian jail or a Philippine one? Anyway, the choice wouldn't be his. "I've been chasing you for five years, you bastard. I knew I'd find you in the end. Just for formalities sake, even if I can't get you back to Belgium, I want the satisfaction of arresting you. With your permission, sir?"

He looked over at the Chief.

"Nick Barker, or Simon, or whatever your name is, I am arresting you on multiple counts of underage sex, rape and buggery."

He carried on with the formal wording while Simon stared into space stony-faced.

As the senior police officers left the hospital it was beginning to get dark. The black SUV with tinted windows pulled up outside the hospital at the same time the policemen were leaving.

"Wait here while I check things out," Jake said.

The others wore police uniforms, it would make things easier. They always carried official clothes 'just in case'. Chief Alveira and his companions passed Jake in the corridor on their way out. By the time Jake got to the room the two officers at the doors were relaxing, glad that their superiors had gone. The door was slightly ajar and as Jake walked by he could see that Simon was alone.

The guards paid Jake no attention. He walked on by and out of a side entrance further along. He reported back to his comrades.

"It's just the two men by the door. He's in the room on his own."

The four men tried to look as official as possible as they entered the hospital.

"We've got orders to take the prisoner."

"Nobody told us," said the braver of the two looking at the other.

The larger man moved forward towards him and whispered quietly.

"Look, my friend, we're going to take him out of there whether you like it or not. You can say you thought we were sent to get him. Look around you, there are plenty of people who will say that four policemen came to get him."

By way of reinforcement, another of the men joined him.

"I think you know what will happen if you resist, boys, don't you?"

He opened his jacket just a fraction to reveal his .35 caliber revolver—a very powerful weapon up close. The two men nodded quickly.

"I knew you'd see it our way. Thanks for your cooperation."

He deftly palmed a small brown envelope into the shaking hand of the nearest man.

"Don't worry; we'll take him out in cuffs to make it look good for you."

He patted him on the shoulder and walked into the room to shake a grinning Simon by the hand.

"Thanks lads, I owe you. What's the plan."

"It's all taken care of," Jake said.

"It's a good job I have friends in immigration—even then it cost a fortune."

"What do you mean?" Simon said.

Jake sighed, as if he had to explain something simple to a child.

"We have to leave the country, I mean right now. In a few hours it'll be impossible to leave. They will be watching out for you."

Simon was bewildered.

"You're on a watch list now. We can sort that out, but we have to leave before they issue a hold departure order against you. It would be much more difficult then."

"But I have nothing with me, clothes, passport, all my stuff."

"We'll worry about that later. Right now, we have to get out of here."

The four 'guards' and Jake escorted their 'prisoner' out of the nearby side entrance and into the back of their waiting SUV. They pulled away smartly as soon as the last door closed.

"Here's your passport, and your wallet, and some more money I found in your room," Jake said, taking a package from his bag and passing it to him.

"I've packed a bag with all the clothes from your room. It's in the back of the car. We don't have any choice, dear, it's now or never."

Simon looked at the things Jake gave him. He was impressed. He didn't think Jake had it in him. He put his wallet and passport in his jacket pocket.

"Where are we going?" he eventually asked.

"Let's wait 'til we get to the airport," Jake replied.

He didn't want the other guys to know where they were going. It was better for all of them.

Ten minutes later the car pulled up in the departure area of Ninoy Aquino International Airport, Terminal One. They said a hurried goodbye and thank you to the guards. There was a small restaurant just to the left of the entrance. Simon and Jake settled themselves at a table in the corner and waited. After a short while, an older woman bustled up.

"Hello, Ate," said Jake.

He kissed the woman on the cheek.

"This is Simon."

The short woman smiled and shook his hand.

Very discretely, Jake slid an envelope over the table towards her. She deftly slid it straight into her handbag. It contained two hundred thousand pesos.

"That's my son," said the old lady proudly, indicating a uniformed immigration officer sitting at a nearby table.

"He'll be on duty on the departure gates in thirty minutes. When you go through, go to his cubicle—he'll get you through. Make sure you remember him."

The officer smiled as he rose and left the table.

After the old lady had gone, Jake turned to Simon.

"We're going to Thailand. Come on, we have to go through now, the plane leaves in less than an hour."

There was only a short line to check in their bags, everything was going smoothly so far. The old woman's son barely looked up at them as he stamped their passports and waved them through.

They were nervous as they waited twenty minutes for boarding.

"Why Thailand?"

"I have friends in Phuket. We can take time to work out our next move."

Simon wasn't sure about the 'we'. He liked Jake, and enjoyed their encounters at the Estate, but he never thought it would go beyond that. Jake apparently had other ideas. The boy obviously thought a lot of him to do all this. 'Oh well,' he thought. 'Let's see what happens.'

There were three safes on the Senator's Estate. Chloe had access to two of them with Consuelo's knowledge; the small safe built into the bedroom wall and the larger one in the corner of his office. There was another in the games room at the back of the pool table, behind the scoreboard. The Senator thought she didn't know about this one, but she did.

She overheard him discussing it with Brian one morning. Luckily for her, it opened with just a key and not a combination. When the Senator was out drinking, she'd had it copied.

Consuelo's office was locked. It always was when he was away, but Chloe had a key. After she left the children playing, she let herself in quietly and locked the door. In the tranquility of the familiar office the nightmare of the last couple of days didn't seem real. Tears came to her eyes. She forced herself to put these thoughts out of her mind and get on with her jobs. Of course, she felt frightened and worried for Consuelo, but now her motherly instincts came into play and her priority was to protect her family, her children.

Inside the office was a secret hiding place. Chloe knew she could find keys to the other two safes there. She locked the office as she left and headed straight for the bedroom. There were no maids around and she emptied the wall safe into a carry bag. Next, she took the papers from the safe in the games room before returning to the office with the contents. Once inside the office she locked the door again and emptied the carrier bags onto the desk making one tall pile.

The safe in his office took a few moments to open. It had a combination, and was very sensitive—you had to get it exactly right, and then you needed the key. She eventually added its contents to her collection on the desk. With a sigh, she sat down and picked up the first piece of paper. Enrique told her many times that he registered many of his properties in her name.

When she met with Dominic, he said she should try to establish who owned what and where and if there was cash to keep it in a secret place, not to bank it.

After more than an hour poring over the stacks and re-sorting them she ended up with five piles. There were title deeds of all sorts. She raised her eyebrows as she discovered his ownership of some surprising properties, including casinos and ships.

Most were in the Philippines, but some were in the United States or the Middle East. There were many share certificates and stocks and bonds, cash, in Pesos, Hong Kong dollars and US dollars. In addition, there was a small pile of gold jewelry and precious stones. She made a fifth pile of all the title deeds and share certificates which were not in her name. There was nothing much she could do with them in a hurry. She placed them back in the safe and returned to the desk.

She was no expert, but she was intelligent enough to know that the pile in front of her represented millions of US dollars and that the Senator had acquired most of it in a dubious, if not illegal manner.

She carefully packed it into two of the Senator's briefcases she in a cupboard in his office and hurried to the bedroom with them. On her way back she caught sight of the children playing in the garden. The window was open, so she called out to them to join her in the bedroom. She caught the eye of the maid as she walked along the hallway and waved to her to come. After a brief conversation, the girl walked briskly next door to the adjoining kid's bedroom.

The children bounded into the room excitedly. They were always happy when they were going on a trip. They had their knapsacks on their backs and two maids stood at the door with three larger cases. She would take the brand new Ford Expedition. It wasn't registered to the Senator and if anyone wanted to check the registration plate they would have to visit the cemetery to find the owner. It was a gift from another politician with equally good reasons for hiding his assets.

Two young guards appeared to carry the bags down to the car. Chloe hurried down to the car, keeping a close eye on the two 'special' cases as the boys packed them in the back of the SUV.

By early evening they were nearing Isabella, her hometown. Chloe pulled into a roadside McDonald's to get some dinner for the children: they were getting hungry now. She used the time when they were eating to phone ahead and make arrangements.

Just before Isabella, they reached a small but tidy beachside resort in a quiet seaside cove. Ferdinand, an old school friend, owned it. It had lockable, secure garages for the cars and there was plenty for the children to do. They arrived there early in the evening and were shown to the best beach chalet by friendly staff. Ferdinand was not there, but would be back soon.

Ferdinand and Chloe dated briefly during their teens, and they remained firm friends. She called in to see him whenever she was passing. This time she had a favor to ask of him, a big one, and she didn't know how much she could trust him. However, time was short and she had to take a chance. After getting the essential bags out, she locked the car in the garage.

By the time she got back in the house, the children were asleep on the small but clean beds. They spread out on the single beds in the larger bedroom; Chloe's bedroom was next door.

She left a message asking Ferdinand to call on her when he got back, and sure enough, at ten o'clock there was a knock on the door. She opened the door quietly, so as not to wake the children. Ferdinand slipped in, a bottle of red wine in one hand and two glasses in the other. She smiled; she really could do with a drink to help her relax, or maybe three.

Ferdinand sat down next to her on the couch. Chloe took the glasses from his hand, smiled and held them out while he poured two generous drinks. They talked about old times and laughed for a while. Ferdinand knew of the Senator's problems but thought that it was up to Chloe to raise the subject if she wanted to. She was a close and dear friend and he just wanted to help her in any way he could.

As they were finishing their third glass, Chloe began to feel mellow. She leaned into Ferdinand to rest her head on his chest. For the first time since the arrest, she felt safe. She didn't resist as his right hand cupped her chin and raised her head up for him to kiss her—she needed comfort, and maybe more. She opened her mouth for him; his other hand moved inside her gown and gently cupped her breast, rubbing her now erect nipples.

His mouth left her lips and started to kiss her breasts, which were now exposed. The gown fell away at both sides revealing her superb body. She lifted his head up to kiss him again, and so that she could open his pants and get her hand inside. It had been a while since they'd made love, but he was slow and gentle, and the familiarity was reassuring.

The children were asleep next door; she tried to be quiet as Ferdinand entered her body. Her moistness helped his smooth penetration. They moved together in a relaxed way until she felt him stiffen, the pulsing of his ejaculation came too soon for her. She kept him inside her and kissed him until she felt that he was ready again. This time when he finished she was completely satisfied.

They lay talking for a long time. After a while, she decided to tell him her plans. She sensed she could trust him now. He listened attentively, and occasionally nodded in agreement. Just after midnight he kissed her passionately one last time. Her eyes followed him up the path as she gently closed the door.

The Senator had been busy. He spoke to Dominic first thing. They agreed to spend the morning on the phones so when they met in the afternoon they would have a better idea what they were up against. The lawyer would come to the jail soon after lunch. He wanted to bring along a couple of colleagues who were specialists, and Consuelo agreed.

When Consuelo called him, he'd already been in his office for thirty minutes. This was going to be a busy day for him. Although still quite young, he was very experienced and he kept his eye on politics. He knew who were likely to be the Senator's political friends and enemies, and made a list of both. Armed forces personnel and police were listed separately. It was now nine. His secretary had arrived sometime in the last thirty minutes, he could hear her outside the door tapping away on her computer.

By lunchtime, he finished making the calls to the supposedly friendly politicians and military men. He was not pleased with the results but he had to finish. His colleague who had been ringing the enemy camps and the two lawyers who would accompany him to see Consuelo should arrive at any time. The meeting may go better if they could at least agree the way forward amongst themselves. Dominic's offices had a small boardroom. The secretary had tidied it ready for them during the morning. By lunchtime, the four men sat around the old and stained table, each with the results of their research held in front of them.

Consuelo had no shortage of detractors in the province and in Manila. If they were sure that the Senator would never be able to hurt them or their families, they would do all they could to help the police to nail him. Five Senators publicly called on Consuelo to resign, and the new President quietly let it be known that anyone who showed any support for Consuelo would not prosper under his regime.

The constitutional lawyer told the others that Consuelo could become the President, notwithstanding the murder charges. However, because he was arrested before inauguration, he was not immune from detention and prosecution. The criminal lawyer was a bit more positive. Consuelo was not present when the murders were committed and there was no direct evidence that he ordered the job.

The downside was that there was a growing mass of circumstantial evidence, and many damning witness statements, with more likely to appear over the coming days and weeks. Dominic sat in silence and listened to each report. They all confirmed what he'd already worked out for himself.

It seemed to him that there was only one positive fact; the Senator had a great deal of money. Dominic could have told the Senator everything that was said in the last thirty minutes himself, but he wanted the reinforcement of the other lawyers when he talked to Consuelo about his options. There were only two routes open to his client—fight or flight.

Dominic favored the flight option. He didn't tell the other lawyers about the 'escape' offer made to him the night before; there was no need for them to know, the fewer people who were aware of it the better. This was the course of action he would recommend to his client this afternoon, after the others had left. He was sure the Senator would take it. Dominic knew him well enough to know that by now he would be clutching at any straws.

The Senator had strong connections all over the world and plenty of money salted away in obscure countries, but he would have to arrange things quickly and quietly. The Senator must decide today, the plan must be put into action immediately. There was nothing more to be said. It was nearly time to visit the Senator.

The three lawyers arrived at the jail soon after lunch. The Senator recognized the two other lawyers as they came through the door. He was comforted to have a criminal defense lawyer and constitutional specialist who were acknowledged experts. He made a mental note to thank Dominic later and reward him well.

The assembled lawyers went through their earlier comments again for the benefit of the Senator, who seemed crestfallen and distracted as the meeting progressed. *He's close to losing the plot,* Dominic thought. The desperation became obvious on his faces as Consuelo started to realize there was little hope of c good way out of this. Unfortunately, he found little comfort.

They talked of defenses, finding supportive witnesses and alibis for a while, but Consuelo knew that his options were limited. The mood of the meeting grew quieter as the afternoon wore on. The lawyers hurriedly made calculations as to how many witnesses would have to disappear for the cases to go away. Even for lawyers, the figures were staggering; the costs were going through the roof.

Consuelo sighed and sat back. He dismissed two of the lawyers, thanking them for their advice, and was now alone with Dominic.

"Have you brought what I asked for?"

Dominic looked around, checking that there were no guards in sight, and then he opened his case.

Consuelo smiled and nodded at the sight of many bundles of $100 bills. Consuelo took out half and hurriedly stuffed them under his bed, out of the sight of the guards. They quietly discussed his plan for the next hour. Dominic told him that the Government would make sure he was convicted and sent to jail for life. He heard about the promise of a pardon from the current President and warned him that she was already telling people privately that it wouldn't happen.

Dominic carefully explained the options and told his client that there was no other possible course of action. He must get out of the jail as quickly as he could by any means that he could. The Senator had to choose, and he had to choose now.

Consuelo didn't need to give it further thought. He wanted to be out of there and quickly, and he told Dominic so. The jailbreak was the only option.

"I'm no fool, Dominic. It's obvious, if I don't get out of here quickly, I probably never will.

"Yes, I think that's correct. It's better to face the reality and deal with it, sir."

"I must leave the arrangements to you, my friend. I have the money. It's offshore. I have a bank account in the Cayman Islands. I'm going to write a letter so you can take control of it. I'll authorize you to take what you need, plus another million for you."

Dominic raised his eyebrows in surprise, and thanked him.

"I need a day to sort out the payments and the people, Senator, but after that, it must happen quickly. You've got to get out the day after tomorrow at the very latest."

He put his hand on Consuelo's arm,

"You'll soon be out of here, my friend. Keep your spirits up."

The Senator smiled. There was some light at the end of the tunnel now, perhaps. By eight o'clock he was feeling tired. He slept with an easier mind that night; he wouldn't be spending much longer in that dismal place. Chloe was travelling back to Manila the next day. She would meet him in the evening; he had spoken to her earlier. She sounded more positive now, maybe the worst was over.

Ferdinand and his sister were watching the children playing on the beach from the bamboo kubo while they drank their morning coffee. They were happy to have the children there.

Their mother told them over breakfast that they'd stay at Frederick's resort while she went to Manila so they were excited. Ferdinand planned to take them on an adventure, an exciting trip, she said.

By noon, Chloe was sitting in the tiny first class area of the first plane of the day from Laoag to Manila. She'd get there midafternoon, and she had a lot to do.

A black diplomatic car waited for her in Manila. The sleek Mercedes with the crest of the Afghan embassy on the doors drove up to the steps of the plane as soon as it had come to a stop. It whisked her away at great speed. Alexi greeted her at the door of the palatial embassy. He could see straight away that she was exhausted so he showed her to her rooms.

Before he left he sat down next to her and held her hand.

"My dear, I must be frank. I can't help Enrique. He has too many enemies, there's nothing I can do for him. I can only help you."

Chloe nodded.

"I know Alexi, it's ok. I already worked it out for myself. Don't worry. I must think of my children now."

He kissed her gently on the forehead and left her to sleep.

The Senator spent most of the day trying to ring Alexi. He knew he could count on his friend to help him flee the country and to give him sanctuary in Afghanistan. He left so many messages begging him to have a plane waiting for him at Manila airport. He had to hope and pray that his friend wouldn't let him down. He kept trying until it was time to prepare for Chloe's visit.

Dominic arrived at the Afghan Embassy to see Chloe exactly at the appointed time. This was his first time to come there. He was amazed at the ornate decors and carpets. Golden statues and large oil paintings adorned the long corridors and spacious rooms—it was a whole different world. Chloe was awake by then and came to meet him; she guided him into a plush drawing room.

She moved over to the couch and sat next to him. This would be a difficult meeting. She needed his trust and understanding. All she could do was be upfront with him and hope he'd understand. Her plan wouldn't work without him. He listened quietly as she explained how much pain and suffering she had gone through, her fears for the children and their future.

It wouldn't be long before someone would try to involve her in her husband's problems, especially if she became active in trying to help him by providing alibis and bribing witnesses. She'd already decided that she wouldn't allow this to happen. Her children must come first, regardless of the consequences. Her best course of action must be to leave the country immediately. There was no viable alternative.

Earlier, she called Alexi's favourite wife, Yasmin. The two girls became close over the years that the two men had been doing business. Yasmin immediately persuaded her husband to rescue their friend. He would get her to Afghanistan by tomorrow. It was dangerous to wait any longer.

Dominic listened quietly while, with tears in her eyes, she told him of her new plan. He was surprised at how quickly things were moving, but he certainly understood. He'd underestimated Chloe. He knew she was bright and resourceful, and today she had proved to him that she was realistic and protective of her family.

Twenty minutes earlier, Consuelo tried to call him, and he was still trying, but his phone was switched off. After they finished talking, she took him to the private office with a computer with internet access and a fax machine. Dominic set about his work. Chloe had just a few more arrangements to make now. The next call on her list was Ferdinand.

By late afternoon, thirty million pesos was in Dominic's account at the Bank of the Philippine Islands in Makati. Dominic knew the manager well. After a long phone call, the senior bank staff got busy making secure arrangements for him to pick up the money at five p.m.

The friendly manager arranged for two guards to accompany Dominic and the money for the rest of the day. It was difficult to keep the movement of such a large sum of money quiet within the bank. There was always a danger of robbery by employees with unsavory connections. You couldn't be too careful.

An hour later, Dominic was back at the Embassy. The two bank guards waited outside the gates as Dominic entered for a second time that day. This meeting with Chloe was much shorter. Chloe received him in her room this time and they sat quietly and drank hot tea. Without saying a word, he passed her a small package about the size of a matchbox. It was sealed with scotch tape. She placed it straight into her handbag. Dominic left shortly after with five million pesos in his case.

He took a call from the Senator at about seven that evening.

"What's happening, Dominic? I've been trying to ring you for two hours."

Dominic noticed the curtness in his voice.

"It's ok, Senator. Don't worry, everything's fine. Just relax, sir. This will be your last night, everything's prepared. Chloe has arranged transport with your friend Alexi. After breakfast tomorrow you must be ready to go. Just do what the guards tell you."

Lying came easy to Dominic.

Chloe was a practical woman. Emotions were flowing through her body like a fast running river and she was close to tears, but she knew what she had to do and would do it. She offered to catch a scheduled flight to Afghanistan but Alexi wouldn't hear of it. One of his private planes was leaving in the early hours of the morning with the gold. It would be waiting at the International Airport in Manila at about four a.m. She would be on it.

She packed for the journey and forced herself to bathe and dress. Her hands were trembling as she prepared. The next few hours were going to be the most difficult time ever for her. The ambassador arranged a car to take her to the prison. She was grateful; she couldn't handle dealing with a taxi driver right now.

The car pulled up at the prison gates thirty minutes later. The long walk to the Senator's prison cell seemed to take forever. Chloe took a deep breath and forced herself to smile at him as the guard opened the door for her. She held him for a long time; he couldn't see her tears.

A short while later the hotel delivered dinner, just as arranged. Her husband looked pale and worn, but his confident manner was starting to come back and he seemed optimistic. She was pleased to see a little of the old spark return to him as they sat down to eat together. It was a great effort, but she managed to put her thoughts of the future out of her mind and smiled while she ate.

When the meal was over, they spoke in quiet tones of his 'release'—he preferred that term to 'escape'. She reached across the small table and held his hand, telling him that everything was prepared and all would go smoothly. He should relax and have a good night's rest.

They discussed the plans for tomorrow. He was to dress in casual clothes and have breakfast as usual in the morning. Soon after breakfast, a senior officer would come to his cell to take him away, he just had to follow instructions. He would soon be enjoying his freedom.

He brightened visibly as Chloe explained the detail of the plan. She forced herself to join in with him in laughing and smiling. He started to talk about his plans for the future. He wanted to mount a defense to the claims and was already, in his mind, planning an eventual comeback to what he saw as his rightful place as the President of the country.

She did her best to smile, laugh, and nod in the right places. It was a strain, but she was doing as best as she could. *He must be the only person in the world who believed that he could ever return safely to the country, let alone as its President*, she thought to herself. Strangely, she felt happy at this time to go along with him and try to keep him in this pleasant mood.

After they had finished their meal, he walked around the table and kissed her passionately, and for a long time. When he pulled away he led her to the bed area in the corner that had sheets hung around it by way of curtains. This she didn't expect. It was the last thing she wanted, but there was nothing she could do. She held the smile while she could, but as he looked away, she dropped it. It was difficult enough to have a meal and indulge in conversation with him, let alone...this!

She sighed in resignation as he held her tight. Consuelo opened her blouse and moved her bra upwards—his fingers were already rubbing her nipples. There was no resistance and the Senator lay her down and slid his hand up under her skirt. She lay down with her eyes closed and her legs gradually moving apart. There was no time for foreplay. Consuelo was sure that his wife would understand, just this once. She kept her eyes closed as he lifted her dress higher. *Thank God it's the wrong time of the month for me to get pregnant*, she thought to herself.

Chloe winced with pain as he entered her forcefully, and without lubrication. Out of habit, she pushed up to meet him and forced him further into her. Thankfully, he didn't last very long, but when he'd finished he lay on top, still inside her. She could do nothing except stroke his back and hope he would move soon.

The Senator became emotional. He clung to her and offered a small prayer of thanks. He was lucky to have someone like her. They lay together; she didn't want to upset him by getting up quickly. Finally, he rolled off and lay next to her on the small bed; she took this as a cue that it was ok to move.

There was a small mirror in the bathroom area and she tidied herself as best she could. As she left his cell she looked at her watch, it was nearly midnight, she was behind schedule. She kissed him again as she stood at the cell door, and told him she'd see him again soon. Tears were running down her cheeks, she couldn't help it. He hugged her and told her to go, she still had much work to do.

The senior of the two guards closed the door behind her and locked it. As before, he escorted her away from the cell, but after they had rounded a corner and were out of sight of the Senator they took a different direction, they weren't going towards the exit. He guided her into a row of empty cells. At the end was a small room, the door was open. He guided her inside.

The two men in the cell were the relief guard that would take over from the night guard at eight a.m. These men would give the Senator his breakfast and take care of all the other details. After everything was discussed and agreed, the two plain clothed men escorted her out of the prison.

The Embassy car was just around the corner with the driver asleep in the reclined driving seat. Chloe opened the driver door to wake him and to ask him to open the trunk. As the trunk clicked open and the lid slowly lifted the three figures huddled around it. There was a bulging McDonald's carrier bag in the corner of the otherwise empty trunk. Chloe lifted it out and handed it to one of the men.

"This is for the Governor."

Then she reached into her handbag and found the small package that Dominic had given her earlier. She passed it to the other man who quickly pocketed it. Neither of them said a word. They walked away without a goodbye or a handshake. This was not the kind of business you shook hands over. She watched them walk away. Tears flowed freely now, she could stop trying to control herself now. As far as she was concerned, it was over.

On her way back to the Afghan Embassy, she called the head waiter at the Dusit Thani hotel. It was half past midnight, but luckily, he answered. Through her tears, she asked him to make sure that the Senator got all his favourite food for breakfast in the morning. Chloe was still crying when they arrived back at the Embassy, but she must soon depart for the airport.

CHAPTER ELEVEN

"Come on, kids," shouted Ferdinand.

He was waiting with his sister by the white van.

"Hurry up or we're going to be late."

The kids were laughing and playing in the sand. Their bags were packed and they were all ready, but they were having fun on the beach. They came running when he called them. Ferdinand started the engine while his sister strapped the children into the back seats. She climbed into the passenger seat, and they were on their way.

"Where are we going, where are we going?" shouted the eldest.

Ferdinand laughed.

"We're going on a plane ride."

They arrived at Laoag airport with time to spare and cleared customs quickly. His sister waved at them from the viewing platform with tears in her eyes. It was a hot day. The small figures shimmered in the hazy heat. They disappeared up the steel stairs into the plane, still waving at her.

Nothing was going to dampen Tom's spirits tonight. He'd checked in and had two hours to wait. There were few duty free shops open at that time, but he did find some. He was hunting for presents for Lucy and Dennis. Many of the seats in the crowded lounge were taken up with people resting or sleeping, but finally he managed to find an empty seat. When he was settled with a tall latte in front of him, he called Lucy.

"Hello, sweetheart."

"Oh, darling, thank God you rang. I was worried, are you ok?"

"Yes I am, sorry, a lot has happened today."

He decided not to tell her the news about the Senator until he was there. There would be plenty of time to sort things out when they were together.

"I saw mum this afternoon. She sends her love to you. I told her she can come and see us soon."

"That's great. Your mum's nice. I like her."

"Well, she certainly likes you. I think she likes you more than me."

"Maybe she does."

They both laughed at that thought.

"How's Dennis?"

"He's fine, he likes the adventure. I haven't told him anything yet about his dad."

"Well, maybe it'll be easier when I'm there. Let him get used to me for a few days."

Lucy went quiet for a few seconds.

"I've spoken to Paul. I told him we're finished."

"That's good sweetheart, I'm glad that's over, and it can't have been pleasant."

"I didn't tell him where we were going, or about you."

"That's probably just as well for now, sweetheart. There will be plenty of time to sort all that out later on."

Lucy went to bed with Dennis for a second night, but she couldn'.t sleep. She watched television while Dennis slept. In a quiet moment, she told Dennis that Tom would be joining them soon. He seemed to accept that without any questions. Maybe she was worrying too much about how Dennis would adapt to the new situation. Children were tough and coped well, as long as they felt safe and loved. She didn't want to say anything until Tom was there to support her.

The doorbell rang at nine fifty. Her heart leapt into her mouth; he was ten minutes early. Tom was dressed casually, with his usual waistcoat. Framed in the doorway she thought he looked like a catalogue model. He came into the room and gave Lucy a warm hug and a peck on the cheek. They agreed they'd be careful in front of Dennis for a while. They would see how things went before being too obvious about their relationship.

Dennis was hungry now, and he kept on to his mom and eventually they all set off to go down for breakfast. As the three walked down the two flights of stairs to the restaurant, Lucy grabbed Tom's hand and gazed longingly at him for a few seconds. She knew that everything would be all right now, her man was here. Dennis was speeding away down the stairs, anxious to get some food inside him as soon as possible.

"Let's find a zoo or a park today—we don't want Dennis getting bored, do we?"

Lucy was as pleased as she could be. Paul had never in his life put Dennis first in that way, she thought. She was even more certain now that she'd made the right decision.

Alexi decided to travel home with Chloe and the gold. The truck pulled up at the entrance to the small area of the international airport reserved for private planes. The area was deserted except for two weary officers who were operating the gates. He wound down the window as they both approached.

"What are you carrying, sir?"

Their interest increased when they saw they were dealing with foreigners.

"Just office equipment for my country."

Alexi handed over his diplomatic passport, and that of his driver.

"You'll need to open the crates for us to see."

Alexi got down from his cab.

"I don't think so. Look at my passport. It carries diplomatic privilege, and so does anything I carry."

The two men looked at each other but did not move. Alexi sighed.

"Look, my friends, you can either ring your supervisor and get into trouble for harassing a diplomat, or you can let us through. It's late at night and I'm tired."

He reached for his wallet.

"Let's settle this. How about you go home a bit richer and I carry on with my work."

He had US$1,000 in each hand.

The men smiled, bowed slightly, and handed the passports back before turning and strolling away.

Chloe was only thirty minutes behind them. The streets of Manila were still busy at two a.m. as her limousine quietly pulled out of the Embassy compound. Her passport was examined and stamped by a lone, tired officer who didn't recognize her. He was still thinking how he would spend his bonus. She proceeded to the plane at the same time as her baggage was taken aboard. As she climbed the steps, she saw Alexi waiting at the top to greet her. She felt safe now and relaxed as the plane rose into the night sky. Looking back at the airport buildings and the Manila skyline in the distance, she wondered when or if she would see her native land again.

The flight to Afghanistan was smooth. Chloe slept for most of the time—she was emotionally and physically exhausted. She was a strong woman but the events of the last few days were taking their toll.

A Rolls Royce limousine was waiting for them at the small and drab airport in Kabul. Luxurious date palms and coconut trees lined the route from the airport to Alexi's home. She opened the window—the air was middle eastern air was hot and humid. They arrived at Alexi's mansion just in time for breakfast. Chloe's friend, Yasmin, was waiting. She opened the door as the car purred to a halt.

For the first time in days, Chloe now had a genuine smile on her face. Her smile broadened as she saw her children come running out of the door and towards her with their arms outstretched. She hugged them very tight. She felt complete now.

"Are you guys ok?"

"It's fun being with Uncle Ferdi," said the eldest. "We do lots of stuff. Can we stay here mummy, please? It's great here!"

"We'll see, we won't be going anywhere for a while, anyway."

"Yay," they shouted in unison.

The door opened wider and Ferdinand walked through. She ran towards him and hugged him.

"Thank you so much," she said, kissing him firmly on the lips. She didn't care who was watching now.

They held hands as they walked inside. Breakfast was late, but relaxed. It lasted more than two hours and was accompanied by champagne. When she did eventually feel like moving, Yasmin showed Chloe to the suite that had been prepared. There was a maid waiting to help her unpack, but Chloe told her to come back later.

She was used to luxurious surroundings, but it was nice to experience the opulence of Yasmin's home. Her feelings of panic were subsiding. Fear had been growing within her steadily since the arrest. Her life had been turned upside down.

The children asked if they could go to the garden and play. Chloe readily agreed. It made her happy to see them so carefree and contented. The mansion was filled with children—Alexi had three wives

After Yasmin left, Chloe turned her attention to Ferdinand and thanked him again. She looked into his eyes and kissed him, this time more passionately. Quietly she locked the door and they slowly undressed each other. Everything seemed so natural with Ferdi. Afterwards, they lay together in the massive bed and sunk into the soft mattress. She put from her mind the memories of her last, painful and unwanted sexual encounter. Their lovemaking was slow and satisfying. They slept for several hours in the giant bed. Midafternoon, they were roused by a loud knocking on the door. The children had returned, and were hungry again. Chloe and Ferdinand quickly threw on robes and let them in.

Afternoon tea was a tradition, with cakes, pastries and sandwiches. Alexi had grown to like it when he was at Oxford, but he and Yasmin did not join them. Yasmin felt they needed some time alone together. She was a wise girl, which was how she managed to stay Alexi's favourite wife.

Chloe felt strange as she sat down. They looked for the entire world like a happy family.

"When do you have to go back?

"Yasmin already organized a plane to take me back at ten o'clock tonight."

Chloe leaned over to him and put her hand on his leg.

"Are you sure you can't stay longer?"

It was not so much a question as a plea. He smiled as Chloe called Yasmin—the pilot wouldn't need to work tonight.

The guards on the Senator's cell block changed soon after dawn. Shortly afterwards the waiters from the hotel arrived with his breakfast. Two waiters were let into his cell and, together with the new guards, they brought dishes, plates and cutlery. He smiled when he saw his favorite breakfast being laid out, the champagne really topped off the meal. He gave them a generous tip. The eggs Benedict steamed and the smoked salmon looked very fresh and appetizing, and tasted just as good.

Chloe already told him everyone assisting the escape had been 'taken care of', but he still readied some small packets of hundred dollar bills from his secret hoard so that he could show his gratitude personally. Nearly all of the money that Dominic had left him with was still in his case. He had only used a small amount of it. It seemed he wouldn't need to use it inside the jail now. It would come in handy when he was out.

There was only one overnight bag full of clothes and the briefcase with the money. He took some of the clothes out of it and stuffed the bundles of dollar bills inside.

He had not yet finished the meal when tiredness came over him, he started to feel strange. *Maybe it's the champagne*, he thought, and he was a bit wary about the escape plan. Things could go wrong. He just had to hope and pray.

The knot in his stomach was painful now. It was as if he'd eaten some needles and they were sticking into him. He got up off the bed thinking he may feel better, hoping that it would ease the pain—it didn't. Now he was beginning to feel sick as well. He walked back to his breakfast table to get a glass of water, and he only just managed to get back to his bed to sit down. The strength had left his legs.

He drank the water, but it had no effect. The pain in his stomach was getting worse. He was starting to feel really ill. He stood up, but his legs gave way, and he collapsed onto the floor. There was no point trying to get up, his legs would no longer carry him. He cried out for help but his voice sounded weak and distant to him; nobody came.

He started crawling towards the bars of his cell but was sick before he got there. There was blood coming up with his food. As he reached his cell door, he shrieked with pain as his stomach began to dissolve. He cried out to get the guards attention. One guard came up, said he'd get help and ran off. Consuelo lay on the floor in agony, praying that the prison doctor would arrive soon, but the guard, of course, had no intention of getting a doctor. When he was out of the Senator's view he slowed down, sat back down with his comrade, and continued their game of cards. They wouldn't have long to wait.

Chloe had made her decision yesterday with a hard heart. She didn't regret it, but she couldn't help thinking about what was happening to Consuelo. The disgraced Senator was unlikely to find sanctuary in any other country legally or illegally. His one and only powerful foreign friend Alexi had turned him down. She couldn't face a life in hiding or on the run, even with plenty of money. What sort of future was that for her children?

Chloe told Dominic that the Senators meals were sent in from the local hotel. The prison Governor didn't take much persuading. It would be easy to put the blame on others. It could have been anyone in the kitchen of the hotel, or the waiters who delivered the meal, or even the delivery driver, or his assistant. Of course, the guards would be suspects as well, but no one could prove anything.

Consuelo could no longer move. He was wishing with every bone in his body that he couldn't feel anything, either. Blood was trickling out of his mouth, and he'd soiled his trousers with bloody feces. His pathetic moans grew weaker. The guards waited a further ten minutes until after the noises had stopped.

As they reached the cell, the pungent smell of the regurgitated food and evacuated bowels hit them. They were both long in the prison service and had seen some pretty bad sights, but this was one of the worst. Consuelo was on the floor, his face frozen in a frightened grimace, a pool of blood had formed under the edge of his open mouth. Wide-open eyes stared at them accusingly.

However, necessity overrode their revulsion and they covered their mouths. They opened the cell, stepped over the body and moved towards the bed. It didn't take them long to find the money stashed in a zipped side pocket. They had their pay.

They divided the bundles, pocketed them, and then without wasting time locked the cell leaving everything as they had found it, with the exception, of course, that Consuelo's hundred thousand dollars had gone with them.

They ran off to call for the prison doctor and raise the alarm.

Yasmin heard the news on CNN before lunch but wanted to choose her time to tell Chloe. She found her later in the afternoon in the garden, watching the children playing. Ferdinand was in their room taking a nap. Chloe was walking through an orangery.

"Chloe, I'm so sorry my dear. Enrique is dead."

Chloe nodded almost imperceptibly without looking at her. Yasmin thought this strange.

"You don't seem surprised. Are you ok?

"Yasmin, my dearest friend, there was no other way. I tell myself he would understand and forgive me."

Yasmin held her hand and said nothing.

Lisa Carriega phoned the Governor of the jail early in the morning to find out when the Senator was to be arraigned.

The Governor was just preparing a press release about the Senator's death. This was as good a way as any to release the news.

"My dear, the Senator is dead. He became ill this morning and died before anything could be done."

Lisa couldn't believe what she was hearing, but she quickly recovered.

"Can you give me some details? How could it have happened?"

"I can't say much yet, my dear. We can't believe it ourselves. Right now it looks like a burst stomach ulcer or something like that, but we are waiting for test results. We just can't be sure yet."

"Is there any chance that it was something more sinister?"

The Governor laughed. "Oh, I doubt that, my dear. You journalists are always looking for conspiracy theories. Life is usually much simpler."

"Well, sir, is there any possibility of deliberate food poisoning?"

"I haven't heard that suggested, my dear, but I'm sure there will be lots of rumors. There always are when someone of the Senator's stature passes suddenly. The Senator refused prison food, he was having his own supply sent in, so if there is any question of food poisoning, it certainly can't be blamed on our food."

Lisa cut the call short when she realized the time. She had to get her piece written for the evening edition, her second major scoop in a week.

The monsoon rains started the following morning. The streets were flooded, even in Makati, the business center of Manila. Paul sat in Starbucks on the corner of Makati Avenue and Buendia, below the Pacific Star building. It was mid-morning, after the morning rush and before the lunch crowd so it was not that busy.

The Philippine Star devoted the first six pages to the previous day's events. He was happy to see photos of the beleaguered Senator embellishing the striking prose of the editorial on the front page.

Paul was determined that he wouldn't come out of this with nothing. Last night he phoned the newspaper and by late evening an attractive young reporter was passing over a million pesos for original photos of the cave, the Senator being pushed into the police vehicle, and an exclusive interview with the man who blew the whistle on the murdering Senator. Lisa rushed back to the editorial office—this story must catch the morning edition.

After she left, Paul sat alone with his Cappuccino. This was the first time he'd had time to sit and think for many days. He was trying to make sense of losing Lucy and Dennis. It was surprising how much he missed them. He would have to deal with it, but not now, it could wait for another day.

ABOUT THE AUTHOR

Arthur is a late developer. He wasted his time earning money as a lawyer for most of his life until he discovered his true vocation—spending money and writing.

Born and raised in Somerset in the UK, he has travelled expensively (not a spelling mistake!) and has finally settled in Hong Kong where he can get a decent Fish and Chips and the policemen look like they do in London.

He has four amazing children in different parts of the world—and a wonderful partner, Lance.

You can contact Arthur and learn more about him in several ways—he always answers emails—unless you want to borrow money:

Website: http://www.arthurcrandon.com
Blog: http://www.arthurcrandon.com/blog-blog-blog.html
Email:
mailto:arthurcrandon@yahoo.com?subject=Enquiry from Deadly Election Ebook
Facebook:
http://www.facebook.com/arthurcrandonauthor
Twitter: http://www.twitter.com/arthurcrandon
Pinterest: http://pinterest.com/arthurcrandon/
Wattpad: http://www.wattpad.com/user/arthurcrandon
Instagram: deadlyelectionbook
Amazon: http://amzn.to/19cKjsP
Goodreads: http://bit.ly/17S1guI